THE MECHANICS

THE BOSTON BRAHMIN SERIES: BOOK FIVE

BOBBY AKART

THE MECHANICS
THE BOSTON BRAHMIN SERIES: BOOK FIVE

Bobby Akart

DEDICATIONS

There is nothing more important on this planet than my darling wife, Dani, and our two princesses, Bullie and Boom. With the love and support of Dani and the never-ending supply of smiles our two girls give us, I'm able to tell you these stories.

Also, a special dedication to America's first responders—the men and women of law enforcement, firefighters, emergency medical technicians, and hospital personnel. These are the underappreciated brave Americans who run toward danger rather than from it.

Freedom and security are precious gifts that we, as Americans, should never take for granted. Thank you, first responders, for willingly making sacrifices each day to provide us that freedom and security.

ACKNOWLEDGEMENTS

Writing a book that is both informative and entertaining requires a tremendous team effort. Writing is the easy part. For their efforts in making The Boston Brahmin series a reality, I would like to thank Hristo Argirov Kovatliev for his incredible cover art, Pauline Nolet for her editorial prowess, Joseph Morton for bringing my words to life in audio format, and the Team—whose advice, friendship and attention to detail is priceless.

Thank you!

Choose Freedom!

ABOUT THE AUTHOR, BOBBY AKART

Author Bobby Akart has been ranked by Amazon as #25 on the Amazon Charts list of most popular, bestselling authors. He has achieved recognition as the #1 bestselling Horror Author, #1 bestselling Science Fiction Author, #5 bestselling Action & Adventure Author, #7 bestselling Historical Fiction Author and #10 on Amazon's bestselling Thriller Author list.

Mr. Akart has delivered up-all-night thrillers to readers in 245 countries and territories worldwide. He has sold over one million books in all formats, which includes over forty international bestsellers, in nearly fifty fiction and nonfiction genres.

His novel *Yellowstone: Hellfire* reached the Top 25 on the Amazon bestsellers list and earned him multiple Kindle All-Star awards for most pages read in a month and most pages read as an author. The Yellowstone series vaulted him to the #25 bestselling author on Amazon Charts, and the #1 bestselling science fiction author.

Mr. Akart is a graduate of the University of Tennessee after pursuing a dual major in economics and political science. He went on to obtain his master's degree in business administration and his doctorate degree in law at Tennessee.

Mr. Akart has provided his readers a diverse range of topics that are both informative and entertaining. His attention to detail and impeccable research has allowed him to capture the imagination of his readers through his fictional works and bring them valuable knowledge through his nonfiction books.

SIGN UP for Bobby Akart's mailing list to receive a copy of his monthly newsletter, *The Epigraph*, learn of special offers, view bonus content, and be the first to receive news about new releases.

Visit www.BobbyAkart.com for details.

INTRODUCTION

THE ORIGINAL MECHANICS and THEIR ROLE IN THE AMERICAN REVOLUTION

In The Boston Brahmin series, The Mechanics are modern day insurgents—patriots battling a tyrannical government. However, they are watched over by the ghosts of the past—the original Mechanics, insurgents who carried out the activities of the Sons of Liberty.

I encourage you to review the Appendix to learn more, found by clicking the link below. In the Appendix, you will find a brief history of the use of insurgent activities which have successfully overcome a more powerful adversary. Afterwards, you will be returned to the beginning of THE MECHANICS, as The Boston Brahmin series continues.

GO TO APPENDIX A

PREVIOUSLY IN THE BOSTON BRAHMIN SERIES

Dramatis Personae

THE LOYAL NINE:

Sarge – born Henry Winthrop Sargent IV. Son of former Massachusetts governor, godson of John Adams Morgan and a descendant of Daniel Sargent, Sr., wealthy merchant, and owner of Sargent's Wharf during the Revolutionary War. He's a tenured professor at the Harvard Kennedy School of Government in Cambridge. He is becoming well known around the country for his libertarian philosophy as espoused in his *New York Times* bestseller —*Choose Freedom or Capitulation: America's Sovereignty Crisis*. Sarge resides at 100 Beacon Street in the Back Bay area of Boston. Sarge is romantically involved with Julia Hawthorne.

Steven Sargent – younger brother of Sarge. He is a graduate of the United States Naval Academy and a former platoon officer of SEAL Team 10. He is currently a contract operative for Aegis Security—code name Nomad. He resides on his yacht—the *Miss Behavin'*. Steven is romantically involved with Katie O'Shea.

Julia Hawthorne – descendant of the Peabody and Hawthorne families. First female political editor of the *Boston Herald*. She is the recipient of the National Association of Broadcasting Marconi

Radio Award for her creation of an Internet radio channel for the newspaper. She is in a relationship with Sarge and lives with him at 100 Beacon.

The Quinn family – Donald is the self-proclaimed director of procurement. He is a former accountant and financial advisor who works directly with John Adams Morgan. Married to **Susan Quinn** with daughters **Rebecca** (age 7) and **Penny** (age 11). Donald and Susan coordinate all preparedness activities of The Loyal Nine. They reside in Brae Burn Country Club in Boston.

J.J. – born John Joseph Warren. He is a direct descendant of Dr. Joseph Warren, one of the original Sons of Liberty. The Warren family founded Harvard Medical and were field surgeons at the Battle of Bunker Hill. J.J. was an Army battalion surgeon at Joint Base Balad in Iraq. While stationed at JBB, J.J. saved the life of a female soldier who was injured saving the lives of others. He later became involved in a relationship with former Marine Second Lieutenant Sabina del Toro. He finished his career at the Veteran's Administration Hospital in Jamaica Plain, where he also resides. He is affectionately known as the Armageddon Medicine Man.

Katie O'Shea – graduate of the United States Naval Academy who trained as a Naval Intelligence officer. After an introduction to John Adams Morgan, she quickly rose up the ranks of the intelligence community. She now is part of the President's Intelligence Advisory Board. She resides in Washington, D.C. Katie is romantically involved with Steven Sargent.

Brad – born Francis Crowninshield Bradlee, a descendant of the Crowninshield family, a historic seafaring and military family dating back to the early 1600s. He is the battalion commander of the 25th Marine Regiment of 1st Battalion based at Fort Devens, Massachusetts. Their nickname is *Cold Steel Warriors*. He is an active member of *Oathkeepers* and the *Three Percenters*.

Abbie – Abigail Morgan, daughter of John Adams Morgan. United States senator from Massachusetts since 2008. A political independent, with libertarian leanings. She resides in Washington, D.C. She has been chosen as the running mate of the Democratic nominee for president. She briefly became romantically involved with her head of security, Drew Jackson, aka *Slash*, on the Aegis team.

THE BOSTON BRAHMIN:

John Adams Morgan – lineal descendant of President John Adams and Henry Sturgis Morgan, founder of J.P. Morgan. Morgan attended Harvard, obtaining a master's degree in business and a law degree. Founded the Morgan-Holmes law firm with the grandson of Supreme Court Justice Oliver Wendell Holmes Jr. Among other concerns, he owns Morgan Global, an international banking and financial conglomerate. Extremely wealthy, Morgan is the recognized head of The Boston Brahmin.

Walter Cabot – direct descendant of John Cabot, shipbuilders during the time of the Revolutionary War. Wealthy philanthropist and CEO of Cabot Industries. He is part of Morgan's inner circle. Married to Mary Cabot.

Lawrence Lowell – direct descendant of John Lowell, a federal judge in the first United States Continental Congress. Extremely wealthy and part of Morgan's inner circle. Married to Constance Lowell.

Paul Winthrop – descendant of John Winthrop, one of the leading figures in the founding of the Massachusetts Bay Colony, his family became synonymous with the state's politics and philanthropy. The Winthrops and Sargents became close when Sarge's grandfather was governor of Massachusetts and his lieutenant governor was R. C. Winthrop. The families remained close and became a valuable political force on behalf of The Boston Brahmin. They have a French bulldog called Winnie the Frenchie. Married to Millicent Winthrop.

Arthur Peabody – Dr. Arthur Peabody is a plastic surgeon in private practice. He is the youngest of the Boston Brahmin at age fifty-five. His wife is Estelle, affectionately called Aunt Stella. They are Julia's aunt and uncle. They're direct descendants of the Hawthorne and Peabody lineage.

General Samuel Bradlee – former general and Secretary of

Defense. A direct descendant of Nathaniel Bradlee, one of the key participants in the Boston Tea Party. He is Brad's uncle.

Henry Endicott – great-grandson of former Secretary of War William Crowninshield Endicott. The Endicott family name is synonymous with warfare throughout the world as one of the largest manufacturers of advanced weapons systems in America. His third wife, Emily, is younger than some of his children.

OFFICERS OF 1st BATTALION, 25th MARINE REGIMENT:

Gunny Falcone – Master Gunnery Sergeant Frank Falcone. Under Brad's command for years. A loyal member of the Mechanics. Stationed at Fort Devens. Primary on-base recruiter of soldiers to join the Mechanics.

Chief Warrant Officer Kyle Shore – young. Expert in sniping. Recorded two kill shots in Afghanistan at just over 2,500 yards. Stationed at Fort Devens. Also recruits members of the Mechanics.

First Lieutenant Kurt Branson – Boston native. A loyal member of the Mechanics.

SUPPORTING CHARACTERS:

Agent Joseph Pearson – special agent working for the Federal Protective Services—a division of Homeland Security. He first appeared at Fort Devens to meet with Brad in April. A subsequent meeting at Fort Devens with Brad following the cyber attack became very contentious. He is now the special liaison to the Citizen Corps governor of FEMA Region I—James O'Brien. His office is located on High Street in Boston.

Citizen Corps Governor James O'Brien – former president of the Boston Carmen's Union—one of the oldest and largest public service employees' unions in the city. O'Brien is a staunch supporter of the President and is known to have organized-crime connections. He is a fierce political opponent of Republican Governor Charlie Baker. He was named the new governor of Region I. His office is located on High Street in Boston.

Governor Charlie Baker – Governor of Massachusetts. First Republican in decades to be endorsed by the left-leaning Boston Globe newspaper.

Marion La Rue – Member of the International Brotherhood of Teamsters. Called upon by union leaders in Boston to undertake special union *activities*, including the orchestrated walkout of MBTA bus drivers during the St. Patrick's Day festivities.

Ronald Archibald – Newly appointed town chairman of the board of selectman in Belchertown, Massachusetts, a small town just to the west of Prescott Peninsula.

J-Rock – Jarvis Rockwell, leader of the unified black gangs of Dorchester, Roxbury, and Mattapan in South Boston. He rose to power after the death of his unborn child during a race riot in Copley Square. He is recruited by Governor O'Brien to loot the wealthy neighborhoods of Boston.

Joaquin Guzman – Head of a Central American drug cartel known as *Mara Salvatrucha*, or MS-13, which predominantly operates in the East Boston ghettos. He is recruited by Governor O'Brien to loot the wealthy neighborhoods of Boston.

John Willis – also known as *Bac Guai John*, or more commonly as the *White Devil*. He is the only Caucasian in Chinatown and the undisputed head of the Ping On gang. Over time he rose through the ranks and became the leading oxycodone importer from South Florida—a three-billion-dollar-a-year industry. He has entered into an alliance with The Loyal Nine.

General Mason J. Sears – descendant of Richard Sears, an early settler of the Massachusetts Bay Colony in the seventeenth century. General Mason J. Sears, USMC, is the current Chairman of the Joint Chiefs of Staff, and has been designated by the President to implement the Declaration of Martial Law. He is an insider for John Morgan and The Boston Brahmin.

Joe Sciacca – *Boston Herald*'s chief editor.

Malcolm Lowe – John Morgan's trusted assistant. Former undersecretary of state during Morgan's tenure as Secretary of State. He *handles* sensitive matters for Mr. Morgan.

Sabina del Toro – former Marine second lieutenant deployed to Iraq, assigned to the 6th Marine Regiment under the 2nd Marine Division based at Camp Lejeune. The 6th was primarily a peacekeeping force deployed throughout the Sunni Anbar province, which included Fallujah, just west of Baghdad. Sabs, as she prefers to be called, was seriously injured protecting children from a car bomb blast. She lost her left arm and left leg as a result of her heroics. She was in a relationship with J.J. She died in *Martial Law*, book three, during a confrontation with local residents.

ZERO DAY GAMERS:

Andrew Lau – MIT professor of Korean descent. A brilliant mind that created the Zero Day Gamers as a way to utilize his talents for personal financial gain.

Anna Fakhri – MIT graduate assistant to Professor Lau, of Arabic descent. She prides herself on her "Internet detective work." She speaks multiple Arabic languages.

Leonid "Leo" Malvalaha – MIT graduate assistant to Professor Lau, of Russian descent. He is very adept at creating complex viruses, worms, and Trojans used in cyber-attack activities. He speaks fluent Russian.

Herm Walthaus – newest member of the Zero Day Gamers. MIT graduate student. Introverted, but extremely analytical. Stays abreast of the latest tools and techniques available to hackers.

AEGIS TEAM:

Nomad – Steven Sargent.

Slash – Drew Jackson. Former SEAL Team member who worked briefly for private contractors like Blackwater. Born and raised in Tennessee, where his family farm is located. He has excellent survival skills. He was assigned to Senator Abigail Morgan's security team that works with her Secret Service detail.

Bugs – Paul Hittle. Former Army Special Forces medic, who left the Green Berets for contract security work. He owns a ranch in East Texas, provided to him as compensation for his service to Aegis.

Sharpie – Raymond Bower. Former Delta Force, who now operates a lucrative private equity fund venture with former classmates from Harvard. He resides in New York City.

PRIMARY SCENE LOCATIONS

100 Beacon – Renovated residential building located in the heart of the Back Bay area of Boston. Located on the lower end of the Boston Common, just to the south of Cambridge and the Charles River, the top three floors of the eleven story building were renovated as a veritable fortress. The top floor housed Sarge's residence, and the Prepper Pantry. The floor below it, was intended to provide housing for The Loyal Nine and The Boston Brahmin. The ninth floor contained an armory, a small medical trauma center, a jail cell, and large storage area. The rooftop provided three hundred and sixty degree views of the city, and overlooked Storrow Drive and Cambridge.

73 Tremont – historic building in downtown Boston located at 73 Tremont Street. (Pronounced "trem-mont") Formerly a historic hotel, the building was purchased by John Morgan to house the top floor offices of The Boston Brahmin. 73 Tremont overlooks the gold dome of the Massachusetts State House and Boston Common.

Fort Devens – is a United States military installation located in northern Massachusetts. It is the home to First Battalion, 25th Marine Regiment, headed up by Lt. Col. Bradlee. It is also the location of a Federal Bureau of Prisons Medical Facility.

Prescott Peninsula (1PP) – The largest land mass in the Quabbin Reservoir, Prescott Peninsula was completely surrounded by the reservoir and was largely unimproved except for an abandoned radio astronomy observatory where the old town of Prescott Center once stood. The observatory was renovated by the Quinn's to create a state-of-the-art bug-out location, known as 1 Prescott Peninsula, or 1PP. Bungalows were built around 1PP to house The Boston Brahmin and the soldiers from Fort Devens who were tasked with protecting 1PP.

Quabbin Reservoir – the largest body of water in the State of Massachusetts. Located in the central part of the state, it was formed by the creation of dams and dikes in the 1930s, and became federal government owned and was largely undeveloped. The largest land mass, Prescott Peninsula, was completely surrounded by the reservoir and was largely unimproved except for the abandoned radio astronomy observatory which was renovated to create 1PP.

Quabbin Visitor Center – located on the southernmost shore of the Quabbin Reservoir, the Quabbin Visitor Center is a federal style building built to house a museum, offices and a Massachusetts State Police barracks. It was commandeered by Ronald Archibald and the townspeople of Belchertown, MA.

Belchertown, MA – is a small town in Hampshire County on the western shore of the Quabbin Reservoir, west of Prescott Peninsula. The population of fifteen thousand was now reduced to five thousand. Citizen Corps Governor O'Brien appointed Ronald Archibald as the town chairman of the board of selectman.

99 High Street – the former offices of FEMA Regions One, and current offices of the new Citizen Corps Governor, James O'Brien. The building is located in downtown Boston, overlooking Boston Harbor to the east.

630 Washington – the site of the famous Liberty Tree. At the time of the Revolutionary War, a great elm tree stood in front of the grocery store located here. All the great political meetings of the

Sons of Liberty, and their insurgent arm known as the Mechanics, were held in this square. Now, it is the clandestine meeting place of the modern-day Mechanics.

PREVIOUSLY IN THE BOSTON BRAHMIN SERIES
BOOK ONE: THE LOYAL NINE

The Boston Brahmin series begins in December and the timeframe of *The Loyal Nine*, book one in The Boston Brahmin series, continues through April. Steven Sargent, in his capacity as Nomad, an Aegis deep-cover operative, undertakes several black-ops missions in Ukraine, Switzerland, and Germany. The purposes of the operations become increasingly suspect to Steven and his brother, Sarge. It is apparent that Steven's actual employer, John Morgan, is orchestrating a series of events as part of a grander scheme.

Sarge continues to teach at the Harvard Kennedy School of Government. He begins to make public appearances after publishing a *New York Times* bestseller *Choose Freedom or Capitulation: America's Sovereignty Crisis*. During this time, he rekindles his relationship with Julia Hawthorne, who is also celebrating national notoriety for her accomplishments at the *Boston Herald* newspaper. The two take a trip to Las Vegas for a convention and become unwilling participants in a cyber attack on the Las Vegas power grid. Throughout *The Loyal Nine*, Sarge and Julia observe the economic and societal collapse of America.

The unraveling of society in America is evident as the chasm between the haves and have-nots widens, resulting in hostilities between labor unions and their employers. There are unintended consequences of these actions, and numerous deaths are the result.

Racial tensions are on the rise across the country, and Boston becomes ground zero for social unrest when a beloved retired bus driver is beaten to death during the St. Patrick's Day festivities. In protest, a group of marchers descend upon Copley Square at the end of the Boston Marathon, resulting in a clash with police. The protestors are led by Jarvis *J-Rock* Rockwell, leader of the unified black gangs of Dorchester, Roxbury, and Mattapan in South Boston. The march quickly gets out of hand, and J-Rock's pregnant girlfriend is struck by the police, resulting in her death and the death of their unborn child.

The Quinn family—Donald, Susan and their young daughters— are caught up in an angry mob scene at a local mall, relating to the Black Lives Matter protests. Donald decides to accelerate the Loyal Nine's preparedness activities as he gets the sense America is on the brink of collapse.

The reader gets an inside look at the morning security briefings in the White House Situation Room. Katie O'Shea becomes a respected rising star within the intelligence community while solidifying her role as a conduit for information to John Morgan.

John Morgan continues to act as a world power broker. He manipulates geopolitical events for the financial gain of his wealthy associates—the Boston Brahmin. He carefully orchestrates the rise to national prominence of his daughter, Senator Abigail Morgan.

As a direct descendant of the Founding Fathers, Morgan is sickened to watch America descend into collapse. Morgan believes the country can return to its former greatness. He recognizes drastic measures may be required. He envisions a reset of sorts, but what that entails is yet to be determined.

Throughout *The Loyal Nine*, the Zero Day Gamers make a name for themselves in the hacktivist community as their skills and capabilities escalate from cyber vandalism to cyber ransom to cyber terror. Professor Andrew Lau and his talented graduate assistants create ingenious methods of cyber intrusion. At times, they question the morality of their activities. But the ransoms they extract from their victims are too lucrative to turn away.

The end game, the mission statement of the Zero Day Gamers, is succinct:

One man's gain is another man's loss; who gains and who loses is determined by who pays.

But who else loses in their deadly game? *Cyber Attack*, book two in The Boston Brahmin series, begins with the Zero Day Gamers testing their skills by taking over control of an American Airlines 757. Throughout *Cyber Attack*, the Zero Day Gamers conduct various cyber intrusions, including compromising a nuclear power plant in Jefferson City, Missouri. But one of the Gamers, in an attempt to impress a young lady, makes a mistake. His cyber snooping into the laptop of Abbie Morgan following the Democratic National Convention is discovered.

Meanwhile, over the summer, the Loyal Nine increase their preparedness activities. Through some legislative maneuvering, John Morgan acquires Prescott Peninsula at the Quabbin Reservoir in central Massachusetts. The Quabbin Reservoir is the largest body of water in the State of Massachusetts. Located in the central part of the state, it was formed by the creation of dams and dikes in the 1930s and became federal government owned and was largely undeveloped. Prescott Peninsula is completely surrounded by the reservoir and was largely unimproved except for an abandoned radio astronomy observatory where the old town of Prescott Center once stood. The entire acquisition encompasses nearly forty square miles. He immediately tasks Donald and Susan Quinn with renovating the property into a high-tech bug-out location for the Boston Brahmin.

While Donald, Susan, J.J., and Sabs focus their attention on Prescott Peninsula, Sarge is making a name for himself on the speaker's circuit as a straight-talk libertarian. His relationship with Julia Hawthorne has grown, and they continue to observe world events with an eye towards preparedness.

After the hack of Abbie's computer, through some excellent cyber forensics on the part of Katie O'Shea, the Zero Day Gamers are located and contacted by Steven Sargent and Malcolm Lowe, acting on behalf of John Morgan. The three orchestrate a ruse upon Andrew Lau and his team of cyber mercenaries for hire.

Morgan has determined that America is descending into collapse, both socially and economically, and is in need of a reset. The Zero Day Gamers are the perfect tool to accomplish this purpose.

Morgan has conducted several private meetings with the President, culminating with a face-to-face discussion in August. The two agree—a reset is necessary, and each will play a vital role in bringing America to its knees only to build the country back in their respective images. These two powerful political players navigate a complex game of chess, not realizing the unintended consequences on the people of America.

As *Cyber Attack* closes its final chapter in early September, Andrew Lau is forced to make a choice. Does he watch his young proteges die by a gunshot to the head at the hands of Morgan's men, or does he push the button that will result in the end of life as we know it?

PREVIOUSLY IN THE BOSTON BRAHMIN SERIES

BOOK THREE: MARTIAL LAW

Lau makes his choice, and his sophisticated cyber attack causes a cascading collapse of the Western and Eastern Interconnected Grid representing ninety percent of America's electricity. Only Texas, whose grid is not connected to the rest of the nation, is spared.

The Loyal Nine are scattered throughout the country. Each faces their own set of unique circumstances and challenges.

John Morgan, despite his meticulous, well-thought plans, makes one critical mistake—he loses track of his daughter's whereabouts. Despite his efforts, Morgan is unable to call off the cyber attack. This leads him to frantically arrange a trip to Florida to extract his daughter and bring her to safety. Just before, and immediately following the grid collapse, he communicates with Abbie's chief of staff to insist that Abbie meet him at Camp Blanding.

Abbie Morgan is in Tallahassee to give a campaign speech. Under the watchful eye of her ever-present protector, Drew Jackson, Abbie addresses a packed crowd at the Donald Tucker Civic Center. Then they are thrust into darkness. Within moments, thirteen thousand people are informed, via text messages and cell phone calls that America has been attacked and the power grid is down.

Drew, Abbie, and some of her entourage attempt to travel several hundred miles east to Camp Blanding, where John Morgan will meet them in his helicopter. First, they have to flee the inner city of Tallahassee, where nearly one hundred thousand people have congregated for the concert and a college football game.

During this night of terror, Drew and Abbie fight their way through looters, marauders, and the throes of Hurricane Danni. Within thirty miles of their destination, they run out of fuel near the small town of Lulu. This small community has been ravaged, not by the hurricane, but by escaped inmates from three of the worst prison facilities in Florida.

Daylight approaches, but the feeder bands of Hurricane Danni continue to obstruct visibility. With a borrowed car from an elderly victim of the inmates' violence, Drew and Abbie make their way to the rendezvous point. Within fifty yards of the helicopter, and safety, they are overrun by a group of attacking inmates. Drew pushes Abbie to the safety of her father, but he is savagely beaten and left for dead. As Drew reaches toward the helicopter, shouting, Abbie and Morgan leave him behind, much to the devastation of Abbie, who had fallen in love with Drew.

In Boston, Sarge and Julia are having drinks on the rooftop of 100 Beacon, having a deep conversation, when the transformers begin to explode. As the lights go out in waves throughout Boston, they immediately recognize this as a possible grid-down collapse event.

They immediately begin to implement their preparedness plan. First, they secure their perimeter. Next, they establish various means of communications and information gathering.

The first call Sarge makes is to John Morgan, who at the time is traveling to the heliport by private car. Morgan's orders are clear: gather up the Boston Brahmin and keep them safe. Sarge knows that this is his call to duty. But something else bothers him about the conversation. Morgan's words weigh heavily on his mind —*widespread, long-lasting.* For the past seven years, somehow Sarge knew this moment would come. What bothers him is the fact that so did John Morgan.

Sarge successfully gathers up the executive committee of the Boston Brahmin, but it does not go without incident. During his last pickup, Sarge is involved in a high-speed chase, with gunfire, through Chinatown. He unknowingly leads them right to the front door of 100 Beacon.

Steven and Katie are in Washington together, enjoying a few beers and shooting pool at a local hangout near the White House. As the grid collapses, they also recognize the need to get out of the major population center and return to Boston. But for Katie, work calls. She ignores her instructions to report to the Situation Room in the White House. She cannot, however, ignore the phone call from John Morgan with instructions to contact General Mason Sears, the chairman of the Joint Chiefs. Katie makes a choice to remain with Steven and loyal to her friends.

Katie is prepared for a bug-out scenario, and the two embark on a road trip through the Poconos toward Boston. They quickly learn that bugging out isn't easy, even when you are armed and prepared. They are attacked near a toll-booth exit and Steven is almost killed. Katie repels their assailants and nurses a badly injured Steven back to health.

But now their car is destroyed. Their gear and communications are lost. They only have their handguns and limited ammunition. They have to enter survival mode in a world without rule of law. Finding a car dealership, they commandeer a Range Rover and begin their trip northward. But another unexpected confrontation occurs.

Within miles of the last encounter, they see a young girl running in fear from a group of men who are chasing her through an industrial park. Steven and Katie give chase and save the girl, leaving four dead bodies in their wake.

At various junctures of their trip, the two meet people familiar with Sarge and his book. Some have tattoos of the Rebellious Flag—five red and four white vertical stripes. Several use the phrase *choose freedom* as a way of showing solidarity. Steven begins to see that Sarge's message is resonating throughout the country.

Finally, driving a FedEx delivery truck, the two make their way to Boston and the safety of 100 Beacon only to find it under assault by four Asian men. Steven, who quickly morphs into *Nomad*, despite his injuries, takes out the four attackers. The only thing standing between them and the top floors of 100 Beacon is a group of frightened residents firing wildly out of the front entrance. Not a problem for Nomad.

At Prescott Peninsula, the detailed preparedness plan implemented by Donald and Susan Quinn is on full display. They had successfully built a state-of-the-art bug-out facility on the old radio observatory site. J.J. and Sabina had grown close over the past several weeks and were officially a *couple*. Along with the Quinn's young girls, the four are enjoying a quiet Labor Day weekend away at the Quabbin Reservoir facility.

When the power goes out, the four are enjoying drinks and dinner in front of 1PP. Because of the lack of surrounding, ambient lighting, they don't realize the grid is down. Once they discover the situation, they begin to implement their preparedness plan.

Their first arrivals come in the form of the Morgan Sikorsky helicopter. Abbie is still upset over the loss of Drew and mourns for several days. As she calms down, Donald introduces Abbie and John Morgan to the sophisticated 1PP facility, which includes a gold and silver vault worth hundreds of millions of dollars.

Brad beefs up security at Prescott Peninsula. After a visit from a representative of Homeland Security, he senses that the President is about to declare martial law. Brad goes rogue and rallies the Mechanics led by Gunny Falcone, Chief Warrant Officer Shore, and First Lieutenant Branson. They systematically divert assets and like-minded troops to Prescott Peninsula. They are nearly at company strength in gear and numbers.

In the process of building up the military assets at Prescott Peninsula, Brad has to send a platoon to Boston. He gathers up the Boston Brahmin from 100 Beacon to take them safely to 1PP. Sabs, over J.J.'s objection, takes up the slack and joins the security detail at the gated entrance to the Quabbin Reservoir complex. In a confrontation with locals, she is shot.

J.J., with the assistance of Susan and Donald, tries valiantly to save his new love, to no avail. Sadly, Sabs dies on the table, together with his unborn baby, of which he has no knowledge. Susan and Donald wrestle with telling him, but the arrival of the Boston Brahmin and the upcoming address by the President puts the issue off for another day.

On the fifth night following the collapse, the President is set to speak to the nation through whatever means of communications are available. Susan overhears a conversation between two of the Boston Brahmin that leads her to believe there is something nefarious going on. Abbie, who has been having nightmares, finally comes to the realization of what happened the morning they left Drew behind. He was shouting, "He knew, he knew." *What did that mean?*

The President addresses the nation, but not with an uplifting message of hope and perseverance. It is divisive, condemning, and declarative. Through executive orders, the President quickly sets up a massive militaristic occupational force called the *Citizen Corps*. In conjunction with regional FEMA governors, the Citizen Corps will establish local Citizen Corps Councils that will fall under the control of the President and FEMA.

Then the President instructs General Sears to read the Declaration of Martial Law, which suspends the constitution and essentially revokes all freedoms guaranteed to American citizens by the Bill of Rights. *Freedom, liberty, and independence are lost.*

After General Sears reads the declaration, he receives a phone call from John Morgan. The four words that General Sears hears from John Morgan are plain and simple—yet chilling.

The end begins tomorrow.

As book four, False Flag opens, Sarge stands atop 100 Beacon alone, reflecting on the President's Declaration of Martial Law. In just a matter of days, the country was rapidly descending into collapse. He was surprised at how rapidly the President reacted to the events, and the level of governmental overreach contained in the Declaration.

But Sarge's thoughts were interrupted by a series of massive explosions as the Kendall Station Power Plant malfunctioned. The blasts rocked the city, and caused the collapse of the Longfellow Bridge. The deaths and casualties were numerous.

Julia insisted on helping the injured by volunteering at Massachusetts General Hospital. Unknowingly, she and Sarge assisted with a severely burned patient—Andrew Lau. Later, Katie and Steven discover that Lau is alive.

Prescott Peninsula, and 1PP, was now inhabited by The Boston Brahmin and their wives, the Quinn family, Abbie, and a platoon of Marines dispatched by Brad. J.J. was still distraught over the loss of Sabs, and insisted upon going back to 100 Beacon. News of the Kendall Station explosion gave him an excuse to leave.

As part of the President's Declaration of Martial Law, the former

FEMA regions were re-designated to fall under the purview of the newly created Council of Governors appointed by the President. With the expansion of the Citizen Corps, the President named former Carmen's Union President, James O'Brien, as the new governor of Region One, which consisted of Massachusetts, and upper New England. His offices were in the FEMA location at 99 High Street overlooking the Boston Harbor.

O'Brien is thrilled at his new appointment, but not out of pride. He is an opportunist. He sees the collapse as an opportunity to enrich himself, and his friends. He also intends to right many perceived social wrongs. He surrounds himself with men willing to work outside the law to achieve this purpose.

The White House assigns for Federal Protective Services Agent, Joe Pearson, to be the liaison between O'Brien and the President. Pearson, who has had heated conversations with Brad on two prior occasions, is prepared to assist O'Brien achieve his goals.

However, for the more nefarious jobs, O'Brien enlists the employment of an old friend, and notorious Union thug, Marion La Rue. La Rue orchestrated the walkout of the union transit workers during the St. Patrick's Day event last March. The walkout inadvertently led to the death of a black man named Pumpsie Jones, which caused social unrest throughout the city.

Pearson is tasked with training forty-four of O'Brien's trusted union associates. The first order of business is to raid all of the Massachusetts Guard Armories across the state. Via inside information, The Loyal Nine are aware of the details of the raids, and provide a surprise for O'Brien's men. Throughout the night, Steven and Katie coordinate ambushes of O'Brien's men using The Mechanics. They apprehend O'Brien's men and imprison them at Fort Devens under Brad's watchful eye.

O'Brien, thinking the men betrayed his trust, looked for an alternative to carry out his plans. He instructs La Rue to arrange a meeting with Joaquin Guzman, head of the El Salvadoran MS-13 gang, and Jarvis Rockwell, a/k/a J-Rock, heads of the unified black gangs in Boston. Their task is a simple one — loot. They are provided assurances that no one under O'Brien's command will impede them as they enter the wealthiest neighborhoods of Boston and take what they want.

Meanwhile, The Loyal Nine seek out an ally of their own to counteract O'Brien. They meet with John Willis — The White Devil, head of the Asian gangs in Chinatown. A celebrity of sorts, having been interviewed extensively by Rolling Stone magazine, Willis is hesitant to to deal with Sarge, Julia and Steven at first. But an alliance is formed for the purposes of thwarting MS-13 and the black gangs of Dorchester, Mattapan, and Roxbury.

The Loyal Nine also begin to organize their modern day insurgent arm — The Mechanics. Meeting under cover of darkness at the location of the original Liberty Tree, 630 Washington Street, Sarge and Steven rally their trusted militia. Steeped in historic precedent as the predecessors to the Sons of Liberty, The Mechanics are ordinary Bostonians who are answering the call of duty to protect and defend the Constitution and the United States.

At 1PP, Morgan, who is exhibiting signs of stress, grows concerned that the President is ignoring his phone calls. Morgan advises the President that it is time to consider rebuilding the country but he is rebuked by the President, who responds "You'll make your money now let me finish what I started." The President is surly and combative, prompting Morgan to contact General Sears suggesting the nation was in a constitutional crisis. He seeks to remove the President from office, but Sears refuses such drastic action as a coup d'état.

Following the shooting death of Sabs at the front gate, the residents of Belchertown, located just west of Prescott Peninsula, became enraged. They insisted their newly appointment Chairman of the Board of Alderman, Ronald Archibald, take action. For Belchertown, supplies are quickly running out and there haven't been any new provisions from the Federal government in weeks. They are panicking. Partly out of revenge for the death of their neighbor, but mostly out of need, they concoct a plan to attack the inhabitants of Prescott Peninsula and confiscate their provisions.

O'Brien begins to suspect that Brad is working against him. After a brief period of mistrust (courtesy of Brad) in Agent Pearson, O'Brien enlists Pearson's support in contacting the White House for reinforcements in the form of a United Nations occupying force. Along with La Rue and Pearson, O'Brien watches as tanks, and artillery, together with thousands of U.N. soldiers roll off the ships lined up in Boston Harbor. "Boys, now I've got my army," he quips.

The Loyal Nine come together at Prescott Peninsula for the first time since the cyber attack. Their first order of business is trade notes on the events which led up to the power outage, and to make a determination of who is responsible. The conclusion becomes obvious — John Morgan.

Without notice to Abbie, Sarge is tasked with confronting Morgan with these facts. While Abbie and Steven watch, Morgan and his godson, Sarge, engage in an epic debate about the use of the cyber attack as a means to reset America from its downward path into economic and social collapse.

As the argument intensifies, Morgan suffers a stroke. J.J. is called in to assist and is successful in savings Morgan's life. After surviving the ordeal, and contemplating his future, Morgan calls in his trusted friends, Cabot and Lowell. Then Sarge is summoned to Morgan's bungalow. The conversation went like this:

"Come, sit with me, Henry," said Morgan, who took a deep breath before continuing. "I promised your father that you would do great things. I promised to be your guardian, your mentor, and protector. For all of these years, I have ushered you through life, keeping a watchful eye over you as if you were my son."

"Yes, sir, I know," said Sarge, who was welling up with emotion.

"I am not a dying man, but I am tired. A tired man can do nothing easily, and we still have work to do, Henry." Morgan attempted to push himself up again, and he was assisted by Sarge.

Morgan continued as he addressed the room. "I thank God that I have done my duty in upholding the ideals and vision of our forefathers. I've done all of the business I am capable of doing on this earth." He turned his attention to Sarge.

"Patriotism is not enough, Henry. I see compassion in you I never had. You recognize that our fellow man must not be forgotten."

Morgan again looked into the faces of the Boston Brahmin. "I intend to live, my friends. You can't dispatch me that easily.

"We must finish what we started, but it requires a younger man. It needs a different vision, one capable of looking beyond the creation of wealth, but to the creation of a new nation. My role now is that of teacher—the grand master to the student." He turned his attention to Sarge and struggled as he reached out to grasp his shoulder.

"It is time for me to step aside. The Boston Brahmin must be led by the next generation of patriots. Henry, I am entrusting you to take the reins and accept your destiny as the new head of the Boston Brahmin."

The Mechanics begins now …

EPIGRAPH

An invisible army spread itself over nearly the whole of Spain like a
net from whose meshes there was no escape for the French soldier
who for a moment left his column or his garrison. Without
uniforms and without weapons, apparently the guerrillas escaped
easily from the column that pursued them, and it frequently
happened that the troops sent out to do battle with them, passed
through their midst without perceiving them.
~ French Count Miot de Melito, 1814

We attack an enemy who is invisible, fluid, uncatchable.
~ Col. Roger Trinquier, WWII

That's the insurgency strategy. You can't fight against an unseen
enemy.
~ Professor Bruce Hoffman, Georgetown University

Be so subtle that you are invisible. Be so mysterious that you are intangible. Then you will control your rival's fate.
~ Sun Tzu, *The Art of War*

Now you're messin' with a son of a bitch.
~ Dan McCafferty, Scottish Minstrel, 1975

Yea, though I walk through the valley of the shadow of death I shall fear no evil, because I am the meanest son-of-a-bitch in the valley.
~ George S. Patton

Pride goes before destruction, a haughty spirit before a fall.
~ Proverbs 16:18

PART I

OCTOBER

CHAPTER ONE

Saturday, October 1
1:11 a.m.
Prescott Peninsula
Quabbin Reservoir, Massachusetts

It was now October, and the autumn chill of the New England air began to set in. So did reality. The fire, dying down now with only a few glowing embers, had served its purpose. It provided warmth, light, and a distraction when the voices of his friends needed to be compartmentalized away from his thoughts.

"It is time for me to step aside. The Boston Brahmin must be led by the next generation of patriots. Henry, I am entrusting you to take the reins and accept your destiny as the new head of the Boston Brahmin."

Sarge's mind replayed the words of John Morgan over and over again. *Entrusting. Destiny.* He knew this day would come. But not now, and certainly not under these circumstances.

Sarge finished off the last of the Moulin-à-Vent Beaujolais and studied the red Solo cup as he chuckled to himself. *A hundred-dollar bottle of wine in a ten-cent cup. King Henry the VIII, I am not. Where's my silver chalice?*

His thoughts were interrupted by Donald, who tossed his cup into the fire as he slid off the top of the picnic table. "Well, guys, it's been real, but I'm gonna turn in."

Sarge lifted himself out of the Adirondack chair and hugged his friend. In normal times, he would lean on Donald heavily as he managed the massive global financial holdings of the Boston Brahmin. He doubted his life would ever be *normal* again.

"Good night, buddy," said Sarge as he hugged Donald. "It's been a helluva day."

"No kidding." Donald laughed. "There's a lot to talk about, and I'm sure Mr. Morgan will want to be a part of our conversations if he's up to it. Listen, there's a whole lot more that I don't know than what I do know. Make sense?"

"It's pretty damned overwhelming," replied Sarge. "Where the hell do we start?"

"Let's not worry about it now," Donald replied. "Global finances are not a high priority at the moment. We'll get a handle on things on the fly."

Sarge patted his friend on the back and led him out of the circle of chairs that surrounded the fire. They walked toward the steps of 1PP.

Sarge leaned in and whispered into Donald's ear, "Do you think he'll tell us everything?" One of the lingering doubts in Sarge's mind was whether the secretive John Morgan was truly ready to turn over the reins of leadership and power.

"He has to sooner or later," replied Donald. "This was inevitable. It's just that the circumstances suck."

Sarge stopped and looked Donald in the eyes. "I'm gonna need you to guide me through this. I can only imagine how vast their holdings are."

Donald laughed and replied, "No worries, Sarge. It's only money. If you squander a few hundred million here and there, who cares, right?"

"Thanks for the vote of confidence, *Mr. Quinn*," Sarge said, using his best impression of Morgan. "Good night."

"Good night, Henry," Donald replied, using his best John Morgan Brahmin accent.

Sarge shook his head and returned to the remainder of the Loyal Nine gathered around the dying fire—Julia, Steven, and Katie.

"There's a little more wine, honey," said Julia as he approached. She held up the last of the bottles the group had polished off during the evening. There might be a few headaches in the morning from the celebration. Steven had suggested popping a few corks of champagne, but Sarge quickly put that idea to rest. He was not sure whether this was an event to celebrate. Not only because of the stroke that led to the decision. But Sarge also knew that the eyes of the Boston Brahmin would be upon him during this period of transition. Sarge was accepting his new role reluctantly, and a champs-fueled celebration was inappropriate.

"I'm good, thanks," he replied. He was tired and desperately wanted to speak with Julia alone. They'd been surrounded since the announcement earlier, and he needed his best friend to analyze the events with him.

Sarge eased back into the chair and sat in silence, staring at the last of the burning embers. Inwardly, he hoped that Steven and Katie would go to bed.

The quiet had the desired effect. "Well, I guess we'll hit the bunks too," announced Steven. He stood and helped Katie out of her chair. Sarge started to rise and Steven stopped him. "No, please sit, your highness. Allow me, your humble knave, to kiss the ring of the king once more." Steven bent on one knee in front of Sarge and attempted to kiss his hand.

"Screw you, knave!" Sarge swatted at Steven's head several times, and he easily avoided the blows like Sugar Ray Leonard in the boxing ring. The girls laughed, clearly enjoying the playful banter between the brothers.

"As you wish, your highness," said Steven. "Will you join us on the hunt in the morning? We are in search of the wildebeest who roams the forest." Steven stood and struck a *Game of Thrones* pose.

"Maybe," replied Sarge.

"Or perhaps your highness would prefer to sleep in with the fair maiden here and create an heir to the throne?"

"Away with you, knave, before I give the order." Sarge laughed. "Off with his head!" Sarge stood and gave his brother a hug. He also hugged Katie.

"Congratulations, Sarge," she whispered in his ear. "Good luck." Katie broke their embrace and she walked off into the darkness toward the bungalows. Sarge smiled and nodded at his brother, who was standing awkwardly alone. He watched them for a moment as Steven gradually turned to a ghostly figure disappearing into the darkness.

CHAPTER TWO

Saturday, October 1
1:30 a.m.
The Quabbin Visitor Center
Quabbin Reservoir, Massachusetts

Ronald Archibald paced the floor in front of his handpicked lieutenants. He had no military or law enforcement experience, but he stood alone as the leader of the Belchertown raiding party. Joseph Pearson had offered little assistance in the planning of the raid on Prescott Peninsula. The raid was Archibald's baby, and he intended it to be a success.

Archibald had successfully recruited and trained nearly three hundred men for the task. Lack of intelligence about the current inhabitants of Prescott Peninsula was a concern, but he was confident in his ability to overrun them with overwhelming force and surprise.

His troops, as he called them, consisted of ordinary citizens from the surrounding areas. They included the local pharmacist, an auto mechanic, an unemployed car salesman, and a retired postal worker. They were different in most respects, from their occupations to their race and gender. But they all had one thing in common—they were hungry, for food and revenge.

The day before, Archibald had whipped them into a hatred-driven frenzy. The residents of Belchertown were now convinced that the enemy consisted of the unknown faces on Prescott Peninsula. These mysterious opponents had food and supplies to save their families. Archibald convinced his *troops* to risk their lives to attack and claim the supplies for the benefit of the town. Archibald did not reveal to his troops, however, that the enemy was likely made up of seasoned military personnel. That minor detail would have doomed the mission to failure before it started.

"Okay, gentlemen, let's get down to business," announced Archibald, calling the group to attention. "Let's take a look at the map and go over the plan one last time."

He grabbed one of the men and whispered, "Raise the Allen brothers on the radio. Tell them we're on time. They'll know what to do."

The assistant nodded his head and left the room.

Archibald turned his attention to the room and walked in front of a bulletin board hung on a wall. Above it, on a particle board shelf, sat a stuffed beaver, an owl, and an otter. Under their watchful eyes, Archibald rapped his knuckles on the map.

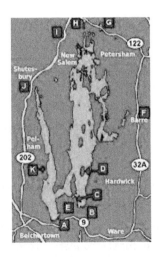

"We've gone over this, but this will be the last time, as we'll be giving the order to start this party. Sunrise is around 5:00 a.m. and everyone needs to be in position."

Archibald turned and looked at his men. The murmur of nervous conversation died down when he spoke. He pointed to the letter *A* on the map.

"This is the Visitor's Center, which will be used as our fallback position and for wounded triage."

The group began to whisper again, and Archibald quieted them down. He could sense their trepidation. "Gentlemen, make no mistake, we will take some casualties. I hope not, obviously, but for our families to survive, we must take risks. In the lobby, we have our most capable health care providers and all the medical supplies we could muster. While the success of our mission is paramount, the lives of our friends and neighbors are just as important. If you or the man next to you gets wounded, come back here immediately for medical attention."

Archibald laid out the plan, first pointing to the letter *E*. "I will be taking up a command and control position here, on Quabbin Hill, at the Observatory Tower. Those of you assigned to the power boats will convene here, at the launch that I've marked as letter *C*. Gentlemen, you will be the second phase of the attack."

He moved across the map to point to the left side identified as Pelham. "Just south of Pelham, at letter *K*, the pontoon boats will be at the ready to cross this narrow stretch of the lake onto the west shore of Prescott Peninsula. You will be the third phase of the attack."

Next, he slapped his hands at the top of the map, on top of the letter *J*. "This is where we get their attention—the front gate. Jimmy Fulks was murdered there. The front gate is where the battle begins."

The men in the room cheered, clearly ready for the task at hand. He allowed the celebration to go on, and then he moved to calm them. He pointed to the other letters on the map designated *B*, *F*, *G*, *H*, and *I*. "We have established roadblocks at these remaining locations. We don't want them to be able to call in any reinforcements. *Mano a mano*, right, gentlemen?"

"Yes, sir!" they shouted as they patted each other on the back.

"Okay, before I send you out to get into position, does anyone have any questions?"

One hand rose in the rear of the room. "I do, sir."

"What is it?" asked Archibald.

"We've never discussed letter *D* on the map. What is that for?"

Archibald looked at the tiny island in the middle of the Quabbin Reservoir and grinned. "I've got a special surprise in store for these people, and our men who will be carrying it out have been in place for a couple of days. It has already been set into motion, my friends."

CHAPTER THREE

Saturday, October 1
1:35 a.m.
Mount Lizzie
Quabbin Reservoir, Massachusetts

"Showtime," said Will Allen to his younger brother, M.C. He was cold and tired. They had spent forty-eight hours camping on the Quabbin Reservoir. Their first stop was Mount Zion to their north, gathering up a skiff full of timber rattlesnakes. The Allens camped on the island the first night, then in the early morning hours of Friday, they rowed past Walker Hill and along the eastern shore of the Quabbin Reservoir until they reached Mount Lizzie.

Prior to 1939 when the flooding of the Quabbin Reservoir began, Mount Lizzie was the home of the small town of Greenwich. The oldest of the four towns flooded by the Quabbin Reservoir project, Greenwich was incorporated in 1754 under land grants to immigrants of Scottish and Irish heritage following the Indian Wars.

Once known as the Plantation of the Quabbin, the name of a revered Nipmuc Indian, the town was renamed for the Scottish

Duke of Greenwich. This was a once thriving town, boasting the first church in the area, the first post office, and one of the first public libraries. Progress, in the form of the Quabbin Reservoir, flooded the historic town eight days after its one hundred and eighty-fourth birthday.

Today, it was one of the smallest islands in the reservoir, but it stood the tallest at an elevation of nearly nine hundred feet. During the day on Friday, the Allen brothers made camp at the summit of Mount Lizzie and observed the activities on the eastern shoreline of Prescott Peninsula through binoculars. They kept their boats and the cargo hidden from view on the east side of the island. They also kept quiet, as voices carried on the water. They were only a mile away from the shore of Prescott Peninsula and the uninhabited Little Quabbin Hill island to their southwest.

"I'm ready," said M.C. "I'm more than ready to get this over with and get home to the missus. This better be worth it, brother."

"It will be," replied Will. "You're hungry, aren't you?"

"Yeah, hungry enough to eat them rattlers."

"Then let's do this," said Will. "It'll take a couple of hours to make our way around the island. Thank God there ain't a moon tonight. We'll use the dark skies and Little Quabbin Hill for cover. Then we'll work our way up towards that point." He directed his brother's attention to the pronounced stretch of shore that was nearest Little Quabbin Hill.

"How far do we have to carry the snakes before we release them?"

"I'm not sure, probably a mile or so," replied Will. "It'll take us a couple of trips. C'mon. We need to get in position for the signal."

The two men folded up their camping gear and headed down the eastern slope of Mount Zion to their flat-bottom aluminum boats, which were pulled onto the rocky shore. Although their skiff had a trolling motor, in order to approach undetected, they would have to row the entire distance—not an easy feat when pulling another boat full of dozens of large rattlesnakes.

Over the next two hours, they made their way across the half-mile stretch of lake undetected. The Allens sought cover on the banks of Little Quabbin Hill while they rested. They could easily row the last few hundred yards in less than fifteen minutes. Their orders were to wait for the signal.

M.C., out of boredom, broke the silence. "How will we know when it's time to get started? What's the signal?"

"Don't worry. We'll know."

CHAPTER FOUR

Saturday, October 1
1:52 a.m.
Prescott Peninsula
Quabbin Reservoir, Massachusetts

Julia broke Sarge out of his half-conscious, hypnotic state. He got a chill and attempted to shake it off.

"Honey, are you ready for bed?" asked Julia. "Maybe we should produce an heir to the throne?"

Sarge rolled his neck and released some tension. He took a deep breath, exhaled and sat back in the chair. He realized that he had been on edge all day. This was his first opportunity to relax—alone with Julia.

"Let's polish off this bottle and talk," he said.

"Are you okay?" asked Julia. She poured the last of the wine into her cup and handed it to him. She reached over into Katie's chair and grabbed Sarge a blanket. The temperature was in the upper forties.

Sarge smiled and reached over to hold her hand. "Yeah, it's been a long day and my brain is tired. I've wanted to talk with you alone, and we've never had the chance."

"Suddenly, you're a very popular guy."

"I know, Julia, and my mind has been racing all day. I've known Mr. Morgan my entire life, but I've never really contemplated what he does every day." Sarge covered himself with the blanket and took another sip of wine. He allowed the fruit flavors to soak into his mouth before swallowing it. Julia studied him and allowed him to continue.

"Am I still a professor? Do I go to work every day at 73 Tremont? Does any of that matter anymore now that the country has been thrown back into the 1800s?"

Julia reached for her wine and emptied the cup, which she put in the pile of empty wine bottles. "No wonder you're brain-dead. It's difficult to answer any of those questions or establish a game plan when the world is collapsing around us. Since the cyber attack, we've been *reacting*. Right?"

Sarge allowed the statement to soak in. For the past four weeks, their lives had been a whirlwind of activity—acting in response to a particular situation rather than creating it or controlling it.

"That's a great point," said Sarge. "Our survival instincts kicked in, and we hunkered down. Fate keeps throwing us curveballs and …"

"We hit it right back at 'em," added Julia, finishing his sentence.

Sarge nodded in agreement. "It may be this way for a while, but at some point in time, we need to rebuild our lives." He stretched out his body and clasped his hands behind his head. "I've had quite a bit of wine, and as you know, I can get real philosophical at times."

"Really? Nah." Julia laughed.

"You know me," said Sarge, adding in his best Southern drawl, "I do my best thinkin' when I'm drinkin'."

Julia nudged the pile of empty wine bottles and laughed.

"Hey, I didn't drink all of those!" protested Sarge. She reached over, and he held her hands, which were soft and warm. "You and I have always talked in terms of fate, destiny, and even karma."

"That's true."

"I guess, deep inside, I've known this was my destiny," said Sarge. He stared up at the stars. The new moon allowed faint objects such as galaxies and star clusters to shine unimpeded. *We're such an insignificant part of the universe, yet we are the center of our own.*

"You're not afraid, are you?" asked Julia, indicating unease for the first time that day.

Sarge quickly eased her concerns. "Oh, no, not at all," he replied reassuringly. "I've got a job to do and a whole lot of lives to be responsible for. I'm not sure where to start."

Julia was briefly quiet and then spoke. "Sarge, Mr. Morgan is not going to leave you out here flailing on your own. It could be worse, you know. He could be dead."

This reality struck Sarge like a ton of bricks. *He could be dead.*

"I'd really be crappin' my pants then," Sarge said with a chuckle.

"Sarge, he's going to be very supportive of you. You're the chosen one, so to speak. He will not set you up for failure."

"I know, I know. It also seems like the others were on board. Cabot and Lowell gave me the impression they were pleased with Mr. Morgan's decision."

"I agree," said Julia. "As I talked with them, and especially Mrs. Lowell, they were enthusiastic in their praise for you and your abilities. Mrs. Lowell hasn't been happy during this entire ordeal until now."

"How about our guys, the Quinns, J.J.?" Sarge's voice trailed off.

Julia let go of his hand and sat up in her chair. "They love *and respect* you, Sarge. We've never had a defined hierarchy, but it was always assumed that you were our fearless leader."

"Ha-ha, the fearless leader who is over here shakin' in his boots," said Sarge. He laughed with Julia at his self-deprecation.

"I think it's natural to be apprehensive, Sarge. But you know everyone will support you as you take on this new role. We all have our roles, and now you have the ability to be the final decision maker on everything. You hold the power and the purse strings."

"Julia, I'll control billions of dollars in assets worldwide. I'll be able to pick up the phone and call world leaders. Hell, Morgan has a direct line to the President. All of that power and responsibility rests squarely on my shoulders now." Sarge also sat up in his chair and started to contemplate the magnitude of his new role.

"We can do great things, my love," encouraged Julia. "Let it all soak in and don't look at this as some daunting, overwhelming task. You've been given the unique opportunity to shape world events in your vision."

Sarge thought about this. *What is my worldview? I used to lecture about this at Harvard. Now I feel like Sarah Palin in her first ABC interview with Charlie Gibson—dumbfounded.*

"Absolutely," said Sarge. "Our country, hell, the world faces a serious catastrophe. I'm taking the reins of the Boston Brahmin at an opportune time. I don't think we can solve this crisis by using the same way of thinking that helped put us here in the first place."

"Now you're talkin', Sarge. You have to be optimistic about this opportunity you've been given. Besides, you can always cry about it later."

CHAPTER FIVE

Saturday, October 1
4:52 a.m.
Prescott Peninsula
Quabbin Reservoir, Massachusetts

"Alpha One, this is Bravo Two. We've got a vehicle approaching the front gate, sir," said Corporal David Morrell into his comms. Morrell led a six-man patrol that guarded the front gate and perimeter fence on a twenty-four-hour basis. Because of the unusual hour and the heightened state of awareness his team was practicing, Morrell felt it necessary to notify his immediate superior officer, Chief Warrant Officer Kyle Shore.

"Roger, Bravo Two. Is it hostile?" asked Shore, still groggy from the early wake-up call.

"Unknown, sir," replied Morrell. "The vehicle is approaching slowly. I've called in two men from the shore patrol to assist, if necessary."

"Roger that, Bravo Two. Stay on mission. Alpha One en route," replied Shore.

The vehicle came to a halt one hundred yards from the

protective cover of the HESCO barriers at the front gate. Morrell gestured for the two soldiers to flank him left and right and take cover positions. They waited. In the distance, he heard the sounds of four-wheelers approaching.

"This is private property!" shouted Morrell to the stopped and idling vehicle. Because the headlights blinded him, he couldn't discern the make or model, although it appeared to be a pickup or SUV.

He shouted again, "Stop. This is private property. Exit the vehicle with your hands over your head and state your business!" There was no response.

Then the vehicle began to roll forward, slowly crunching the gravel under its tires. The truck was closing on the entrance. *Seventy-five yards. Fifty yards.*

Morrell crouched lower behind the barrier. He shook his head and frowned.

"I don't like this," he mumbled to himself. The four-wheelers were approaching from his rear. The truck was inching closer. He had to make a decision.

"Light it …" he yelled until the sound of his voice was muted by a massive explosion. The pickup truck's payload of fifty-five-gallon drums containing oil, gasoline, and shrapnel was detonated by shots fired from a high-power rifle in the distance. The first two rounds punctured the drums, and the third round ignited the mixture.

A deadly barrage of broken nails, screws, bolts, and ball bearings tore through the gatehouse, obliterating the windows. The soldier closest to the gatehouse was killed instantly. The approaching Marines were knocked off their four-wheelers from the blast. The soldier to Morrell's right was safely behind the fortified mesh container designed by HESCO for this type of blast.

Morrell received shrapnel wounds to his left arm, which he'd used to shield his face from the blast. He was bleeding but was able to continue.

"Alpha One, this is Bravo Two," shouted Morrell into his radio. He repeated, "Alpha One, this is Bravo Two."

"Roger, Bravo Two. I'm two klicks out," responded Shore. The radio erupted with activity. Orders were directed to all of the patrols as responses came fast and with a clear sense of urgency.

"Charlie Two, this is Charlie Six. Over."

"Go for Six," a voice squelched back on the radio.

"This is Charlie Six. Vehicle approaching through the woods at fence post five. Repeat. Vehicle approaching at fence post five. Over."

Morrell crawled to check on the young private who survived the blast. He was huddled behind the barrier, holding onto his M4 with a death grip.

"Are you hurt, soldier?" asked Morrell. The sound of several four-wheelers could be heard in the distance.

"Not too bad, sir," replied the young man. He wiped the blood off his face with the sleeve of his wounded left arm.

"Let me see this," said Morrell as he examined the arm. The soldier winced with pain as he turned his arm over and back. "You'll be fine, soldier. I've got the same problem." He showed the young man his shrapnel-torn left arm.

Morrell looked to his left and saw Shore dismount from the ATV and approach him in a low crouch. He could see the worry on his CO's face. Things weren't right. Shore checked in by radio with the other patrols along the front gate.

More four-wheelers were approaching from 1PP, as it was all hands on deck. Shore instructed them to reinforce the western boundary of the front gate. He turned his attention to Morrell.

"What happened?" he asked.

"Sir, the truck stopped about a hundred meters out," replied Morrell. "I instructed it to stop, and then it began rolling forward again."

"I thought I heard gunfire," said Shore as he continued to look nervously back and forth.

"Yes, sir. They punctured and then detonated an explosive device contained in the back. It was dark, sir, and I was blinded by the headlights."

They were interrupted by the squawk of the radio. "This is Bravo Six. Vehicle is approaching slowly. Now half a click. Permission to open fire!" the soldier shouted.

"Hold your position," replied Shore. "They are out of range at this point. Draw your aim on the vehicle's tires. Repeat. Shoot the tires."

"Roger that, Alpha One. Range now two hundred meters, sir."

"Open fire. Shoot the tires!" yelled Shore. The rapid fire of the soldier's automatic weapon filled the air. Then another explosion lit up the sky to the west, and a fireball quickly ascended above the tree line.

"Bravo Six, this is Alpha One," said Shore into his radio. Morrell caught Shore's glance. There was silence for a stressful moment. Shore repeated the request. "Bravo Six, Alpha One. Over."

"Go for Six."

"Sitrep."

"Vehicle exploded, sir. Roughly two hundred meters from our position. No casualties, sir."

Shore leaned against the barrier and responded, "Stay frosty, Bravo Six."

"Roger that, Bravo Six out."

More soldiers arrived at the front gate, and Shore quickly dispatched them along the front entrance. The sun was rising in the east and visibility would improve.

The wounded soldier spoke up. "Sirs, you might want to take a look at this."

Morrell and Shore turned their attention from the radio and looked over the HESCO barriers. There was movement across the clearing and beyond the still-burning skeleton of the pickup truck. Armed men were scurrying from tree to tree, taking up positions across the gravel entry road.

Shore alerted the others on the front gate patrol. "Bravo Six, Charlie Three, this is Alpha One. Over."

"Charlie Three. Go, Alpha One."

"Go for Six."

"We're being approached by hostiles," instructed Shore. "We are under assault. Lethal force authorized. Repeat. Lethal force authorized."

"Roger that. Charlie Three out."

"This is Bravo Six. Hostiles approaching—" ***crack crack crack*** "—moving through the woods ... four-wheelers approaching. Open fire!"

More Marines were arriving from 1PP, and they were immediately directed to lend support to Bravo Six along the western fence line.

"Sir," interrupted the soldier, grabbing Morrell's attention. "They're moving closer." Morrell looked up and saw the approaching armed men moving quickly through the woods and into the clearing.

Shore gave his orders. "Open fire!"

Morrell lifted his M16 over the barrier. The large weapon thumped in a quick report as it poured round after round into the approaching attackers. The bullets tore through their bodies, leaving bloody masses of death in the gravel. The young soldier followed his lead and began firing upon the remaining assailants hidden in the woods. Their rounds ripped flesh and shredded the bark of the trees that were being used for cover.

Humvees were approaching from the south as Shore moved away from Morrell to greet them. From the turret, a gunner lit up the forest across the way. The fifty-caliber rounds from the Ma Deuce ripped saplings in half and cut down the retreating men with ease. Shore called for them to cease fire, and additional troops were posted along the two-mile long perimeter fence and the front gate. Except for the smoldering trucks and the smell of spent rounds, the scene became eerily still.

But then a high-pitched whine could be heard in the distance. Morrell looked up, thinking it was a drone. The noise grew louder.

"Sir, are those drones?" asked Morrell.

Shore looked up and then around their perimeter. "No," he replied. "Those are boats!"

CHAPTER SIX

Saturday, October 1
5:01 a.m.
Prescott Peninsula, 1PP
Quabbin Reservoir, Massachusetts

It was Rebecca's scream and not the blast from the front gate that woke Donald from a deep sleep. His dreams had been vivid lately, and the subconscious sound of an explosion would not necessarily stir him awake. The shrieks of his seven-year-old daughter did.

"Susan, did you hear that?" asked Donald, still groggy and unsure of what happened.

Now Penny was awake and holding her sister on the fold-out sofa bed across the room in their small bungalow. Both were crying. Susan bolted upright and immediately ran to comfort their daughters.

"It sounded like a bomb," replied Susan. The girls' crying increased as Donald quickly got dressed. He strapped on his leg holster, which contained his .45.

"Stay here." Donald leaned down in front of the girls and wiped the tears from their cheeks. "I need you guys to calm down and be big girls, okay?"

They both nodded, but the tears continued to flow. Donald touched Susan's cheek and lifted a finger to his lips to be quiet.

He exited into the crisp, dewy morning at the same time Steven and Katie emerged from their bungalow. Sarge was already in the clearing, instructing Abbie and several of the Boston Brahmin to return to their tiny houses.

It was still dark, but the sun was peering over Mount Zion to their east. It was also quiet except for the sounds of four-wheelers and crunching gravel in the distance.

"Sounded like a bomb exploded near the front gate," said Sarge.

"Roger that, bro," added Steven. "We need to get everyone inside the bunker."

"I agree," said Donald. Four partially dressed Marines emerged from their sleeping quarters. "But first, we need to get 1PP secured."

"I'm on it." Steven jumped in. He turned to the Marines. "Listen up, I want everyone suited, booted, and strapped. Full kits, gentlemen."

The Marines quickly returned to their quarters and grabbed their tactical vests filled with six thirty-round magazines and body armor plate inserts that could stop an AK-47 round at point-blank range. They included a drop pouch for spent magazines. Their kits also contained flashlights, batteries, zip-tie handcuffs, and their favorite knives. Finally, a concealment holster containing their preferred sidearm rounded out the bulky vest.

"What can I do?" asked Sarge.

"You and Julia—" Steven started before he was interrupted by Donald.

"Nothing," he said. "You two need to get inside and in the bunker now. GO!"

"But we can—" started Julia.

"You can do nothing," said Donald. "We can't risk you getting hurt. Get inside while we secure the grounds and bring the Brahmin to the bunker one family at a time. Now please go!"

Susan stuck her head out of their bungalow door. "Donald?"

Donald grabbed Sarge by the arm. "Sarge, wait." He turned to Susan.

"Susan, grab the girls' packs and bring them now!" he ordered. "I want you to go with Sarge and Julia."

J.J. joined the group. Steven and Katie were now wearing their kits and directing the soldiers to their positions.

Donald turned to Julia. "I need you to get Sarge in the bunker and get the girls safe as well. Susan will need to help J.J. with any possible casualties."

"Okay," replied Julia as the Quinn women arrived at her side.

"Steven," said Donald, "I need you and Katie to escort them inside and then come back for the rest. Let's take them across the clearing one by one. Start with Abbie and Mr. Morgan."

As Steven and Katie escorted the contingent on the wraparound porch, Donald caught his breath and gathered his thoughts. He had an emergency plan in place for a possible attack on 1PP, but they'd never practiced it. Mr. Morgan didn't want to cause concern among his elderly friends. Donald regretted his acquiescence now, but as long as everyone followed his directives, it would work out fine.

J.J.'s voice brought Donald back to the present. "What can I do?" J.J. put his hand on Donald's shoulder, reassuring him he wasn't alone now.

"Thanks, J.J.," replied Donald. He motioned toward the Morgan bungalow. "Come with me. I want you to help Mr. Morgan inside and get him comfortable in the bunker. I don't know if we'll have casualties, but you and Susan need to be ready."

"Got it," said J.J.

Katie and Steven jogged toward them as Donald gently knocked on Morgan's door. A frightened Abbie poked her head through the narrow opening.

"Are we being attacked?" asked Abbie.

"We don't know, but we're gonna follow protocol and get everyone into the bunker."

Abbie opened the door wider to allow Donald and J.J. to come in. Steven and Katie took defensive positions outside the door. Their radios came to life with a lot of chatter. Steven muted his volume and inserted an earpiece. He looked at Katie, who nodded and did the same.

"DQ, we need to move this along," said Steven as he stuck his head through the doorway.

"Okay," replied Donald, turning to Abbie. "We don't know yet, Abbie, but we need to move quickly. J.J. will help you guys get inside and settled. Watch over your father carefully and immediately notify J.J. or Susan of any issues. Please hurry."

Abbie and J.J. helped Morgan get dressed and escorted him across the compound. Donald moved from door to door to the other bungalows and ordered the Boston Brahmin to get dressed and ready. Naturally, everyone had questions, but he had to minimize any conversations.

In between evacuations, he called Brad on the satphone.

Brad answered immediately. "This is Colonel Bradlee," he barked.

"Brad, this is Donald. We've had an explosion at—"

Brad cut him off. "We know, Donald. Get secured. We're on our way."

"Okay, Brad, I'm hearing gunfire now from the front gate. We must be under—"

And then a second explosion drowned out his words. Donald hit the ground and crawled toward the Peabodys' bungalow. Art opened the door and pulled Donald inside.

"Are you all right, young man?" asked Peabody. Stella Peabody sat on the couch, crying, clutching a white handkerchief.

"Yes, sir. Something is happening at the front gate. We need to get you both to safety."

Steven was outside the bungalow. "DQ, are you in there?"

"Please come with me, ma'am," said Donald as he helped Stella Peabody off the sofa. The three left the building and quickly followed Katie towards 1PP. Steven brought up the rear, walking backward as he surveyed the woods.

Just as they reached the steps, they heard the barking of a small dog. Winnie the Frenchie had been left behind in the Winthrops' bungalow.

"Her barking will draw attention to the compound," said Donald. He looked at Steven. "We've gotta get her inside."

"Really?" muttered Steven as he surveyed the woods and ran to retrieve the French bulldog.

Once the contingent was inside, Art Peabody insisted upon helping. Donald sent him upstairs to the widow's walk with a radio and binoculars. The sun was rising now, and visibility would be better for him. The widow's walk was built with reinforced steel panels to provide ballistics protection. The height gave them a tremendous advantage over anyone attempting to breach the 1PP compound.

Donald stood in front of the windows and stared intently toward the woods. The Marines were tucked behind stacks of sandbags at each corner of the building. Less than ten minutes had elapsed since the first explosion and the second one. In that brief time frame, Donald had successfully emptied the bungalows and brought everyone to the more secure 1PP facility. He let out a deep breath and some tension with it.

Susan approached Donald from the kitchen, carrying a bottle of water. He immediately drank half of it before securing its cap.

"Now what?" she asked.

"We watch and wait," Donald replied.

CHAPTER SEVEN

Saturday, October 1
5:18 a.m.
Prescott Peninsula
Quabbin Reservoir, Massachusetts

Donald and Steven took up positions on the front porch of 1PP as they monitored the radio transmissions. The gunfire had stopped moments ago, but now the roar of motorboats could be heard from their east.

"They're coming at us from all sides!" exclaimed Donald as he ran down the front steps toward the boat launch on the east side of Prescott Peninsula.

Steven shook his head as he quickly followed and then passed him on the trail. He and Brad had assessed the security issues surrounding Prescott Peninsula back in mid-July. Securing the two-mile entrance to the land mass was easily fortified with a security fence and the barriers at the front gate. But the massive shoreline concerned both men at the time. An attack by sea did not surprise him.

In addition to the constant perimeter foot patrols who utilized the ATVs for rapid response, Steven had created an armageddon navy of sorts. Following the advice of his longtime associate and friend Drew Jackson, Steven contacted Stroker boats, a boat manufacturer near Knoxville, Tennessee.

Over the summer, a dozen bass boats were outfitted for a situation like this one. The boats were modified to include ArmorCore bullet-resistant fiberglass panels. Together with the Kevlar-reinforced hoses and hydraulic systems, the Strokers proved to be excellent patrol gunships that passed as fishing boats.

Steven arrived at the boat launch as several Marines were preparing the boats for battle. At the end of Egypt Brook, a small stream that emptied into the Quabbin Reservoir, Donald had constructed a hidden boat dock, which was obscured from view within an inlet. Before this, the modified fishing boats had not been seen on the vast reservoir.

"What've we got?" asked Steven. He caught his breath as he looked out of the inlet to the southwest.

One of the Marines, a lance corporal who was directing the removal of the pedestal-mounted boat seats, replied, "We have reports of as many as three dozen boats approaching from the south-southeast. There are multiple launches on both sides of the Winsor Dam. Hey, be careful with that, soldier!" One of the Marines had lost his footing while attaching the swivel-mounted fifty-caliber machine gun onto the pole where the fishing seat was.

"Did you say three dozen?" asked Steven.

"At least," he replied. "We may be outnumbered by four or five to one." The lance corporal turned his attention back to the task of readying the boats.

"Hell, yeah!" Steven laughed as he removed his sweatshirt, revealing a gray T-shirt that read *I Don't Care*. "I'll take point!" He bounded down the bank onto the floating dock and waited for the first boat to be ready.

"Hey, Steven, hold up!" shouted Donald as he followed Steven down the bank. He caught up to him and lowered his voice so as not to alarm the other soldiers. "Do you think this is a good idea for you to man one of these? You're seriously outnumbered."

"No worries, DQ. We may be outnumbered, but we're not outgunned." Steven turned the Ma Deuce around on its swivel mount. Steven looked at the Marines awaiting orders on the bank. "Who's with me?"

"Damn it, Steven!"

Ignoring Donald's protests, Steven reached into a storage compartment and grabbed the high-powered Steiner marine binoculars and surveyed the water. Boats were coming at a high rate of speed around nearby Little Quabbin Hill, swamping two fishermen in a skiff paddling across the water. The skiff overturned and the men were scrambling to crawl back inside without getting run over.

"Poor idiots," mumbled Steven under his breath.

"Steven, I have to let Sarge know about this!" yelled Donald.

Steven turned and pounded his chest three times with his fist and then outlined the words on his T-shirt—*I Don't Care.*

"Let's go, dammit!"

Steven got behind the console and brought the twin 2.5-liter Mercruiser outboard motors to life. With two hundred eighty horsepower each, the Merc motors could easily achieve seventy miles per hour speeds with the additional equipment and ballistic protections added.

Because two-thirds of the Marines were now manning the front gate, only six of the boats had the ability to field two-man crews. Wisely, Steven waited until all six vessels were ready to go.

"Listen up," said the lance corporal assigned to the boat dock. He gave the crews a briefing. "Our patrols at the southernmost point have fired upon several boats already. They diverted east and north of our position. More boats are approaching along the back side of Little Quabbin Hill to our south and Mount Pomeroy to our east."

"They don't know about us," added Steven, who was bursting at the seams for some action.

"That's right," said the lance corporal. "I have twelve more Marines being pulled from their posts to assist. They will be ready for a second wave of attacks. In the meantime, fan out and chase them out of our waters!"

"Damn straight," shouted Steven as the other engines roared to life.

"Remember, no friendly fire," the corporal instructed. "It'll be easy to have bullets flying in all directions."

"Shock and awe, gentlemen!" proclaimed Steven as he pushed them away from the dock. He strapped into the gunner's position by placing his feet in the modified water ski boots bolted to the deck. This provided grip and counter-leverage against the g-forces of the boat turning in the water.

The driver gunned the throttle and Steven's head snapped back. His hat flew off his head and he instinctively turned to mark its position. As they roared out of the inlet toward the southeast, he had the luxury of an open field of fire. He made use of it.

The Browning M2s mounted on the boats provided the gunner a short recoil. The heavy fifty-caliber cartridge had a fairly long range of two thousand yards and incredible stopping power. While capable of producing over forty rounds per minute, this was not sustainable. Steven knew that the Ma Deuce was most effective, and accurate, using six- to eight-round bursts.

As Steven grabbed the spade-handle grip of the eighty-pound M2, he knew that the distinct jackhammer sound it produced would have a chilling effect on those on the receiving end of its wrath.

Steven turned to his driver and pointed toward the northern tip of Mount Lizzie. "There!"

The Stroker picked up speed and lurched toward the island and three approaching boats. Steven looked up to assess his opponents. The boats appeared to be open-bow runabouts similar to a Sea Ray or Wellcraft. The Stroker was quickly closing on the three boats, which were clustered in a V formation.

"Big mistake," Steven muttered as he opened fire. He fired eight rounds in a staccato blast of power. The lead boat, a twenty-three-foot bowrider, erupted into flames and exploded. The other two boats veered to avoid the carnage and lost control. The high-speed, abrupt turn of one of the bowriders threw all four passengers into the lake. Their boat roared to the north, unmanned. The other inboard vessel veered southward in retreat, and Steven quickly adjusted his aim, filling its stern with holes. The engine failed, and the boat immediately began to sink.

Suddenly, bullets whizzed over their heads, and Steven instinctively ducked. To their east, a gunman was emptying an AR-15 magazine in their direction. His boat was bobbing in the wakes created by the flurry of boat activity. When his mag emptied, he saw that he had missed his intended target. The man dropped into the V-hull of the Ski Pro Extreme and his driver roared around Mount Lizzie.

"Chase those guys!" shouted Steven as he regained his footing.

The twin Mercs roared to life once again and started after the competition ski boat.

"Veer right, veer right!" shouted Steven, pointing at a large drifting tree trunk in their path. He put a death grip on the M2 as his driver avoided destroying their props.

Their boat quickly leveled out and continued in pursuit. The boat planed on top of the lake, its propellers under the surface as it vaulted forward after the more agile ski boat. They were a quarter mile behind the Ski Pro, but closing. Steven released a couple of bursts from the M2.

GRRAKKA, KKAKKAKK, KKAKKAKK, KKAKKAKK.

The movement of their boat through the water and the turbulence caused by the Ski Pro's wake prevented any accuracy with the heavy weapon.

"Closer!" Steven shouted.

The Ski Pro deftly maneuvered through the string of tiny islands at the northernmost end of Quabbin Reservoir until Steven lost sight of them. He held his fist high, indicating to his driver to stop. Steven stumbled forward as the boat's momentum unexpectedly halted their progress.

The Stroker listed back and forth as their wake caught up with them. Steven was on alert. He'd studied the maps of the lake in anticipation of this scenario. Locals would know the waters better than he would.

He turned to his driver. "We're sittin' ducks out here in the open. I don't like it. Let's drift up along Mount Russ to our left. Maybe they'll make their move first."

The driver put the throttle in idle and slowly made their way northward. They eased closer to the shallow waters of Hip Brook Pond and Newton Pond. The water was bizarrely still considering the sounds of gunfire that echoed across the lake's surface behind them.

Then a flash of light—the reflection off something metallic— caught Steven's eye. He saw the bow of the Ski Pro easing around the northern point of Mount L.

"There!" He pointed at the boat as it revealed itself further and his driver throttled forward toward them, lifting the bow several feet out of the water. It was the horsepower of the Mercruiser engines and the torque the props created that saved Steven's life that day.

A barrage of bullets ricocheted off of the Kevlar-reinforced hull of their boat at that precise moment. The lucky timing saved both of their lives.

As their boat planed out, Steven opened fire again. But the Ski Pro had quickly maneuvered and headed south again, using Mount L as a buffer.

"Screw it! Turn around, one-eighty!"

The driver whipped the boat to the left and gave it full throttle. They were running parallel to the Ski Pro with Mount L as their buffer. Steven knew he had a chance up ahead and readied the M2. As they reached the end of the island, there was a narrow stretch of lake, roughly twenty yards, between Mount L and Mount Zion.

They approached the divide at over seventy miles an hour. Steven kept his hands steady, pointing the powerful weapon at the gap. When he saw his target, he didn't hesitate. He opened fire.

GRRAKKA, KKAKKAKK, KKAKKAKK, KKAKKAKK.

But the sound of the boat continued. He thought he'd hit it. He gestured for the driver to continue parallel to Mount Zion.

What Steven could not see was the Ski Pro careening out of control, hitting a sandbar just beneath the lake's surface and vaulting into the air. The crashing sound it made as it skidded hard into the shoreline, ejecting its already dead occupants, was unmistakable. Steven knew this battle was over.

The Stroker came to a stop to view the scene. Along the eastern shore of Prescott Peninsula, Marines were engaging the pleasure craft at will. Small-arms fire could be heard echoing across the water, but none of the marauders' rounds found their marks.

On the other hand, the huge eight-hundred-grain bullets of the M2s found their marks often and easily lived up to their reputation as *one-stop shot*. The lake was riddled with burning, sinking boat corpses. The tide had turned against the attackers quickly, but Steven wanted more.

"We've got 'em on the ropes!" shouted his driver. The dozen or so remaining boats were rapidly retreating to the perceived safety of their boat launches. "Look at 'em bolt!"

Steven was breathing heavily from the adrenaline-fueled engagement. Undoubtedly, the battle was over before it got started. *Or was it?*

"On the ropes isn't the same as bleedin' out!" shouted Steven in response. "We need to send a message to them. Let's go!" Steven got into position and pointed toward Winsor Dam.

Although the retreating vessels had a healthy head start, the Stroker caught up to the slower pleasure craft and Steven handily ripped them to shreds. As they got closer to land, they began to take on small-arms fire, and he raised his fist to indicate to his driver to let off the throttle.

One of the hostile boats beat such a hasty retreat that it didn't slow down in time as it approached the earthen Winsor Dam. It hit the bank at full speed and catapulted up the bank and over the other side, sending its passengers flying in all directions.

Steven began to laugh hysterically at the sight of this and added several six-round blasts from the Ma Deuce to top off the victory.

He shouted at them, "Don't come back!"

CHAPTER EIGHT

Saturday, October 1
5:34 a.m.
Prescott Peninsula
Quabbin Reservoir, Massachusetts

As the daylight grew brighter, Shore finally began to relax. He had positioned men along the front perimeter and added more men to the boat launch. The southernmost point was protected by two fortified machine-gun nests outfitted with .30-caliber M1919 Brownings. He was receiving updates from his men at the boat launch on the progress of the six two-man teams on the water. He had several other teams on shore, ready to engage if necessary. He was concerned with putting too many boats on the water. Friendly fire was entirely possible.

His radio interrupted his thoughts. "Alpha One, this is Delta Two. Over."

"Go, Delta Two," replied Shore.

"Sir, we've discovered three pontoon boats tied off along our western shore at Lighthouse Hill, Prescott Hill, and the abandoned Rattlesnake Den launch."

"Dammit!" shouted Shore, which caused Morrell and two soldiers to rush to his side.

"What is it, sir? What did they find?" asked Morrell.

Shore didn't take time for explanations. He gave Morrell instructions instead. "Morrell, take one of the Humvees back to 1PP with the injured man and two others. Make them aware that hostiles are on shore and are possibly headed inland."

"How many, sir?" asked Morrell.

"As many as three dozen," he replied. "Hurry! Go! Raise them on the radio on the way and secure that perimeter!"

Morrell didn't waste any time as he helped the injured soldier into the Humvee and motioned for two other men to come with him.

Shore quickly assessed his manpower. He had pulled the majority of the Marine contingent to the front gate, leaving his west flank vulnerable. *Think!*

He knew Prescott Peninsula like the back of his hand. He had walked every road and explored every trail. He had to hope the attackers didn't know how to find 1PP, so that gave him an advantage. The aggressors, however, had the time advantage and a head start.

Prescott Shutesbury Road ran the length of Prescott Peninsula from the front gate to the southernmost point. The 1PP compound was located half a mile to the east of this wide gravel road. He had to gamble that the attackers were tentative in their approach. They didn't know the lay of the land. They would plan deliberately at the shore, then make their way inland toward 1PP.

"Delta Two, Alpha One."

"Go, Alpha One."

"Pull your entire team back to the east side of Prescott Shutesbury Road. Take positions in the woods, waiting for contact from the west. Spread them out for max coverage."

"Roger, Alpha One."

Shore's Echo Team was much farther south than the landing

zone of the attackers. He wasn't going to pull them and get caught off guard down there.

"Foxtrot One. Alpha One. Do you copy?"

"Five by five, Alpha One."

"Sitrep, Lance Corporal," said Shore.

"Sir, the enemy vessels have been repelled. I am maintaining six of ours on the water to establish a perimeter."

Shore processed the scenario. If the first-wave assault was turned away that easily with six two-man crews, the additional manpower could be redeployed to 1PP. "Foxtrot One, redeploy non-active personnel to 1PP to assist Corporal Morrell."

"Roger that, Alpha One. Foxtrot One out."

Shore now had a minimum of twelve Marines guarding the compound, led by a wounded but capable Morrell, plus the muckety-mucks, who were pretty good with their own firearms, so he'd been told. *Now, I've got to flush out the cockroaches.* The radio interrupted his thoughts.

"Alpha One. Delta Two. Over."

"Go, Two," replied Shore.

"In position, sir. I've instructed two men to cover our six in case they've slipped past us already."

"Well done, Delta Two. Stand by. Over."

"Roger. Delta Two out."

Shore contemplated the risk. He'd already been attacked with two truck bombs along the northern fence line. Several dozen hostiles were killed and others were fired upon before they retreated. He hesitated to pull too many off their posts in light of these events, but he was trying to defend a large area with limited bodies.

I'll box them in.

He jumped on a four-wheeler and rode to the easternmost fence posts to assess the situation. There had been no sightings of hostiles in thirty minutes. He instructed the men on post to spread out and keep a sharp eye. Any signs of movement and he was to be contacted immediately. He handpicked four men.

"Saddle up, soldiers, we're goin' huntin'," ordered Shore. He missed his beloved Barrett rifle. Jungle warfare was not his forte, but he was comfortable he was better at it than the men scared in those woods. The contingent rode their ATVs down to Cooleyville Road and ditched the machines in the underbrush.

"We've got two klicks to cover," started Shore, looking into the eyes of the young soldiers. "We'll either flush the sons of bitches out, or they'll walk out into the open on Prescott Shutesbury Road to our welcoming committee."

"What are the rules of engagement, sir?"

"We're under attack, so we shoot to kill. We're not acting in a law enforcement capacity, attempting to apprehend a fugitive. We are fighting an enemy who has attacked us on two fronts, so far. We have one KIA and several wounded."

"Yes, sir."

"A couple of more things, gentlemen. Use your suppressors. No verbal commands. We'll spread out with two on each of my flanks. Keep constant eye contact on my hand signals. I expect these dirtbags to be bunched together in groups. Be prepared for a straggler or a scout operating alone. Take them out quietly. Gunfire will attract attention. Are we clear?"

"Yes, sir!"

Shore led his team through the woods in a southerly direction parallel to the Quabbin inlet to their right, and Prescott Shutesbury Road and Delta Team to their left. Most of the leaves had turned to vibrant fall colors and some had fallen to the forest floor. They provided a quiet pad for the soldiers to make their way undetected.

For the first twenty minutes, they moved toward Rattlesnake Den Road without incident. As the contingent approached the narrow gravel road, gunfire erupted from the southeast.

"Alpha One. Delta Two. Over."

Shore raised his fist and fell to one knee. His team was now evenly spaced along the north side of Rattlesnake Den Road.

"Go, Two," Shore quietly responded.

"Sir, we took fire from several hostiles at the Egypt Road intersection. Seven KIA. None of ours, sir."

"Roger, Delta Two. Any additional activity?"

"A group of armed men were seen running in retreat toward the western shoreline and the boat launch, sir."

"Roger, Delta Two. Pull your northernmost flank to take up a position at the Barnes Road intersection. We'll pursue them down Rattlesnake Den Road. We'll pull out on your signal."

"Roger that, Alpha One. Out."

For several minutes, Shore waited while the remainder of Delta Team moved into position. He could hear the sounds of frantic voices and heavy feet working their way toward the boats on the western banks of Prescott Peninsula. As much as he wanted to pursue them, he couldn't run the risk of the attackers slipping behind them to the areas already cleared.

When the Delta Team members made contact from the Barnes Road intersection, he waved for two of them to join him. They hustled along the edge of the woods until they reached his side.

"Catch your breath, gentlemen, and listen up. Maintain sight contact with the rest of Delta Team, and fan out like we have here. Do not let anyone cross this road. Are we clear?"

"Yes, sir." The men quickly replaced Shore's men and took up their positions. Shore circled his hand in the air, indicating for his men to join him.

"Okay, gentlemen. We're gonna make our way down Rattlesnake Den Road past Lighthouse Hill. They're headed our way. They'll be scared and tired. Let's take them out if fired upon. But I want a couple of prisoners. Let's find out who is behind this, got it?"

"Yes, sir."

"Okay, two by two on opposite sides of the road. I'll take the lead on the right side. Watch my hand signals. Let's go!"

Shore led his men down Rattlesnake Den Road. Within minutes, they heard the sound of a boat motor roar to life and move steadily away from them. He picked up the pace until he heard the sounds of men running through the woods just ahead of them. He raised his fist and motioned for the men to take up positions on the west side of the road. Four men and a teenage boy entered the opening, and Shore raised his rifle.

"Stop," he shouted. "Hold it right there!"

One of the men turned and fired wildly over Shore's head. He was killed instantly by one of the Marines. The three other men continued across the road, but the boy froze. He was holding a handgun and shaking uncontrollably.

Half a mile down the road, several other men crossed the road, stopped briefly, and then ran into the woods. Another boat motor fired up and the group escaped. Shore approached the boy cautiously with his red dot laser trained on the teenager's chest. More red dots joined Shore's. The boy saw them, dropped his gun, and peed his pants.

"On the ground or in your grave, son. Your choice." Shore was only a few feet away from sixteen-year-old Nathaniel Archibald, son of Ronald, when the young prisoner's knees hit the gravel of Rattlesnake Den Road.

CHAPTER NINE

Saturday, October 1
12:41 p.m.
Prescott Peninsula, 1PP
Quabbin Reservoir, Massachusetts

Brad arrived on the scene barely an hour after the onslaught
subsided. He cursed himself repeatedly for not being there. It was
difficult for him to maintain his duties on behalf of the 1st
Battalion, 25th Regiment and the responsibilities he undertook on
the part of the Boston Brahmin. Since the cyber attack, Brad had
swayed in the direction of his friends—the Loyal Nine. He was
going to have to make a choice at some point. He loved his country
and was proud of his service. He didn't want to abandon his duty
and his post. The uncertainty was tearing at him with each passing
day.

"I think we can give the all clear, Donald," he said as the two men
stood on the front porch in silence. "They seemed to have shot their
wad."

"No doubt." Donald laughed.

Brad continued. "They came at us with a pretty good, three-pronged plan of attack. The problem is their execution sucked, and their men didn't appear to have their hearts in it."

"Your men scared the crap out of them."

"Nothing beats the training of a Marine, Donald. I suppose their leaders, whoever they were, didn't let them know that someone would be over here prepared to shoot back."

J.J. joined them on the porch with a beer.

"Happy hour already?" asked Donald, pointing at the adult beverage.

J.J. provided a faux toast and took another sip. "My day is done. I've stitched up Corporal Morrell and the other soldiers from the front gate. A couple of guys had minor wounds from the Battle of Midway out there." He gestured toward the Quabbin Reservoir.

"That's good news," replied Donald. "Did you treat any of their men?"

"Not yet," replied J.J. Then he laughed, hesitated, and added, "Not yet, anyway. I don't know what Steven and Katie are doing to that kid in there, but I keep hearing a mixture of laughter and hysterical crying. Those two are clearly enjoying themselves too much."

Sarge and Julia now joined the group, each with a can of Beanee Weenee and a plastic spoon.

"Diggin' into the C rations, I see." Brad laughed.

"This is great stuff," replied Sarge with a mouthful of Beanee, but short on Weenee.

"Yeah," added Julia. "These are highly recommended by the Quinn sisters."

"I added some Tabasco to mine," said Sarge.

Steven and Katie walked out of the entrance to 1PP, having overheard the conversation. Steven was wiping sweat off his face with a towel. "Great, you'll be firing off nuclear gas out of that ass later!"

The group erupted into laughter as Sarge's face turned beet red.

"You've got a way with words, brother." Sarge laughed. Steven patted Sarge on the back and the group made their way down the front steps to the picnic tables.

Julia took Sarge's empty can and started to walked inside. "I'll let the others know that we're all clear."

Sarge pecked her on the cheek before she left, and then took a seat across from Steven. Brad was anxious to find out what Steven and Katie had learned from their prisoner.

"Guys, is our prisoner still alive?" Brad chuckled. "Did we violate the Geneva convention?"

"Geneva who?" jokingly replied Steven. Brad knew that in Steven's line of work, rules regarding the treatment of prisoners were different from accepted practices.

"He's still alive—the little prick," said Katie dryly. "He was a tough guy at first, but eventually peed his pants for the second time today."

"Before spilling his guts," added Steven.

"What?" asked Sarge, clearly alarmed that his brother was speaking literally.

"No, Sarge, not like a fish," replied Steven, looking over at Katie. "But I do believe we got everything out of him."

Katie nodded. "He's barely able to drive, but he had access to all of the planning and inner workings of Belchertown. His dad is in charge over there—Ronald Archibald."

"He's the guy you spoke with when you were hunting for Pearson, right?" asked Brad.

"One and the same," replied Steven. "It gets better. Guess who else was intricately involved in this little soirée?"

"Pearson?"

"BINGO, Brad. Your old pal Pearson has guided Archibald every step of the way. The kid said his father suspected you and I were somehow involved in all of this." Steven stood and waved from north to south.

"I'll be damned," said Brad. "I've hated that guy from the moment he stepped into my office last spring. Well, the idiots only succeeded in getting a bunch of their friends killed."

"And a couple of ours," added Sarge.

"Trust me, I don't take that lightly," said Brad. He turned his attention back to Steven. "Did he say what prompted them to come after us?"

"They're hungry," replied Katie. "It's as simple as that."

"So they decided to come kill us and take our food," interjected Julia as she rejoined the group. More of the Boston Brahmin were filing out into the beautiful fall afternoon.

"Let's keep our voices down so the others don't hear us," said Sarge in a whisper.

The group huddled together without trying to be obvious. Most of the Boston Brahmin appeared apprehensive, and several hastily walked toward the comfort of their bungalows.

"They won't interrupt us," said Julia. "I gave everybody a quick briefing before they came out. In the bunker, they weren't able to hear the gun battles all around us. I think it's best that we don't scare them."

"I agree, Julia," said Sarge. He drew her close to him and put his arm around her. "You did the right thing, and I'm sure Mr. Morgan would approve. How's he doin'?"

"He's doing fine, but he didn't buy me sugarcoating it, however. He's already asked to speak with you." Katie looked down and shook her head.

"Okay," said Sarge. "Well, let me get all of the facts before I face the inquisition. Steven, what else did you learn?"

"Really, that's about it," he replied. "These people grew desperate when our friend Governor O'Brien cut off their Citizen Corps food supplies. From what we gathered, the boy's father whipped the townspeople into a frenzy over the shooting of the guy who killed Sabs. Obviously, he used the man's death as a false flag to convince the locals to attack us. That, coupled with the fact they're in dire straits, was what prompted the attack."

"Did the governor intentionally cut them off?" asked Brad.

"I don't think so," replied Steven. "I think it's consistent with what we learned earlier. The governor is hoarding the food and supplies for himself. He's playing God with it all."

"What do we do with the kid?" asked Brad.

"Do we have any indication that he fired on our people?" asked Sarge.

"No."

"And the dead bodies?" said Julia inquisitively.

"I'll have them bagged and taken to the front gate with the others," replied Brad.

"All right," said Sarge. "Let's hold the boy and see how things develop. Perhaps his father will come around looking for his son. Let's make the piece of crap unzip the body bags one by one, looking into the faces of the men he sentenced to death. I want him to wonder if his teenage son is one of them."

"Do you plan on meeting with Archibald?" asked Brad.

"Clearly, this needs to be addressed sooner rather than later," said Sarge. "Thanks, everyone. Let me go meet with the Big Guy."

Brad heard it, but no one else did. Katie said, under her breath, *There goes the new boss, same as the old boss.*

CHAPTER TEN

Monday, October 3
9:40 a.m.
Citizen Corps Region I, Office of the Governor
99 High Street
Boston, Massachusetts

Citizen Corps Governor James O'Brien believed in first impressions. The commander of the United Nations forces arrived during the night and was scheduled to meet with him at noon. He donned his best three-piece suit, intending to convey his importance to the man who would lead his army. Every army had a commander in chief, and that was his job. He was going to make that abundantly clear to this UN general, or whatever his rank was.

He paced the floor while waiting for Pearson and Marion La Rue to arrive. The Seaport District was bustling with activity as the UN troops continued to unload equipment and personnel. Two additional Watson-class ships had arrived, containing a variety of troop carriers, supplies, and soldiers. They had confiscated the Boston Convention and Exhibition Center for temporary housing.

A half million square feet of exhibition space now housed UN soldiers from fifty-three nations around the world.

The parking lots around Seaport Boulevard and Summer Street were packed with *Blue Helmets*, the nickname given the variety of soldiers, police officers, and civilians that traditionally made up a UN Peacekeeping force. O'Brien knew little about their manpower, but he was told by Pearson that the UN had no problem finding willing new recruits for this mission. *Everybody wants a piece of America's ass.*

As he looked down upon the activity, he realized he hadn't been told how many troops were available to him, nor had he been informed of when these *Peacekeepers* would be ready for *his orders*. He was presented a tremendous opportunity, and he intended to seize it.

"Good morning, Governor," announced Pearson as he entered the room. He was also dressed in a suit and tie. Obviously, Pearson intended to make a good impression on the UN commander. *You gotta watch these government snakes. They're always after someone else's job.*

O'Brien slowly assessed Pearson's appearance before responding, "Morning."

La Rue appeared in the doorway, paused and then entered. He had a frown on his face and O'Brien could tell he was troubled. He'd address it later.

"Good morning, boss," said La Rue, who quickly took a seat. Pearson followed his lead.

"As you both know, *I* have a meeting with our new friends from the United Nations today," started O'Brien, standing and looking directly at Pearson. "There will be a number of topics on the agenda, but I need to be brought up to speed on everything. We also need to establish our list of priorities." O'Brien turned to stare out the window with his hands in his pockets. It was too early for a cigar, although he desperately wanted one.

In the window's reflection, he saw Pearson shift in his seat and look towards La Rue, who remained quiet. Nobody was speaking up, so O'Brien forced the issue.

"Dammit, I haven't got all day!" he yelled.

"Governor, the raid on Prescott Peninsula did not go well," started Pearson. "Their assault plans were sound, based on a multipronged approach."

"What the hell happened?" asked O'Brien, who was beginning to feel his blood pressure rise. "I thought you said they had more than enough men to pull it off."

"Governor, they had hundreds of men involved, but they were unable to break through the defenses set up by the Marines."

"You confirmed that Prescott Peninsula is full of Marines?" asked La Rue.

"From what I was told afterward, the men they encountered were not in uniform, but they were well trained and had advanced weaponry. Heavy-caliber automatic weapons, military-style vests, and specially outfitted boats mounted with machine guns."

"Did these Belchertown fools succeed in accomplishing anything?" asked O'Brien.

"Not really, sir," replied Pearson.

O'Brien glared at Pearson for an awkward moment before collapsing into his chair in a heap. He rubbed his temples and shook his head.

Finally, O'Brien spoke. "Did they learn anything Saturday besides how to get their asses handed to them?"

"Nothing, sir," replied Pearson. He hesitated and then added, "They lost several dozen men, and another dozen are missing. The townspeople are pretty pissed off at the whole thing."

"Pissed off!" exploded O'Brien. "Pissed off at what? That they're a bunch of failures? A few hundred armed men can't overrun an island full of widows and orphans? I don't care how many Marines were at the gate or in some fancy boats. A few hundred of their own *obviously* aren't hungry enough to get the job done."

"Abused mothers and their children," said Pearson.

"What?" asked O'Brien, glaring at Pearson.

"Governor, they're not widows and orphans. They're abused mothers and children."

I'm gonna shoot this guy. Right here, right now.

Silence. O'Brien reached in his jacket pocket for his crutch—a cigar. There wasn't one. He began to rifle through the drawers of his desk. Nothing. He was fuming now. He shouted for his nephew.

"Peter, find me a cigar!" he screamed through the closed door. O'Brien shook his head and exhaled.

Peter knocked hesitantly on the door and entered with a tin of Macanudo Petites and a butane lighter. He handed them to O'Brien, who looked at the four-inch-square tin of cigars, which were just slightly larger than a cigarette. His hands shook slightly before he slammed them on the table.

"Peter, what the hell are these?" he yelled, tapping his fingers on the tin.

"Uncle, I mean, um, sir, this is all we have right now," replied O'Brien's nephew sheepishly.

O'Brien rooted around in his pockets and slid his car keys to his nephew. "Go look in the console of my car. Hurry back."

Peter quickly exited while O'Brien pulled a notepad and pen out of his desk. He roughly pushed them at Pearson.

"Make a list, Pearson. The first item is cigars."

Pearson dutifully began the list. "Got it."

"Next item, Prescott Peninsula," added O'Brien. Pearson wrote down item two. "I want to send those blue-helmeted screwballs out there to pay a visit to the widows and orphans. There is more going on at Prescott than meets the eye."

"Yes, sir," said Pearson.

That's more like it—respect. "Let's talk about getting our guys back," said O'Brien. "Marion, have you learned anything else?"

"A lot of heavy equipment was moved out of Fort Devens yesterday," replied La Rue. "I didn't have enough men available to follow them, but they headed west on the Stanton Highway towards the one-ninety."

"Towards Prescott Peninsula?" asked O'Brien. He was starting to put together a pretty clear picture.

"Maybe," replied La Rue. "It makes sense anyway. The base is pretty much abandoned from what we can tell."

"How many men are guarding the prison camp?" asked O'Brien.

"A dozen or so, rotating through shifts. Most stay on base, but some come and go in their Humvees."

"Have our guys seen our friend Colonel Bradlee?" asked O'Brien. He held his hand up to pause the conversation as Peter returned with a cigar and a cutter. He nodded and smiled at his nephew and waved him out with his hand. O'Brien took a deep draw and let out an exhale full of smoke. It immediately relaxed him. Looking at Pearson, he thought, *this cigar just saved your life.*

After lighting his cigar, O'Brien gruffed, "continue."

"Bradlee tore out of the base early Saturday morning with two Humvees and a dozen men," said La Rue.

"What time?" asked Pearson.

"It was around 5, 5:30," replied La Rue. "What time did Archibald start the raid?"

"About the same time." La Rue and Pearson both turned their attention to their governor.

"Well, there you have it, boys," said O'Brien, taking another deep drag on his beloved cigar. "No doubt in my mind that there is a connection. Our Colonel Bradlee has been undermining us from day one."

"Agreed," said La Rue.

O'Brien pointed his cigar at Pearson. "Write that down, Pearson. Put it on the list. Hell, make it item *numero uno*. My cigars can wait. I want that traitor's ass!"

"Sir, would you like me to make some inquiries at the White House?" asked Pearson. "I can see if he can be recalled or something."

Pearson raised a good point. *Why not let the President help us out?* Then he thought against it. "You know what? Better the devil you know than the devil you don't. Maybe we'll have our friends out there take care of it for us." O'Brien leaned back in his chair, contemplating what it would look like to hang that SOB Bradlee right in the middle of Boston Common.

La Rue interrupted the moment. "Jim, may I have a moment alone?"

"Of course, Marion," replied O'Brien. He motioned for Pearson to leave while deciding to include him in the meeting with the UN. It might help his credibility to have the White House liaison present. "Pearson, we're done for now. Come back at noon."

"Yes, sir," said Pearson as he quickly left the room, leaving the notepad on the table.

O'Brien turned his attention to his longtime friend. "What's the matter, Marion? I could see it on your face when you walked in the door."

La Rue stood and walked to the window to observe the UN personnel. O'Brien stood and joined him. The men remained quiet as they observed the activities. The bright morning sun reflected off the UN helmets.

O'Brien tried to lighten the mood. "They look like an army of Smurfs." Both men erupted in laughter.

"They sure do," said La Rue. They watched for another moment and then La Rue added, "My concern is that we're not getting what we hoped for."

O'Brien led them back to the desk, but this time he sat in the chair next to La Rue instead of assuming the power position behind the desk. He and Marion had worked side by side during all of their union activities. O'Brien trusted him more than any man on the planet.

"Whadya mean?"

"Jim, I don't profess to be a military man, you know that. All I know about soldiers is what I've seen on TV." La Rue paused again.

"Go ahead. What's on your mind?"

"I do, however, know men. I have prepared and led men into battle, so to speak. It may not have been a battlefield in the military sense, but we have undertaken missions over the years that required the same type of planning and discipline."

O'Brien studied his friend. He took another drag on the cigar and exhaled over his shoulder. "We've orchestrated many union operations over the years," he added.

"These *Smurfs* are not military personnel. They are thieves, criminals, and thugs. I know these things, Jim. I've dealt with men like them all of my life."

"Why is that a bad thing?" asked O'Brien. "I've got no problem shaking things up around here. We got in bed with the gangs, remember?"

"Of course, but that was different. Our goal then was to disrupt things, which included running people out of the city. The gangs served their purpose. Now we need a military force to follow *your orders.*"

"I agree," interrupted O'Brien, but La Rue continued his thought.

"In watching these mopes for the last few days, I'm of the opinion that they can't be controlled."

"I'm meeting their commander today," said O'Brien. "I'll feel him out about the quality of his people."

La Rue continued. "My concern is that they're gonna be more interested in raping and pillaging and not at all interested in taking on a viper nest of Marines holed up on Prescott Peninsula."

O'Brien drew on his cigar and took in his friend's observations.

CHAPTER ELEVEN

Monday, October 3
12:20 p.m.
Citizen Corps Region I, Office of the Governor
99 High Street
Boston, Massachusetts

O'Brien and Pearson became impatient as they paced the floor of the conference room. They didn't know how many of the UN officers would be present, so they allowed for a dozen chairs around the ten-foot-long faux-mahogany conference table. O'Brien ordered sandwiches and beverages to be brought in. He wanted to put on a good show for his guests. In his mind, this was a momentous occasion, one of international importance.

"Governor, do you want me to go downstairs and see where they are?" asked Pearson. They were now twenty minutes late. "I've been monitoring the entrance to look for an entourage of some sort. So far, nothing."

O'Brien hitched his pants up over his protruding belly, temporarily, before they slid down to where they were. Somehow, he had managed to gain weight during the apocalypse.

"Yeah, go ahead," he ordered Pearson. O'Brien knew nothing about the inner workings or hierarchy of the United Nations. He thought their peace armies were used to shut down rampaging Africans in places like Darfur and Libya or Liberia or some such country. He really didn't give a crap what they did overseas. He was most interested in what they could do for him.

He did know that the President was a big fan of the United Nations. Hell, if the truth were known, he'd rather be king of the UN than President of the United States. He did have international roots after all—*Kenya*, that was.

Before the collapse, O'Brien recalled that the President worked with the UN to expand the size of its peacekeeping force, as they called it. After Ebola had its way with Western Africa and then threatened America, the President had the excuse he was looking for to beef up the UN's military forces. Over the last several years, the White House reallocated budget dollars to the UN. The rationale had to do with beefing up the UN's rapid-response capabilities, which enabled their troops to reach hot zones around the world quickly. *Yeah, hot zones like this one.*

The UN received its troops through agreements with one hundred and twenty-three of its member-states. Based upon the news reports O'Brien could recall, these soldiers were clearly not the cream of the crop. There were allegations of raping and sexual exploitation of women in Somalia.

While in Haiti following the devastating earthquake, UN troops routinely looted food and supplies designated for the Haitian survivors. They used their UN credentials to freely pass over the border with the Dominican Republic. Strong-armed robbery and sexual assaults skyrocketed during this period in the tiny Caribbean nation.

O'Brien trusted La Rue's intuition. Based upon past UN-sponsored atrocities, it was likely this group of Blue Helmets was as bad if not worse than their comrades.

"Governor," said Pearson, immediately grabbing O'Brien's attention, "I'd like you to meet Major General Zhang Wei of the

People's Liberation Army and the commander of the United Nations Peacekeeping force."

O'Brien unconsciously paused, shocked by the sight of the general. Zhang stood five foot six, was fairly thin, and was pushing seventy years old. *This is my general?*

O'Brien regained his composure. "Um, welcome, General. I'm Citizen Corps Governor James O'Brien. Welcome to Boston." O'Brien spoke slowly and louder than normal.

Chinese preferred to be formally presented to a stranger. Because they were taught not to show excessive emotion, the Chinese might seem unfriendly when being introduced. Etiquette prevented them from approaching someone to shake hands, and they customarily remained standing during introductions until their host extended his hand.

O'Brien stepped forward and the two men shook hands. Zhang bowed slightly at the shoulders as he shook O'Brien's hand. "You may call me General Zhang."

"Chung? Not We?" asked O'Brien. Zhang seemed perturbed by this. O'Brien was confused. His first foray into international relations was off to a bad start.

"My family name is Zhang. In China, I am Major General Zhang Wei. In English, I am General Zhang."

You mean General Diva.

"Well, General, it is a pleasure to meet you," said O'Brien. "You can call me Jim. Where is your staff?"

"My subordinates are making arrangements at my directive. That is why I am here to speak with you, Governor."

"Yes, of course, and I have a list to go over with you as well." O'Brien picked up the notepad off the conference table and began to sit down. When Zhang continued standing, O'Brien remained standing. He was now very uncomfortable and off his game. Zhang stood in silence and stared at him.

"General," O'Brien hesitated, and then continued, "would you like to sit down? I've brought in some sandwiches."

Zhang continued to stand. The room sat in awkward silence.

"Would you prefer for Mr. Pearson to leave the room?" asked O'Brien, growing perturbed. Zhang slowly moved to face Pearson.

"I am Major General Zhang."

Pearson picked up on the clue. "I am pleased to meet you, General Zhang. I am Joseph Pearson, liaison to the White House for Governor O'Brien."

Zhang bowed slightly at the shoulders as they shook hands, and Pearson mimicked the action.

Zhang turned toward O'Brien, nodded and sat in front of the plate of sandwiches, although he never touched them. O'Brien caught Pearson's eye, shrugged, and then pulled up a chair.

"General, there are a number of things I'd like to discuss with you. I have a list here."

Zhang raised his hand in response. "In due time, Governor. My first concern is the feeding and housing of the United Nations soldiers. Your arena facility is inadequate. What is your solution?"

"Well, um, what did you have in mind?" asked O'Brien.

"A barracks will be suitable. Do you have an available military facility?"

"You want to take over one of our military bases?" asked O'Brien, not sure if the general was being serious. O'Brien's eyes darted from Zhang to Pearson and back again.

"Yes, that would be sufficient. Or we can occupy a college campus and dormitory. Do you have a college campus?" *Yeah, Harvard. But that might piss the President off.*

"How many troops do you have?" asked Pearson.

"Three thousand seven hundred forty-five, including myself."

Wow, things were looking up. O'Brien's mind was in overdrive now. He needed to keep this Chinese general happy. Maybe he could kill two birds with one stone. One of the birds was gonna be a certain not-quite-a-full-bird colonel at Fort Devens. In the process, he'd get his guys back.

"General, I think we have a military installation that fits your needs perfectly," said O'Brien with a huge smile.

CHAPTER TWELVE

Wednesday, October 5
12:41 p.m.
Prescott Peninsula, 1PP
Quabbin Reservoir, Massachusetts

Brad gave Gunny Falcone and CWO Shore some final instructions and sent them back to Fort Devens. They were his two most trusted men, and the job of decommissioning the base had to be handled properly. He had made a decision. The American military was in disarray and divided. Battle lines, so to speak, had been drawn.

Over the past eight years, the President had systematically replaced conservative, longtime military personnel with those who shared his vision of transforming the military. But his recent activity was only a continuation of a policy designed to insert political correctness into the armed forces. Twenty-three years ago, President Bill Clinton issued an executive order that became commonly known as the *Don't Ask, Don't Tell* policy. Until then, it had been unlawful for a homosexual person to serve in the military. *Don't Ask, Don't Tell* opened the door to allowing openly gay military personnel, a policy adopted in 2011.

During the last five years, a push to allow women to join combat forces on the front line was implemented. These drastic changes to military policy did not come without political risk. The *Don't Ask, Don't Tell* policy almost derailed the Clinton presidency before it got started. A woman in combat was the last straw for many hardcore military leaders.

For them, the current President's relentless implementation of political correctness into military doctrine was a part of his broader goal to neutralize America's military capability. Military analysts uniformly agreed that the implementation of the President's social policies during a period of increased worldwide instability had jeopardized the nation's national security.

As these debilitating social engineering directives were adopted by an administration full of military experts whose vast military experience came from the hallowed halls of Ivy League schools, disgruntled generals and admirals were leaving the military. They were quickly replaced with left-leaning subordinates who had been rapidly advancing through the ranks in the name of cultural diversity. *The first black this* and *the first woman that* became common news headlines. The American left celebrated as they burned the Stars and Stripes.

The warrior mentality of America's armed forces had been replaced, in large part, with the multicultural makeover envisioned by President Clinton and then implemented by the current President.

In this respect, Brad was a fossil—a throwback to World War II. Military duty and honor were in his genes. His family had shed blood for this country, and he was committed to making America great again, even if it meant taking on his fellow soldiers. He made a choice. He was prepared to leave the military to join the fight for renewed independence.

As Steven approached, Brad thought about the ramifications of his decision. Would he be remembered as a soldier who abandoned his post when his country needed him the most? Or would he make his mark by leading America back to its former greatness?

"Hey, Brad," started Steven, holding a roll of maps under his arm, "do you wanna go over this out here or inside?"

"Let's do it down at the docks where we won't be interrupted," he replied, patting Steven on the back and leading him down the trail. As he began walking in that direction, he informed Corporal Morrell of where he and Steven could be found.

Steven followed him down the path to the docks. A squirrel scampered out of their path into the woods, and a snake slithered out of the way as well.

"It's hard to believe we were in a firefight just a few days ago," said Steven. "You'd think these critters would find a quieter place to live."

"Yeah," added Brad. "We're not very good neighbors, are we?"

"No kiddin'. The whole neighborhood has gone to hell."

The two men entered the clearing where the fleet of Stroker attack boats lay relatively still. Only a small westerly breeze created a wake.

"Lance Corporal, we're going to use the fish-cleaning tables to do a little work. Why don't you gentlemen grab some chow and give us an hour."

"Yes, sir!" came the reply as the two Marines hastily made their way to 1PP.

"You gotta love military discipline," said Steven. "It's been a month since their lives were turned upside down, and they still follow orders and do their duty."

"I'm proud of these young men. I gave them the option to haul ass and join their families. Our unit has always been cohesive. In fact, we've had three of our men return to Fort Devens in the last few days. They got their families squared away and wanted to resume their duties."

"Good to hear," said Steven. "I hope to build that same sense of duty and honor with the Mechanics."

"Well, let's get this strategic planning session under way." Brad was anxious to set the course for his men and the Mechanics.

"Okay, let's start local, and then we'll look at the big game plan," started Steven. He rolled out a map of Massachusetts and the greater Boston area. He grabbed a few rocks off the ground and used them to hold down the corners.

"I hate to give up Fort Devens," said Brad. "But logistically, it doesn't make sense. We're spread out too much. If we had another hundred soldiers, then we wouldn't be having this conversation. The region is too unstable for me to travel to other installations and poach their personnel. We have to make do with what we have and refocus our priorities."

"I agree. What's your timetable?" asked Steven.

"Other than a ten-man unit guarding the front gate and the prisoners, all personnel are stationed here. I'm moving four men into a condo unit at 100 Beacon. They will be my eyes and ears in the city and will be available to you as well."

"I'll use them to guard the building and train my guys."

Brad knew it was time to address the elephant in the room. "Lastly, there is the issue of O'Brien's men."

"Just shoot 'em." The men laughed at Steven's repeated use of his patented phrase.

"Trust me, that would be the easy way out," said Brad, smiling. "I don't believe I can bring myself to do that or order my men to execute the thugs either. If released, however, they will go straight back to O'Brien and pick up where they left off."

"And fully implicate you," added Steven.

"Oh, I suspect that ship has sailed."

Suddenly, the men ducked as a hawk swooped down over their heads and picked up a snake in both claws. The powerful wings thrust the bird upward as the snake wiggled to free itself.

"Dammit," said Steven. "That scared me more than those idiots shooting at me the other day."

Brad laughed. "A bird's gotta eat, right?"

"No doubt," replied Steven. He got back on topic. "I've got the same problem with the kid. Although I don't recall seeing him in Belchertown the day Katie and I were there, he can describe us to his daddy and the connection will be made."

Brad gave all of this some consideration. The boy was less emotional and had become mouthy while in captivity. He was well fed and comfortable. But like all prisoners, he was ready to be free again, having forgotten what landed him in the cell to begin with.

"For now, we'll hold onto all of our prisoners until we can come up with a better solution short of letting them loose."

"We may have to deal with the kid sooner," said Steven. "If we don't, his daddy may round up a posse to come looking for him."

"Agreed. Let's talk about the UN forces and their capabilities."

Steven reached for a legal pad and slid it in front of Brad. Brad took a moment to read the three pages of notes.

"Check it out!" exclaimed Brad. "These guys mean business."

"That they do."

"Howitzers, T-72s, and Russian gunships. We can't compete with this." Brad slammed the notepad on the table in front of him. "What about troop strength?"

"Upwards of four thousand military and support personnel. Their artillery and vehicles are dispersed around the Seaport and the Cruise Ship Terminal."

"Where are the troops housed?"

"The Convention Center. They have to be cramped."

Brad removed his cap and ran his hand through his hair. "Steven, I'm not overstating this. This is a real problem for us."

"I get it, buddy. We need to consolidate your boys here and determine exactly how to counteract this."

"We have the upper hand because we know Boston and the rest of the terrain. Your observation people are well placed. But if we get into a battle, I can neutralize the tanks with the Javelins, but we can't miss."

According to Steven's intelligence reports gathered by the Mechanics, there were six Indian Army T-72 tanks, which had rolled out of the UN prepositioning ships.

By sheer luck, Brad had six FGM-148 Javelin portable antitank missiles, which were now stored at Prescott Peninsula. The 76th Field Artillery Regiment was based at Fort Devens. Part of the 4th

Brigade Combat Team out of Fort Stewart, Georgia, the 76th was being trained on the use of the FGM-148 system as the replacement for the older M47 Dragons.

Known as a fire-and-forget missile, it used an infrared guidance system that allowed the user to immediately seek cover after launch. The Javelin was the latest technology. It used a high-explosive, antitank warhead capable of penetrating solid vehicle armor. The missile was able to achieve a high trajectory by attacking the tanks from above.

"How many do you have?"

"Six T-72s, six Javelins," replied Brad.

"What about the helos?" asked Steven. "Got any more toys?"

"No problem there," replied Brad. "I consider this the higher priority. Those gunships could take out this whole complex in a flash. They're fast and agile and difficult to hit with small-arms fire. We've got to hit them when they're sittin' still."

"What do you have in mind?" asked Steven.

"MANPADS."

CHAPTER THIRTEEN

Thursday, October 6
6:00 p.m.
100 Beacon
Boston, Massachusetts

Sarge poured Steven a scotch and fixed one for himself. The brothers hadn't spent any time alone together since the attack on Prescott Peninsula last Saturday. Sarge also realized that he hadn't slept at 100 Beacon in nearly two weeks. Despite its dual purpose as his home and the base of operations for the Loyal Nine, the top-floor residence would always give him a sense of stability. Since Julia moved in with him last winter, the two had become a couple, and this was their home.

Julia was assisting Katie on the tenth floor in fulfilling Donald's *shopping list*. J.J.'s trauma supplies were diminished, and Donald wanted to increase his par levels of ammunition following their encounter last weekend.

The building was now inhabited by the Mechanics. Each of the two-million-dollar units housed two families. Sarge provided them with basic sustenance—beans, rice, pasta, and sauces. They also were given access to medical supplies and personal hygiene items.

In addition to their regular duties, which consisted of fighting the ever-expanding gangs of Boston, they also foraged through abandoned buildings. Sarge wrestled with the definition of looting and the more palatable connotation—foraging. He settled upon a survival standard. If the item was needed for survival and had been abandoned, then it became fair game as an item to be foraged. If the item was clearly a matter of luxury such as valuables, then pilfering it would be considered looting.

In typical short-minded thinking, the gangs focused on valuables during their looting expeditions. They relied upon O'Brien and the Citizen Corps to feed them. But as the Loyal Nine learned after the attack on Prescott Peninsula, either there wasn't enough food to go around or the Citizen Corps was picking winners and losers for the necessities of life. This was one of the topics to be discussed with Steven.

"Hey, check this out," said Steven, smiling. He reached into his rucksack and pulled out a rubber-coated ball with several small glass inserts.

Sarge picked it up and rolled it in his hand. "Have you been playing with Winnie the Frenchie?"

"No, this is way better than a toy. This, my brother, is a Bounce Imaging Explorer."

"Sounds like the name of a spacecraft." Sarge laughed as he began to roll the sphere back and forth on the table. He picked it up and bounced it on the tabletop.

Steven reached into his pack again and pulled out a smartphone-sized device, which he quickly strapped onto his wrist. He pushed a button and the display came to life.

"Check it out." Sarge looked closer at the display and then held the ball up to his eyes. With a swipe of his finger, Steven showed Sarge his eyes on the display.

"It's a camera!" exclaimed Sarge.

"Hell yeah!" said Steven. "Here, watch this." Steven took the

Explorer and rolled it down the center of the Great Hall until it disappeared behind the fireplace that stood in the middle of the room.

Steven swiped across the screen and the device showed him a three-hundred-sixty-degree view of the other side of the room.

"Cool," said Sarge. "Where'd you get it?"

"One of the Mechanics who moved into unit 4A is Boston PD," replied Steven. "When the crap hit the fan, he was on a SWAT team, which quickly disbanded. He kept his tactical gear."

"This has a lot of potential."

"If you have to clear a building, you can see who is armed and detect their position. Our guys will be able to differentiate between hostiles and friendlies."

"It's a throwable tactical camera," added Sarge. "How many do you have?"

"Just the one," replied Steven before adding, "but I've got a line on a whole lot more. They're made here in Boston by a company called Bounce Imaging."

"You're kidding." Sarge laughed.

"Nope. Our man says they're located down the street from Harvard Stadium. I'm gonna send a team down there and see if we can *procure* a few more."

Sarge got up to retrieve the Explorer. *Amazing technology.* He grabbed the Glenlivet off the kitchen island and poured them another round. He took his seat across from Steven.

"I assume you agree with Brad's decision to pull out of Fort Devens," started Steven. He took a quick swig of his drink.

"I do," said Sarge. He leaned back in his chair and draped his arm over the one next to him. "We've had our share of skirmishes, but last weekend was a clear wake-up call. We need to prepare for war."

"Brad and I agree, which is why we sat down yesterday and divided up our areas of responsibility. My forte is black ops, so I'll direct all of the activities of the Mechanics. He will continue to command his Marines except those who are under roof here. They'll handle our security and training of new recruits."

"How is recruiting coming along?"

"Well, this ball is a good example of what we've been able to accomplish. As the word is spreading around the city of our successes and goals, our numbers are swelling."

"How many?"

"Nearly a thousand, with more who are making overtures every day. We may not be able to match the troop strength of the United Nations forces, but at least our guys will be committed to the cause."

Sarge contemplated the rapid growth of the Mechanics. Numbers were important, as long as they were loyal and committed. Increasing the numbers too quickly could result in a spy entering their ranks.

"How are you vetting the new people?" he asked. "Adding someone to what is supposed to be a group of covert operatives has risks. It's like dating. You can't really tell if they're right for you until after a few dates."

Steven appeared to be put off by the question. "First off, they have to be recommended by an existing member. I don't believe in love at first sight, brother."

"I know, Steven," said Sarge. Steven's bristly reply caught him off guard. "We're in a pickle here. We need to increase our numbers, but we also need to maintain what you military guys call operational security."

"We look at a lot of things in addition to relationships. I wanna know what they bring to the table, like experience, weapons, and commitment."

Sarge didn't want to argue with his brother and was puzzled by his change in attitude. This wasn't intended to be a contentious conversation.

"What happens if one of the Mechanics wants out?" he asked, fully aware that this might rile his brother up further. These questions needed to be asked. Sarge had a much greater responsibility now, and he had to make sure that his subordinates, which included Steven, were on the same page.

Steven leaned forward. "We just shoot 'em."

"C'mon."

"Of course not, Sarge. Listen, the situation hasn't come up, but when it does, I'll handle it. Don't worry, bro, I've got this."

"Okay, okay, I know," said Sarge, wanting to change the subject. "What's the first thing on the agenda for the Mechanics?"

Steven seemed to relax as well and poured himself another drink. He started to pour one for Sarge, but Sarge held his hand up and declined another. Steven shrugged and set the bottle down.

"I've got things on the drawing board, both big and small. You and I will meet with our top people at the Liberty Tree in a couple of days. We're going to ramp up our insurgent activities. We're gonna be like a bunch of mosquitos constantly buzzing in O'Brien's ears."

"Guerrilla warfare?" asked Sarge.

"You have been paying attention!" exclaimed Steven.

"I've picked up a few things." Sarge laughed, welcoming the ease in tension between them.

"Guerrilla warfare enables us to move quickly and be more mobile. I've established over a dozen teams for this purpose. Sarge, to ease your fears, these teams are led by trusted guys—most of whom are living in the condo units below us. They handpick their men. New guys are eased into the process by proving themselves during our activities."

"Makes sense," said Sarge, who then attempted to recite the infamous quote from Sun Tzu. "It's the way of the weak against the strong."

"Exactly. When faced with a stronger force to overcome, you concentrate your efforts against its weak points to distract and disorganize the enemy."

"The UN forces are well armed, but they're also despised by the locals," said Sarge. "We can use that to our advantage."

"Winning a guerrilla war requires having popular opinion on your side. The city's population has been decimated. There has been a clear line established between the makers and takers. Right now, the takers outnumber the rest of us, but their hope is fading."

"They're not getting fed," interjected Sarge.

"You've got it. We are going to change that and try to win them over, at least in part. Once we do, I plan on turning the tide against O'Brien."

Sarge became very interested in Steven's plan. "What do you have in mind?"

"It's a combination of shock and awe and the Robin Hood approach."

Sarge laughed. "That's a mouthful."

"The timing is critical to our success. But after it's over, the Mechanics will be on the tip of the tongue of every patriot throughout the region, if not America."

CHAPTER FOURTEEN

Friday, October 7
11:58 a.m.
1st Battalion, 25th Marines HQ
Fort Devens, Massachusetts

The two Humvees roared out of the reinforced front gates that protected the entrance to Prescott Peninsula. Two days prior, several pickup trucks arrived and loaded the body bags containing the dead from the failed raid. The body count was thirty-seven, not counting those floating in the Quabbin Reservoir.

Brad moved quickly to handpick seven Marines to join him. Captain Branson contacted 1PP, advising them of the reported UN convoy heading up Highway 2 near Concord. The five-vehicle caravan was led by a Jeep, two troop carriers, and two armored vehicles. The all-white vehicles with the black letters *UN* emblazoned on the sides raised eyebrows near Hanscom Air Force Base in Bedford, prompting the call to Fort Devens.

Brad instructed Branson to secure the prisoners and close the shuttered windows of the former Federal Prison Camp. If the contingent arrived at the south gate before he did, Branson was instructed to deny entry. Brad would deal with the UN personnel himself.

Under normal circumstances, the UN convoy would arrive at the gate in forty minutes, but Brad instructed Gunny Falcone to leave Fort Devens and create an obstacle to slow their progress. They agreed upon a stretch of Highway 2 northwest of Acton.

Falcone fabricated an accident scene to block the road. The disabled vehicles would require the convoy to return to Acton and then pick up Highway 111, adding forty-five minutes to their trip. Brad would be given plenty of time to get into position.

Brad dispatched members of the Mechanics who lived in the surrounding community to monitor the UN's progress and route. There were several entrances into the Devens complex, and Brad wanted to be ready for all contingencies.

Brad arrived as he received a report that the convoy had turned north on Highway 111 at the small town of Harvard. They were only a few miles away from the Barnum Entrance, where Brad was already waiting.

Ordinarily, Barnum Road, and the large circle it created with the intersection of Highway 111 and East Main Street, was readily accessible to civilian traffic. Brad closed down the road to traffic after the cyber attack by installing concrete traffic barriers and razor wire. Not only did this prevent vehicular access, but it put the local residents on notice that Fort Devens was no longer open to pedestrians.

The businesses in the Barnum Road circle that serviced the base were closed and then looted. The Jack O'Lantern Package store, McDonald's, and Wendy's fell victim to the collapse of society. Much of the available inventory at Gervais Ford had either been stolen or ransacked. Even businesses within hundreds of yards of a military installation were not immune from the onslaught resulting from the aftermath of the cyber attack.

Brad stood defiantly in front of his two Humvees, which leveled their guns on the narrow entrance through the barriers. He'd strategically parked two abandoned vehicles in the roundabout, forcing the convoy to follow the rules of the road and take the entire circuitous route to the entrance. The forced route had the added effect of exposing the UN convoy on all sides. Brad had snipers on the rooftops of the fast feeders as well as Gervais Ford. The blocked exits and the forced entry created a perfect choke point for the approaching UN troops. They were deep into the trap before they could do anything about it.

"Gentlemen, remember our rules of engagement," said Brad into the radio. "Do not fire unless fired upon. As soon as they are contained within the circle, deploy the spike strips at Old Towne Road, pending further orders. Barnum Base out."

"Roger."

As soon as the convoy was fully contained in the roundabout, the lead vehicle came to a sudden stop, causing the other vehicles to bunch up behind the white UN Jeep. Both sides remained silent, and still, for several minutes.

Brad could see the passenger in the lead Jeep on a military phone. *Did they expect us to welcome them with flying baby blue UN flags and the customary marching band? Maybe throwing roses?*

The Jeep began to inch forward and came to a halt in front of the concrete barriers. Brad boldly walked forward, comforted in knowing that his soldiers would rain hellfire on the convoy if they so much as blinked.

A heavyset soldier came out of the doorless Jeep and put on his baby blue beret, indicating he was an officer with the UN contingent. He approached Brad with an envelope.

"I am Major Donald McLaughlin of the United Nations Peacekeeping forces," he said with an Irish accent. "I have orders to enter this facility. May I speak with your commanding officer?"

"I am the CO, Major. Your entry is denied."

The major thrust the envelope towards Brad, who hesitated before taking it. Without removing his eyes from the major, he opened it and glanced at the letterhead. It was written by Governor O'Brien, who now had gold flake letterhead on what felt like construction paper.

Brad attempted to hand it back to the major, who refused to take it. "Your entry is denied, sir. I'm advising you to leave!" Brad raised his voice for added effect. This, however, raised the attention of the UN troops, several of whom disembarked from their vehicles. Brad's men, including those hidden in the trees across the circle, immediately raised their weapons. The number of arms directed at the UN soldiers stopped them in their tracks.

"Major, I am advising you to order your men to remain in their vehicles, or this will not end well for any of you," said Brad.

The major raised his arm and yelled, "Stand down!" His soldiers had already done so, including two that beat a hasty retreat back into their troop carrier.

"Sir," the major started. "We all have our orders here. I am under the command of Major General Zhang Wei of the United Nations. You are holding in your hand a directive from Governor James O'Brien to allow us access to this military installation."

Brad dropped the envelope and its contents on the ground at the major's feet. "Do I need to repeat my request, Major?"

"I am the authority here!" yelled the frustrated UN officer.

"I'm afraid not, Major. This is the United States of America, and Fort Devens falls under the command of the United States Marine Corps. This conversation is over." With that, Brad turned and walked steadily to the front of the Humvees. He intentionally spoke into his comms loud enough for the major to hear his instructions. "On my order!"

The sounds of charging handles being pulled were heard throughout the tense air. The major from Ireland looked around frantically. Behind the trees, through the tall berms of orange daylilies, on the surrounding rooftops, and behind every blade of grass, American Marines drew their aim on his chest and those of his troops.

"This isn't over!" he shouted in Brad's direction.

Brad quickly turned and returned the challenge. "It is for today!"

CHAPTER FIFTEEN

Saturday, October 8
7:00 p.m.
630 Washington Street
Boston, Massachusetts

Once again, Sarge and Steven found themselves convening a meeting of the top lieutenants of the Mechanics. Sarge knew that keeping the same location could lead them to suffering the same fate as the Mechanics who continuously met at the Green Lantern Tavern prior to the Revolutionary War. Their meetings and the locations would have to become more clandestine.

Tonight marked the first time Katie attended a meeting with him. She was also the first woman to be included in the planning stage with the Mechanics. Steven argued with her before this decision was made. She won the argument and further encouraged him to take a greater role in the leadership of the Mechanics.

These are your men. You've got to assert yourself. That's the only way to gain the respect of all those people at Prescott Peninsula.

Katie was having difficulty hiding her contempt for the decision to put *Sarge in Charge*, as she frequently said sarcastically. She insisted that Steven was equally important, especially in light of the circumstances, and that he should've been given shared authority over the activities of the Boston Brahmin.

Steven tried to impress upon her that his relationship with his brother was solid, and they were a team. Each of the Loyal Nine had a role to play, and Sarge would be the guy who worked behind the scenes, politically and financially. Katie continued to bring his attention to perceived slights by Morgan toward Steven and favoritism for Sarge. Although Steven noticed and attempted to push these snubs out of his mind, the whole thing was beginning to wear on him.

"Let me get them started, and then I'll turn it over to you for the details of the operation," said Sarge as he walked up to join Katie and Steven.

"Sounds good," started Steven before he was interrupted by Katie.

"Shouldn't Steven be the sole voice of the Mechanics' leadership team?"

"Katie, of course these men look up to him as their leader," replied Sarge. Steven grabbed Katie's hand and squeezed it. She quickly pulled it away.

"Sarge, you have so much on your plate right now. Maybe it's time Steven's men looked to a single person for their inspiration and instruction."

Sarge stood silently, dumbfounded.

Steven had heard enough and stepped in. "Okay, Katie."

"Steven, this is how we've always conducted these meetings. I give them the *rah-rah* speech, and you go over the nuts and bolts of the operation. I have no problem stepping aside to let you conduct the whole meeting."

Steven was pissed. Katie should've kept her opinion to herself. This was an important night, and now there was a cloud of tension hanging over the three of them.

Katie held her hands up and said sarcastically, "I just thought you'd have more *important* things to do, that's all." *She had to get the last word.*

Sarge stood silently, looking back and forth between them. He put his hands in his pockets and shrugged. "Okay."

Steven leaned in and whispered to Sarge, "I've got this, bro."

Steven walked to the front of the open room and rapped his knuckles on the old wooden desk. The idle talk between the Mechanics died down as they turned their attention toward Steven.

"Everybody, listen up. We need to get started."

Steven took a deep breath and attempted to put the political infighting out of his mind. These were his men. He'd been building relationships with them for years. There was a mutual trust that Sarge did not enjoy with them. Now was his time to shine.

"Gentlemen, it's time to start poking the bear!"

Shouts of *choose freedom* and *hell yeah* filled the room. Each of these men commanded a team of insurgents that had enjoyed success against the governor so far. But now a much greater challenge in the form of the UN forces threatened them.

"We're gonna take them all on," Steven continued. "The Citizen Corps, FEMA, DHS, and now the UN are all threatening our freedoms and the very fabric of this country. We will not let this happen!"

"*Choose freedom!*" they shouted.

"Many of you are ex-military and law enforcement. I've known some of you for years. We come from all walks of life. Some of you are Ivy Leaguers, others are former gang members. Some of you were born with a silver spoon in your mouths, and others grew up with no spoon at all." Heads were nodding throughout the room, and men were slapping each other's backs. The collapse had created a large family of diverse people.

"We've learned a lot in our lifetime. Teamwork is important because if we don't work together, we will fail. In combat, failure can mean death.

"We learned tactics and strategy, discipline, and the importance of chain of command." Steven caught Sarge staring at him intently. *Was this speech for their benefit, his benefit, or mine?*

"Together, we are all learning how to survive, to fight, and to push ourselves far beyond our comfort zone. Many of us have seen the horrors of war while fighting abroad. Many of you have seen the horrors of watching your neighbors starve to death.

"Despite the effect this tragedy has on our great country, one thing we all can agree upon is how fortunate we are to be Americans."

"Yeah!" hollered several voices in the room. "God bless America," yelled another.

"I would rather be an American under these circumstances than a Russian or North Korean or Iranian or ISIS jihadist under any other!"

"Hell yeah! Choose freedom!" they responded in unison.

Steven allowed the cheers to die down and then he looked at his brother and smiled. Sarge remained impassive and cold. Steven shrugged it off and continued.

"Gentlemen, all hell is about to break loose. This governor is intent upon exerting his will over all of us. He has brought to our soil a foreign enemy under the disguise of a UN Peacekeeping force."

"Not gonna happen!" a man in the rear of the room hollered.

"I agree, and that's why we're gathered here tonight," Steven replied. "We have two missions waiting for us to undertake. Once successful, a war will begin for the hearts and souls of our fellow Bostonians and the rest of this country. They will see that our nation was not built on government handouts or with the help of foreign soldiers. Men founded America with independent freedom-loving hearts and minds. Tomorrow, we will send a clear message to the world!"

"Choose freedom!"

"That's right, my friends, choose freedom!" Steven responded.

"We will not fail in our mission. We will prevail. But know this, success is not a goal. It is a by-product of planning and preparation. Now, let's get down to it."

CHAPTER SIXTEEN

Sunday, October 9
Dusk
Seaport District
Boston, Massachusetts

Gunny Falcone navigated the first of three nondescript Ford Econoline vans through the stalled vehicles on India Street as he cautiously approached the Wharf District Park. The three vans would cross the open intersection of Atlantic Avenue about five minutes apart. The Seaport was less than a mile to their south, and it was bustling with activity. This operation was going to be difficult to pull off without being noticed by the UN troops.

The second van would join him at the maintenance entrance to the southernmost of the two Harbor Towers. A pair of forty-floor condominium residences designed by revered architect I.M. Pei, the buildings provided incredible views of Boston Harbor and the Seaport.

The third van would move closer to the Seaport, taking up a position at Rowe's Wharf. This cluster of hotels, shops, and businesses provided ample opportunities to strike the UN gunships, which were parked at Fan Pier Park on the northern tip of the Seaport District.

Falcone and his men understood there was a high probability of capture or even death. They were initiating an unprovoked attack on international troops who were in America ostensibly to lend assistance during the relief effort. Of course, Falcone and his fellow Marines knew better. They also knew the opportunity to undertake this mission was running out. After the altercation at Fort Devens, Governor O'Brien would instruct the UN to use force in order to disgorge the Marines from their base. Tonight's attack would level the playing field.

The third van, carrying four Marines and an equal number of FIM-92 Stinger missiles, would get into position first. The four men would disperse in high and low hiding spots throughout the Rowe's Wharf complex. Using their communications gear, they would coordinate the attack and then focus their attention on a potential counterattack. They would delay and distract the UN troops while the remainder of the team at Harbor Towers completed the op.

The first priority was to take out the Russian-made Mi-24, an attack helicopter equipped with Gatling guns, multiple ejector racks for bomb loads, and the S-8 heat-seeking rocket launchers. This aircraft could single-handedly eliminate 1PP, Fort Devens, and 100 Beacon within a two-hour flight.

"Alpha Leader, Mike One. Over," said the unit leader positioned at Rowe's Wharf. The designation Mike, or *M* in military alphabet code, was used because their mission was to eliminate the Mi-class helicopters.

"In position, Alpha Leader. Mike One out."

"Roger, Mike One," said Falcone. His Tango teams were so designated because their mission was to destroy the Russian-made but Indian Army-provided T-72 tanks. The T-72 had a storied military history dating back to the Afghanistan War that involved the Soviet Army in the eighties. Its reliable design and flexible characteristics made the T-72 a cornerstone of the UN forces' armored fighting vehicles.

Falcone walked onto the balcony of a sixteenth-floor condominium unit at Harbor Towers. The high-rise unit provided him an unobstructed field of view of the Seaport and allowed him to place his teams. The challenge for the Tango team was to reach raised positions in the building without being noticed by any remaining residents. Carrying the forty-nine-pound FGM-148 Javelin antitank missiles up the many flights of stairs was a challenge for his most physical Marines. This southernmost tower was chosen because it had a direct line of sight to the Seaport, and therefore a higher elevation was not critical.

He needed to make contact with another team—Steven's. "Romeo Leader, Alpha Leader. Over."

"Roger, Alpha."

"Sitrep."

"In position, awaiting your go," said Steven.

"Roger, Romeo, you'll know. Alpha Leader out."

Falcone studied the parking areas and open grounds surrounding the Boston Convention Center and other attractions comprising the Seaport District. He hoped any locals were removed when the UN arrived. War, by necessity, resulted in civilian casualties. But the Mechanics were beginning a propaganda war as well, and numerous deaths to noncombatants would get them off to a rocky start.

"Tango One in position."

"Roger that, Tango One," replied Falcone. The remainder of the Tango teams checked in and Falcone knew it was time to light 'em up.

"Mike One, Alpha Leader. You're green light, go."

Falcone lifted the Steiner 20 x 80 binoculars to his eyes and looked through the massive 80mm lenses. As dusk overtook Boston Harbor, the low-light performance provided him an excellent field of view.

Suddenly, the first of the MANPADS—man portable air defense systems—exploded from Rowe's Wharf. The Raytheon designed infrared homing Stinger missile quickly and easily found its mark.

The Mi-24 gunship burst into flames, sending debris in all directions.

Without directives from Falcone, Mike Two fired its Stinger at the Mi-26 troop transport. The after burn of the solid-fuel rocket motor burned brightly in the dim light for a few seconds before a massive ball of flame lifted into the sky. Both choppers had been destroyed in less than a minute.

"Well done, Mike teams. Hold your positions."

"Roger that, Alpha Leader."

Falcone took another quick glance through the binoculars before giving the Tango team its green light.

"Tango One, GO!" he ordered into the comms.

Each Tango Team manned two of the portable Javelin missile systems. Assisting one another in setup and guidance assured accuracy. The thunderous exploding sound of the first missile launch reverberated off the desolate buildings of downtown Boston. Within seconds, the eighteen-pound missile utilized its imaging infrared capabilities and roared toward its first target, a T-72 tank located near the entrance of the Convention Center. Because of its distance, this would prove to be the most difficult shot.

The FGM-148's tactical precision engagement system did not disappoint. The upgraded armor of the T-72's turret created a thicker, nearly vertical front. Due to its *chesty* appearance, it was unofficially nicknamed Dolly Parton by military analysts. It was not a match for the effectiveness of the Javelin warhead. Upon impact, the tank's turret collapsed, and the inside of the tank swelled from the force of the high-explosive blast fragmentation.

"Hit," announced Falcone into the radio. "Go, Tango Two."

Another Javelin missile was immediately launched. Again, with deadly accuracy, a second T-72 was destroyed. Tango Three enjoyed similar results as did Tango One and their next opportunity. The Seaport was now in chaos. UN troops were frantically running from the area of the Convention Center. Vehicles loaded with soldiers raced across the Seaport Boulevard and Congress Street bridge. The Mi-24 parked at Children's Wharf Park was still in flames as its rotors fell off into the Fort Point Channel.

A different result occurred when Tango Two took their second turn. The UN forces, not anticipating an attack of this nature, mistakenly parked two tanks next to each other. Tango Two took them both out with one missile.

Falcone's mission was complete, but he still had the final Javelin at his disposal. He contemplated his options before his thoughts were interrupted.

"Alpha Leader, Tango Three. Over."

"Stand by, Tango Three." *Gotta make a decision here.* Falcone weighed his options. He could take out the bridge at Seaport Boulevard, but there were several other bridges crossing the channel at the UN's disposal. He could pack up and return with the final FGM-148 system for another mission.

Or he could deal a deadly blow to the enemy. The final Javelin could kill hundreds of the UN soldiers still within the Boston Convention Center. It would either destroy their morale while reducing their ranks or stir an already angry hornet's nest. Gunny Falcone was a seasoned veteran, a soldier who had seen many tours of duty in combat. He had seen war firsthand. He'd seen the savagery of evil people inflicted against innocents. He was ready to pull the trigger. *They're not here to help us, they're here to suppress us!*

"This is Alpha Leader. EXTRACT! EXTRACT!"

Semper Fi.

CHAPTER SEVENTEEN

Sunday, October 9
Dusk
Greater Boston Area Food Bank
70 South Bay Street
Boston, Massachusetts

For days, Steven had teams surveilling the Greater Boston Area Food Bank. Trucks loaded with food and supplies were escorted into the facility by UN-manned vehicles, but the team never reported any food distribution trucks being dispatched into the city. Their suspicions were confirmed—Governor O'Brien was hoarding the food, America's most valuable currency.

The Mechanics were positioned on the side streets just south of the eighty-thousand-square-foot warehouse. If the UN soldiers were ordered to respond to the attack on the Seaport District, they would most likely choose Atkinson Street, which was located next to the now-empty Suffolk County Jail, and then jump on I-93 into the city. They were only a few miles from the Seaport District, and it was likely an overreaction by UN officers that would trigger a recall of the personnel to assist.

This mission was full of uncertainty and risk. The payoff, however, could be a game-changer. Not only would the cupboards of the Mechanics be filled, but the ability to distribute the food to Bostonians who might join the cause was immeasurable. Despite the risk, Steven looked forward to the action. He needed to get away from Katie chirping in his ear and the specter of his brother hanging over his head. The Robin Hood mission was just what the doctor ordered.

"Roger, Romeo, you'll know. Alpha Leader out." This was the final transmission between Steven and Gunny Falcone. Within moments, the first explosion rocked the downtown area to their north. At first, the UN soldiers guarding the loading docks stood in shock. After the second blast, as predicted, their radios roared to life.

Steven maintained his position atop the MBTA Transit Parking Garage. This provided him a clear view of the Food Bank's loading docks and the parking lot across the street, which contained six UN Humvees and a troop transport. Two nights ago, two of the Mechanics had maneuvered themselves into the abandoned T-shirt factory immediately across from the Bay Street entrance to the Food Bank. They were able to hear all of the radio instructions provided to the UN security personnel.

"Romeo Leader, Romeo One." A hushed voice came across the comms.

"Go, One," replied Steven.

"By our ongoing headcount, eighteen leaving, thirteen remaining. Over."

"Roger, Romeo One. Out."

Using a strategy he'd employed at the Massachusetts Guard Armory in Braintree, Steven strategically placed two-man teams near the facility a day in advance. They were able to use the cover of darkness to hide in abandoned MBTA transit buses and in the Suffolk County Jail intake center. After the UN vehicles had cleared the area and were committed northbound on the Massachusetts Avenue Connector, he would engage.

The UN trucks quickly took a right turn onto Southampton Street and headed up the entrance to Interstate 93. *Let's roll!*

Steven and two members of his team ran down the back stairs of the parking garage and into the darkening night. The last of the explosions were heard resonating through the skyscrapers of Boston. His mind only registered seven, not eight, as expected. *Did I miss one? Did something go wrong?* It was agreed in advance to maintain radio silence after Falcone's mission was complete. If the UN picked up any continued conversations, they might be alerted to an ongoing attack and respond accordingly. Steven let it go.

"Romeo Four, Five and Six, advance to ready positions."

"Romeo One, Two and Three, be ready."

Steven gave his teams orders as he moved quickly up Moore Street to join Romeo Two and Three behind the MBTA buses. In their briefing earlier, he outfitted everyone with suppressed M4s. They needed to move swiftly and silently. If any of the troops inside the facility were able to warn their superiors, he and his team would be surrounded, and all exit points could be easily blocked. Between the prison walls and the twenty-foot walls upon which the I-93 frontage road had been built, there was no other escape route. They would have to fight their way out against a much larger enemy.

Hidden across Southampton Street in the parking lots of Newmarket Square were nearly two dozen escort vehicles designed to provide the eighteen-wheelers cover and security during their escape. Prearranged destinations had been selected throughout the city where the food trucks could be hidden and the contents offloaded without being detected.

"All teams, on my go, fire on any identifiable targets." Steven hesitated, glanced at the faces of his team, and yelled into his radio, "GO!"

Steven led the way through the gated fence, firing as he ran. The UN troops were caught completely by surprise, and within moments, nearly a dozen bodies lay on the ground in their own blood. As Steven assessed the carnage, he could see muzzle flashes coming from the windows of the Food Bank's upper levels. The crack of the passing rounds caused him to dive for cover under the protective canopy covering the loading docks.

A member of Romeo Three started to send bursts of three to five rounds through the windows where he could see muzzle flashes. Steven felt a hand on his shoulder and moved to the side to let one of his team take a position in front of him. The man was shielding him from incoming fire, allowing him to resume his command role.

More muzzle flashes lit up the second-story windows. Steven's main concern was the fact that they had been discovered. They had to move quickly.

"Romeo Four, remain outside and watch our six. All other teams, let's clear the building. Quickly. We're looking for half a dozen or so hostiles." They didn't have much time. Each team chose a different breach point. Some went into the open warehouse while others followed Steven's lead through the entrance to the Yawkey Distribution Center, named for philanthropist and former owner of the Boston Red Sox Tom Yawkey. Unconsciously, Steven felt for the Bounce Imaging Camera in his vest. "Play ball," he muttered aloud.

All of the teams were in and were making their way through the building. It was oddly quiet. Steven did not hear any radio chatter. *Did they not have any way of communicating with their superiors?*

It was well past dusk, so the teams used white light flashlights mounted to their M4s once they were inside the facility. Steven motioned for two of the squads to move through the first-floor offices. He and two teams bounded up the stairs towards the source of the earlier gunfire.

In the building, there was a central hallway with offices off to the sides. Some of the offices had been converted to sleeping quarters. Some of the rooms had points of entry from the corridor, while others were interconnected via internal doorways. It was a vast and darkening maze.

With Steven watching the hallways, he instructed the two-man teams to clear each of the rooms. Steven organized and sequenced the men to flow through the rooms evenly. Care had to be taken to ensure the team on one side of the corridor did not pass an unclear area on the other.

Where they were able, they moved between the internal doorways. While being cautious, they had to hit the rooms aggressively with the intention of startling their occupants. Steven would follow their progress and act as their cover while the teams breached each room.

The tension was high as—

Spit—spit—spit. "One down," said Romeo Two.

Steven and the two teams continued their march forward. "Two captured," announced Romeo Five. *Two to go.*

Steven and the two teams came together near the end of the hallway, where a large set of double steel doors remained closed. At least two gunmen had opened fire from the second floor. From the head count, provided it was accurate, there would be two remaining hostiles.

Steven eased open one of the doors and saw the room was divided into a break room and computer terminals located in temporary cubicles. The room must have been used for the truck drivers to eat a meal and access their schedules online. It was now fairly dark except for the faint glow of light from outside. This was going to be a tough room to clear.

Steven stepped through the doorway first, attempting to lead by example. Two members of his team followed. Suddenly, there was a muzzle flash and a hail of bullets came from the left side of the room. The burst passed over the top of Steven and stitched along the wall. One of his team was not so lucky as a round struck him in his ballistic plate as well as hitting the bolt assembly of his rifle. The former police officer grunted and was punched back into the wall, winded from the impact. He dropped to his knees and let go of his M4 but rapidly transitioned to his sidearm, which was secured in his kit.

Steven dropped to a knee and started rapidly firing rounds into the left side of the room, shredding several cubicles. Two more members of the team had entered the room and moved along the other outer walls. They soon found one of the assailants—a uniformed UN soldier crouched behind a Coke machine—fully geared up in body armor and a helmet. Steven's flashlight gave away their position and the UN soldier swung his weapon toward them.

Steven approached from the center of the room. *Hips and heads, Hips and heads.* He found his mark and shot the soldier several times through the center of his body. The soldier screamed in pain and fell backward against the wall, and Steven finished him with a shot to the head.

To his left, flashlights lit up the back side of a salad bar.

"Ne tirez pas! Ne tirez pas!" screamed a young French soldier. He was begging, *Don't shoot!*

One of Steven's team announced, "Room clear, no exits." Steven reached down and took the dead soldier's M4, handing it to his man who was shot.

Steven led his team back to the front of the building, but he stationed two men on the rooftop. They were to provide support from above, but more importantly, keep an eye out for UN reinforcements coming from downtown.

Incredibly, none of the UN soldiers had any form of communications. Perhaps the comms were only held by officers, as all of these personnel appeared to be grunts. In any event, Steven was prepared to put Operation Robin Hood into effect.

The remaining members of the Mechanics arrived on the scene and were running fork trucks in and out of the trailers backed up to the loading bay. As one pulled out, a delivery truck was backed into its space. The men, chosen for their trucking and loading dock experience, moved quickly and efficiently. In total, ten tractor-trailer rigs left fully loaded as well as a dozen or more twenty-four-foot delivery vans proudly displaying the Food Bank's mission statement—*hunger hurts, we can help.*

As the last van pulled out of the loading dock, Steven turned and looked at the vast, empty space, except for the bound and gagged Frenchman in the middle of the room.

Pleasure doing business with you, Governor O'Brien.

CHAPTER EIGHTEEN

Monday, October 10
8:10 a.m.
Citizen Corps Region I, Office of the Governor
99 High Street
Boston, Massachusetts

Governor O'Brien was out-of-his-mind livid. He had received initial reports of the assault on the UN forces within moments after the last tank was destroyed. But it wasn't until this morning that he learned of the devastating theft of his coveted food stores. He demanded that Pearson and Major General Zhang meet up in his office first thing. They were both late, which didn't help his state of mind.

He paced the floor, looking at his watch. What the hell was he supposed to do about the lost provisions? They, *whoever they are,* cleaned out a warehouse and stole all of their trucks. How the hell could this happen?

A timid knock on the door accompanied Pearson's arrival. O'Brien dispensed with the preliminaries. He practically charged at Pearson when he entered the conference room. "You're late!"

"Security is very tight downtown, Governor," defended Pearson. "After yesterday, it appears—"

"It appears somebody finally woke the hell up!"

"Yesterday was devastating to us. Major General Zhang is very angry as well, sir."

O'Brien wondered whether he would be able to make it through this morning without strokin' out. "Oh, he's angry, is he?" said O'Brien sarcastically. "I don't give a damn if he's shooting bottle rockets out of his backside. They've been sitting out there for ten days, waiting for a warm bed and a hot cup of tea before beddy-bye. Guess what? They got themselves blown up, and all of my food is gone!"

"Yes, sir, I understand," said Pearson sheepishly.

O'Brien gave him the death stare. "Do you really? Understand, I mean?" he asked. "Let's recap, shall we? I've got no guns. In the process of that debacle, I lost forty-four of my best men. But hey, we found them. Good news! My army finally shows up for duty, and they sit around on their hands. I give them their own military base and the opportunity to be big heroes by bringing back my boys. What happens? They come back with their tails stuck between their legs. Do you think they came back, fired up the tanks, and return to teach that smug SOB Bradlee a thing or two? Hell no! Instead they sat around and talked about it or who knows what. While they are *commis-ah-rating*, somebody blows up all of their stuff and steals my food! How the hell am I doing so far?"

Pearson wisely didn't respond. O'Brien looked at his watch again and then stared out towards Boston Harbor. For the tenth time that morning, he shook his head as his eyes were drawn from one destroyed tank to another. All that remained of his army was a handful of howitzers and a bunch of foreigners who had yet to get anything right.

"Good morning, gentlemen," announced Zhang as he entered the conference room. O'Brien didn't turn to greet him. He was sick of this Chinese protocol, pomp and damned circumstance. *Give me results, and then I'll play your prissy games.*

O'Brien gathered himself and sat at the head of the table, hoping to reestablish the hierarchy amongst the three men. He halfheartedly gestured for the other men to join him. Venting at Pearson helped, but he did not intend to mince words.

"General, how long will it take for you to obtain replacement tanks and helicopters?" asked O'Brien.

"Sixty to ninety days," he replied. Zhang showed no emotion during the exchange. "We are due for a resupply of necessary provisions and food on January 1. The armaments will come at that time."

O'Brien stared at him, shaking his head. "That's a real shame, General. We're losing before getting started. We need weapons, we need food, and we need to find out who the hell did this!"

"Governor, until we are resupplied, may I suggest a different tack?"

"By all means," replied O'Brien, throwing his hands up and leaning back in his chair to near its tipping point.

"I have a significant amount of experience in dealing with rebels and insurgent activity. We can rely upon what has worked in the past and take a different approach to this situation."

"Okay, I'm open for any suggestions that yield a better result than the last seventy-two hours."

"Terrorist fighters such as these can be difficult to beat. My first suggestion is to gain control of the city. Your President has established martial law. Let's enforce his dictates. First, we will establish roadblocks to prevent the insurgents from traveling freely around the city. Second, a strict curfew should be put into place. If we find the curfew is routinely violated, then authorize shoot-to-kill orders for any violation. Third, confiscate weapons. Your second amendment has been suspended, has it not?"

"It has," replied O'Brien. He looked at Pearson, who would probably leave and never come back after this morning. "I like what I hear so far. Continue."

"I will implement a plan of house-to-house searches. We will announce we are looking for deceased or ailing residents. We will reiterate that in this state of emergency, many have perished and disease is an important concern. As we conduct these searches, we will confiscate weapons and look for the insurgents."

"How will you know if they are insurgents?" asked Pearson, finally mustering up the courage to speak. *Lucky for him it was a good question*. O'Brien was still angry.

"They will be well fed, healthy, and stocked with supplies. Under the President's orders, we can confiscate excesses. Am I correct on this?"

"Yes," replied Pearson.

"Go on." O'Brien was starting to feel better.

"Governor, your police activity has been insufficient to prevent this uprising. Sometimes, brute military force is needed to suppress the people seeking to undermine the authority of the government."

O'Brien was feeling significantly better. "Now we're talkin'."

"This is a vast city, and a coordinated effort must be made. Our soldiers are ready, Governor. Their comrades were killed in these attacks. They are prepared to get their just revenge."

"I'm glad to hear that, General," said O'Brien. "Will three thousand or so troops be enough? Wasn't it your Admiral Yamamoto who said *there's a rifle behind every blade of grass*?"

"Governor," Zhang bristled, "first of all, I am Chinese, and Yamamoto was Japanese. Secondly, he never said that. My forces know how to conduct searches and how to confiscate weapons. We don't care how many blades of grass are in your city."

CHAPTER NINETEEN

Saturday, October 15
2:00 p.m.
1 PP
Quabbin Reservoir, Massachusetts

Morgan used the hickory stick cane to assist him as he methodically walked through woods with Sarge. His left side was weak from the stroke, and he was under orders by J.J. to begin a light exercise regimen. Morgan began walking a couple of days ago around the 1PP compound, and now he was ready to venture out into the well-worn trails. He needed to talk with Sarge away from prying ears.

Like most people, Morgan took walking for granted until he suffered the debilitating injury. It required him to focus on the mechanics, especially when using a cane. Coordination was required. He firmly gripped the hickory stick meticulously carved by Donald in his shop beneath 1PP. It was a nice gesture by the young man. Morgan ambled along, holding the cane in his good right hand so that it provided support. As he took a step with his left leg, which was weakened by the stroke, he would bring the cane forward at the same time. He was careful to maintain the weight of his body on the right side. The entire process was strenuous, physically and mentally.

After about fifteen minutes, Morgan pointed to a series of rock outcroppings that resembled a park bench. The soldiers escorting them took up positions out of earshot but close enough to provide protection.

"Let's sit here for a while, Henry," said Morgan as he tilted his head back to soak in the afternoon sun. "Fall is a beautiful time of year."

"Yes, sir."

"Henry, you and I have much to discuss," started Morgan. It had been two weeks since the stroke, which was not an inordinate amount of time, except during a period of collapse. "I am out of touch with world events. Julia is now providing me daily briefings, and Mr. Quinn has kept me abreast of our financial holdings."

"Are they bombarding you with information unnecessarily?" asked Sarge.

"No, I welcome the distraction from this," he replied, beating his cane on the rocks. "I want to stay informed so that you and I stay on the same page. My concern is that I am losing a grip on the political machinations that are critical to the position that I, um, you hold." Morgan caught himself and his voice trailed off. He had to constantly remind himself that he'd passed the torch to Henry.

"Yes, sir. News and financial matters can be summarized in reports. Politics requires direct contact with those involved."

"Precisely, Henry. We need to begin the transition with our contacts around the world and especially within our own government."

"Sir, are you rested enough to make these overtures? Your speech is certainly better."

Morgan adjusted his position on the rock. It was becoming uncomfortable. He nodded in agreement. "I am capable of making the introductory phone calls, and we will begin that process on Monday."

Morgan paused and thought about the time he was handed the

reins of the Boston Brahmin. He remembered that meeting vividly. The Boston Brahmin each introduced themselves and then they told him of their formation dating back to the mid-1700s. They were brought together by their opposition to tyranny and held together by their love of country.

"When I was tasked with managing the affairs of the Boston Brahmin, I did not have the aptitude and prowess that you possess, Henry. I was a good lawyer and financially savvy, but I didn't understand the politics—especially the people side. I used my power like a bull in a china shop. It served me well because most of my decisions were money driven and, after all, most human beings are driven by the desire to obtain more wealth."

"Times have changed to an extent," interjected Sarge.

"They have, temporarily. This provides us an opportunity, one that requires a leader of men. I was able to yield power and influence, but I was never the leader that you are, Henry."

"Thank you, sir. I understand the political game, but I never envisioned being a part of it."

"Henry, you are an American patriot. Like your predecessors, we believe our nation is the greatest in the world and a beacon of hope for others. But as such, we are also subject to the disdain of the jealous. That makes us the perfect target."

"Yet the Boston Brahmin have been able to survive and thrive for centuries. Your wealth and power continue to grow."

Morgan struggled to stand. "Let's walk some more. This rock is rough on my tailbone."

"Okay," replied Sarge, helping Morgan to his feet. "Would you prefer to do this another time?"

"No, I'm fine," replied Morgan, pointing the stick deeper into the woods. "We're behind schedule, and events are transpiring that we need to get ahead of."

"What is going to happen?" Sarge asked apprehensively.

"Nothing imminent, but politics is a complicated game of chess in which your opponent is capable of cheating. When your opponent cheats, you must use your leadership skills to gain alliances and win the game."

The men, teacher and student, continued to walk at a slow, leisurely pace down the path.

Morgan continued. "You possess all of the traits of an effective leader such as confidence, commitment, and intuition. You have excellent communications skills and the ability to inspire. Now, we need to channel these traits toward clear objectives."

"I'm ready, sir."

"Good. The world's economy is collapsing. I'll get to how we benefit from that in a moment. But first, we need to assure our geopolitical allies that the ship will be righted soon enough. Further, we need to make it clear to the Russians that now is not an opportunity to take advantage of our position of weakness."

"How do we communicate that?" asked Sarge. "Our military is in disarray. Our only available response to an attack by their military would be a nuclear strike. Nobody wins then."

"No, we have to back them down with a counterweight—an unlikely military ally."

"The Chinese?" questioned Sarge.

"Yes. Similar to today, during the American Revolution, the colonists faced the challenge of conducting international diplomacy while fighting a war on its own soil. Through the efforts of Benjamin Franklin, our Founding Fathers forged an alliance with the French. The French provided the colonists military support, but more importantly, the threat of an escalation in hostilities between France and Great Britain kept the Brits off-balance."

"It was a maneuver that bought the colonists time," added Sarge.

"Indeed, and we will employ a similar tactic. While the Chinese are not exactly our allies, they are pragmatists. Our government owes them trillions of dollars. They want their money back, but more importantly, they need us as a trading partner. Without U.S. dollars purchasing Chinese goods, their nation collapses."

Morgan stopped them as they reached the opening of the path

onto Prescott Shutesbury Road. He leaned on his cane with both hands and looked at Sarge.

"We'll play on their greed to get them to do our bidding. The Beijing government requires a stable America. Without our dollars, they are unable to sustain themselves financially. If their government becomes unstable, they'll lose control of their population."

"And a revolution will result," interjected Sarge. "They already know this. We just need to remind them."

"Absolutely."

CHAPTER TWENTY

Saturday, October 15
3:00 p.m.
1 PP
Quabbin Reservoir, Massachusetts

"The President cannot learn of my poor health. He must see me as an equal. We started this endeavor on an equal footing, and if he gains the upper hand, it will have a devastating impact on our nation."

Following that fateful evening when Sarge and Morgan argued about the initiation of the cyber attack, Sarge contemplated Morgan's intentions. He came to the same conclusion—the country was in need of a reset. *How far was too far? Is there a limit to how far one may go to achieve their goals?*

"Sir, I've come to understand your reasoning behind the cyber attack. It's not necessary for us to continue our conversation from two weeks ago."

"Every decision I make on behalf of the Boston Brahmin is designed to be for the long-term good of the country and for us financially. The world is ruled by power, but power is obtained by money. The two are interconnected."

"How do we benefit from the collapse of the American economy?" asked Sarge.

"Young man, catastrophes create many opportunities for profit," started Morgan as they approached the rocks where the conversations began. Morgan quickly took a seat and continued. "Our country was on a path to becoming the next Greece. Like so many before them, the Greek government thought it could print money to solve its social and economic problems."

"I presume you had a limited time to act," said Sarge.

"Just prior to the event, I made major adjustments in our holdings," said Morgan. "I made substantial investments in precious metals. I moved out of all stocks except those companies owned by our associates."

"What if the dollar collapses and is replaced by another currency?" asked Sarge.

"That's not likely. The world markets are already in turmoil, but abandoning the dollar would turn everyone against us. We must bolster the world's confidence in our currency once again."

"Are you suggesting we return to the gold standard?"

"Yes. Our financial problems can be traced back to Nixon's abandonment of the gold standard in the early seventies. Before the collapse, it would have been very difficult to transition back. Gold, like any commodity, is assigned a value and subject to inflation and deflation. It cannot, however, be printed out of thin air like our currency. Because our country had insufficient gold reserves to back up the amount of currency in circulation, the dollar would experience a precipitous loss in value."

Sarge nodded his head in agreement. Limiting the amount of money the government could print when the economy experienced a downturn resulted in higher unemployment. With the entire nation out of work due to the collapse, the timing might be right.

"If we transition to a gold standard now, our government could reestablish the dollar as the world's currency and set itself on a course of financial discipline, which would include balancing its budget."

Morgan nodded and smiled. "You see, Henry, pre-collapse, the American people were not ready for such reforms. Half the nation was on the government dole. Politicians, pressured by voters to give them more, didn't have the intestinal fortitude to make the tough decisions to save our country from economic collapse."

Sarge studied Morgan briefly and then Sarge got it. The major stumbling block to economic and monetary reform was ideological. If this obstacle could be overcome, a return to the gold standard could become a realistic possibility.

"For this to happen, we would have to reintroduce gold and silver as the currency of choice," said Sarge.

"Julia has shed some light on this subject," said Morgan. "She is receiving reports from around the country that marketplaces are being established in small communities. In addition to barter, the preferred method of payment is gold and silver. As world markets settle or bottom out, the dollar value can be established in a gold equivalent. The best time to institute a gold-money ratio is when the market value of the dollar is at its lowest."

Morgan paused to regain his strength and then continued. "If we could achieve that, it would spark the acquisition of gold at an unprecedented rate. There would be a tremendous increase in gold mining, processing and other ancillary industries related to the production, sales, and storage of gold."

"Makes sense. This is why you acquired so much gold and filled the vaults below 1PP."

"There's more, Henry," started Morgan. "The Boston Brahmin acquired two companies just before the collapse—Newmont Mining and Barrick Gold. We now control seven of the ten largest gold mines in the world, which generate seventy percent of the world's production."

"Wow."

"Yes, Henry, wow." Morgan laughed. "In addition, we've acquired depositories worldwide. As this transition is made, we have the ability to manipulate gold prices in the same manner OPEC has manipulated oil prices for decades. Once the gold standard is firmly ensconced into the U.S. monetary system, we can use our expanded wealth to control geopolitical events."

"I must say, this was very risky," said Sarge. "What if the President doesn't agree to place the nation on a gold standard? It is clearly contradictory to his political beliefs. No administration has printed more currency than his."

Morgan paused and turned to Sarge. "JFK once said there are risks and costs to taking action, but they are far less than the long-range risks of comfortable inaction. For too long, freedom-loving Americans sat idly by while an ever-expanding government inserted itself into our lives. You know this. This economy was collapsing before our eyes. It needed a drastic jolt."

"I've come to agree with you, sir. I see the plan as a very big calculated risk. But the goals we hope to achieve may be impossible to reach."

"I disagree, Henry," said Morgan. "Impossible is just an excuse. Anyone who tells you that something is impossible to achieve has probably failed in their own attempts. Our Founding Fathers undertook the impossible. Not only did they defeat what was arguably the greatest military power of their time, but they forged a new nation built on the greatest founding document in history—the Constitution."

"What if the President stands in your way?"

"Then he has to go," Morgan said as he stood and began walking toward 1PP. He was visibly tired.

"Well, elections are in three weeks and he'll be gone after the inauguration," said Sarge, who caught up with Morgan.

"No, he won't. The President will act to suspend elections under the authority of his martial law declaration."

Sarge stopped in his tracks. "We have to stop him. He can't do that."

Morgan also stopped and planted his cane firmly on the ground. "We can't stop him, nor should we."

"Why not?" asked Sarge.

"Revolutions cannot succeed unless you have the will of the people on your side. This can take time, or it can come in a hurry. There were several events that led up to the Battles of Lexington and Concord in 1775. Their names are well known—the Boston Massacre and the Boston Tea Party. But these trigger events occurred in 1770 and 1773 respectively. The seeds of liberty were sown many years before that." Morgan continued his walk and motioned for Sarge to follow him.

"To effectuate change in a hurry, there must be a catalyst," said Morgan.

"Like the cyber attack?" asked Sarge.

"In part. But the President will naturally enjoy a period where the people rally behind him based upon promises of disaster relief and protection. When the American people begin to see that he can't deliver, they will turn on him."

"It's happening already," interjected Sarge. "The government doesn't have the resources to deal with an event of this magnitude. The people are losing confidence in his promises, and they're becoming angry."

"How do you think they'll feel when he usurps his constitutional authority and suspends elections for the purposes of remaining in office?" asked Morgan.

"They'll be angry."

"Yes, they will. We have to accomplish two things very quickly, Henry. First, we have to introduce you as the leader of a movement. A movement intent on helping your fellow Americans while reestablishing our nation's greatness in the vision of the Founding Fathers."

"Okay, what's the second thing?"

"Every movement, every revolution, has an event to rally around. There was the Boston Tea Party. The attack on Pearl

Harbor rallied the nation into accepting World War II. The attacks of 9/11 allowed us to take the fight to terrorists abroad."

"We have to wait for a seminal moment," added Sarge.

"We do, and we'll know when it happens. Be ready, young man."

CHAPTER TWENTY-ONE

Wednesday, October 19
10:00 a.m.
Home of Governor Charlie Baker
Swampscott, Massachusetts

There were many perks that awaited Governor Charlie Baker following his successful gubernatorial campaign and subsequent inauguration delivered to a joint session of the legislature in January 2015. But unlike most chief executives of other states, he did not receive a fancy governor's mansion. Despite efforts to establish one in the past, Massachusetts did not have an official governor's residence.

The Shirley-Eustis House in Roxbury, a Georgian mansion built by the former British royal colonial governor William Shirley, had been one option, but it was rejected in the 1950s because of its ties to the former British governor. The Endicott Estate, offered up by the family of the infamous member of the Boston Brahmin, Henry Endicott, was rejected by Sarge's grandfather as being too costly to be renovated. As a result, the tradition of the Massachusetts governor residing in their own homes continued.

Since he had no official residence, the expression *corner office* was typically used by the media when referring to the governor's mansion. Today, Baker conducted a very important meeting in the corner office with members of his administration.

"Gentlemen, and lady." Baker chuckled, nodding as he addressed his lieutenant governor, Karyn Polito. "I am pleased that all of you have received my letters and found your way here today. Arguably, this get-together is in violation of the President's executive orders. To protect ourselves, my wife has provided finger foods and refreshments. That officially makes this a gathering of old friends." The room laughed as they toasted coffee cups.

"Governor, I think I speak on behalf of everyone in this room in saying we are pleased that you reached out to all of us," said his longtime friend Daniel Bennett, the Secretary of Public Safety and Security. "Communications are not as swift as we're accustomed to, but the letters did the job."

"Thank you, Dan," said Baker. Baker was dressed in jeans and a long-sleeve blue shirt. True to his casual nature, he propped his feet up on a leather ottoman as he sat. Despite the weighty issue to be covered, Governor Baker wanted his cabinet to feel at ease. He was going to ask them to commit the functional equivalent of treason—not an ordinary topic of conversation.

"Our state is in shambles. News and information are scarce, but the reports I hear, especially out of Boston, is that we are on the verge of anarchy. Dan, would you like to bring the group up to speed."

For the next few minutes, Bennett, a former prosecutor, provided the group a summary of events from around the state, including the raids on the Massachusetts Guard Armories. His presentation culminated with the activities of Citizen Corps Governor O'Brien and the UN forces.

"Is this happening all over the country, or are we just blessed to have a misfit like O'Brien in charge of our fair state?" asked Polito. Baker held his hands out to allow Bennett to answer the question.

"I've been in contact with law enforcement from nearly all of the jurisdictions in our Region I and most in the northeastern states," replied Bennett. "Most cities with populations over fifty thousand have descended into chaos. Residents have abandoned their homes and sought refuge in rural areas but are being shunned by the locals. Small communities are circling the wagons, protecting their own and their resources."

Baker spoke up. "In our state, like most others, there is no semblance of order. These Citizen Corps appointees don't have the means or the desire, apparently, to assist the citizenry. Their primary goal has been to help themselves to abandoned valuables and to loot those properties that were secured under lock and key."

"In addition," interrupted Bennett, "they are using known criminal elements to do their bidding. Any goodwill developed following the President's address was short-lived. It's every man for himself out there."

"I think it's time for the people's duly elected government to come to their aid," said Baker, taking another sip of coffee before leaning on the edge of his favorite leather chair.

"What do you have in mind, sir?" one of the group asked.

"We should do what we were elected to do—govern," replied Baker. "I want to reconvene the General Court of Massachusetts." The term *General Court* was the formal name for the Massachusetts legislature, used since the founding of the Massachusetts Bay Colony in 1628.

Every member of the group began speaking, some to each other and others began to pepper Baker with questions.

"At the State House?"

"Do we still have the legal authority?"

"Is it in contravention of the President's declaration?"

"Is it safe?"

"Okay, okay, everyone," shouted Baker, attempting to regain control of the meeting. "I know you all have questions and opinions. I've thought this through for weeks. Recent events convinced me to act. I hope you will agree."

Baker stood up and approached the credenza where his wife had set up a tray of snacks and coffee. He poured himself another cup. The cabinet had dutifully calmed down, and Baker continued.

"The first order of business is to contact the state adjutant general. We need to determine if he has viable law enforcement capability. He can use members of the Massachusetts State Defense Force to augment the National Guard. I'll ask him to set up quarters at the State House. Safety is a concern, and a show of force should deter any reprobates who attempt to disrupt our session. On the other hand, I don't want to have so many security personnel in place that the people are afraid to attend the session.

"Next, there is the matter of notification to the legislators. It'll take some time to reach two hundred senators and representatives, and their trip to Boston will be perilous. But I'm confident that the State Defense Force will assist us."

Polito raised her hand and quickly asked a question. "Charlie, do you intend to propose and pass legislation? We have procedures to follow and also would need a quorum."

"Karyn, I'm not sure what we will accomplish from a legal perspective. I'm still unsure of what my powers are vis-à-vis the President's Declaration of Martial Law. I do know that the people are looking for real leadership, and right now the Citizen Corps is not providing it. When I took the oath of office less than three years ago, I made a promise to the citizens of Massachusetts when I said *we won't let you down*. Well, I meant it."

Baker sat in silence, allowing the words to soak in. His proposal was bold. In his heart, he thought this would provide his constituents a boost, a glimmer of hope that their elected representatives cared about them. He wanted to do the right thing.

CHAPTER TWENTY-TWO

Friday, October 21
11:00 a.m.
Prescott Peninsula
Quabbin Reservoir, Massachusetts

"Mom!" exclaimed Penny. "This is the best twelfth birthday party ever!" She and Becca jumped to reach the giant soap bubble created by Donald from his perch atop a picnic table. The Quinns didn't prepare for a birthday party and gifts when they put together the preparedness plan for Prescott Peninsula. So they improvised.

Donald had created a variety of bubble wands using something as simple as a couple of twigs and a shoelace for small bubbles, to a whale-size bubble-making device that resembled a hangman's noose for a giant.

He found two long branches and cut them to equal lengths. He then took apart a worn-out mop head and used the yarn to create a top string tied between the two ends. Finally, tied to each end of the branches was a stretch of yarn roughly twice the size of the top string, weighted down by multiple layers of duct tape at the bottom. This created a large loop.

Susan concocted a bubble mix recipe. She called it her *world-class stir-and-go bubble mix*. She mixed a bucket of hot water with a cup of Dawn dish soap. She then added half a cup of cornstarch and baking powder. She mixed it all together, and the concoction was complete.

"This is incredible," said Julia. "They're having a blast!"

"Yeah, thanks, Julia," said Susan, who was proud of the DIY birthday gift. "The hardest part was teaching the wand operator the necessary coordination to create bubbles."

"He makes it look easy."

"Donald has been practicing. The process is simple, at least in theory. With the two branches, or wands, held together, you dip the string into the bucket. As you lift the wand out of the bucket, you slowly spread the handles apart to let the bubble form. With just enough breeze, like today, you spread the wands apart, the bubble forms in the loop, and voilà, you have giant bubbles and happy girls."

"I love it, and I love the girls," said Julia. The ladies laughed as Donald lost his balance attempting to make the *biggest one ever*. The exhibition was beginning to draw a crowd of Boston Brahmin as they arrived early for the morning meeting.

"You should have a couple of dozen," pried Susan, breaking the silence. *Call it woman's intuition.*

Julia remained quiet and then giggled. She whispered into Susan's ear, "I hate you." Then they both laughed. "Do you have a pregnancy test?"

"I knew it," Susan whispered back. "I'll discreetly get you a First Response. Do you know how far along you are?"

"I'm a month late. I thought maybe it was just stress. My last period ended around August twentieth. I'm always regular, so I've never kept a calendar."

"Did you guys have sex around September first?"

"All weekend, including the night the lights went out." Julia giggled.

"Well, you certainly were in the prime window of opportunity, so to speak." Susan laughed. She added, "I suspect there will be a lot of babies born at the end of May next year."

"I haven't told Sarge yet, and I'm not a hundred percent sure how he'll feel about it. I think he'll be happy, but these aren't exactly the best times for giving birth and raising babies."

The girls squealed with delight as Donald pulled off a whopper of a bubble. The breeze caught it, splitting it into two smaller bubbles, and the girls chased them in hot pursuit.

"I don't know. Right now seems like as good a time as any," said Susan.

Sarge snuck up behind Julia and hugged her around the waist. She and Susan exchanged smiles. Sarge nuzzled her neck for a bit.

"You smell better today than you did yesterday," teased Sarge. Julia broke away and took a swat at him, but missed to the left. Julia dropped her arms, inducing Sarge to let his guard down, and then she landed a punch to his left shoulder.

"You smelled yesterday too, Mister Man." Today was their shower day. Sarge allowed Julia to shower first to take advantage of the available hot water.

"Good morning, Susan," greeted Sarge. "Is Donald testing out some new secret weapon?"

Susan laughed. "Nah, it's the new prepper bubble bath. You strip naked and he bathes you with the bubbles. Whadya think?"

"I think we should volunteer my brother to be the first bather." Sarge looked at the ground for a moment, thinking about the strained relationship that was festering between them.

Steven and Katie were spending the majority of their time at 100 Beacon. This was by design. Steven was leading daily insurgent activities with the Mechanics. They'd become a royal pain in the ass to the Citizen Corps and their new partners, the UN troops.

Julia rubbed Sarge's shoulders. She knew something was troubling him. The mention of Steven's name accompanied by Sarge's reaction confirmed what she suspected. Julia would discuss it with him, and the results of her pregnancy test, when the time was right.

The daily briefings were conducted by Donald until Mr. Morgan's stroke. Sarge had increased his role in the process over the last three weeks. Whenever he was at Prescott Peninsula, more often than not, he briefed everyone. Today, there was a lot of ground to cover, and Sarge would lead the meeting.

"Girls, it appears Daddy is out of world-class bubble mix," said Susan. "Why don't you girls come with me into the kitchen. Aunt Stella wants to bake some birthday cupcakes."

"Chocky!" squealed Becca.

"It's my birthday, and I want vanilla," replied Penny, giving up the chase for the last bubble.

"How do both sound?" asked Susan.

"Swell!"

"Okay, both of you inside to get cleaned up for your baking lesson." The girls turned towards the door and then, in unison, returned to hug their dad around the neck.

"Thank you, Daddy, we love you!" said Penny. Donald knelt and hugged the girls. Julia was moved by the moment and then she noticed Sarge was beaming with a smile. *Just maybe he'll be a hundred percent Baby on Board.*

Sarge waited while everyone got settled. He was pleased that Mr. Morgan joined them this morning. Patriot activity was ramping up around the country, and he was encouraging Sarge to think towards an overall game plan, not just Boston and Region I.

"Good morning, everyone," he started. He looked at Julia and smiled. "Julia, with her innovative Digital Carrier Pigeon network, has been able to keep abreast of events across the country as well as around the globe. Regionally, the Citizen Corps governor, James O'Brien, has clamped down on the citizens of Boston in particular. Through the use of a United Nations occupying force, curfews have been implemented, roadblocks established, and now door-to-door searches have been initiated under the guise of assistance to survivors. In reality, our reports indicate that the troops are more interested in weapons confiscation and looting."

"Can't they be stopped?" asked Mrs. Cabot. "Where are the police?"

"I'm afraid *they* are the police now," replied Sarge. The group mumbled to themselves, and Sarge was quick to add a positive spin. "I understand your concern, but there is an upside. The majority of law enforcement have joined our ranks. Under Steven's leadership, we've undertaken several covert actions that have been, quite frankly, and pardon my tongue, driving O'Brien and his new friends crazy."

The group erupted in laughter, and Morgan nodded approvingly.

"That said, we do not take the power our anointed governor wields and the potential harm this UN force is capable of for granted," Sarge continued. "History shows us that a tyrannical ruler is capable of many things. For example, during the rise to power of the Soviet Empire, Vladimir Lenin decreed the creation of a group of ruthless soldiers and operatives called the Cheka. The Cheka were granted broad police powers and tasked with the elimination of any form of dissent within the communist system.

"Lenin launched what would later be known as the Red Terror, in which every Russian population center had a Cheka office of operations using surveillance, infiltration, nighttime raids, imprisonment, torture and execution to silence opposition to the authority of the state.

"Some of these people were active rebels, some were outspoken political opponents and journalists, others were merely average citizens wrongly accused by neighbors or personal enemies. The Cheka created a society of fear and suspicion in which no one could be trusted and little criticism was spoken above a whisper for fear of retribution."

"That kind of intimidation can't happen here, can it?" asked Dr.

Peabody. "I mean, where is our military in all of this? Doesn't the UN have to follow our directives?"

"All very good questions, Art," replied Sarge. "I am of the opinion that this kind of activity is exactly what our President wants. By quickly announcing the onerous Declaration of Martial Law, he taunted freedom-loving Americans into reacting angrily. It worked, and as a result, he used the outcry as the impetus for injecting the United Nations Peacekeeping force into the equation."

"And our military?" Peabody persisted. Sarge looked to Brad, who nodded, allowing him to restate a conversation the two men had earlier.

"Military leaders and the soldiers who serve under their command are people just like us," started Sarge. "They have political leanings and opinions just as we do. Many are oath keepers and promised to uphold the Constitution. In some cases, their conscience tells them to disobey orders, but they remain on post. Others have left the service of what they consider to be a tyrannical commander in chief. Naturally, some agree with the President and have used this as an opportunity to advance his political agenda."

"Do you have an opinion as to how strong our military remains as a fighting force?" asked Cabot, looking in the direction of Morgan. Morgan again nodded and tilted his head towards Sarge. *Sarge is in charge.*

"Yes, sir, we do," he replied. "Brad has been in contact with his counterparts throughout the country. Our active military troop level is at thirty percent of its pre-collapse numbers." The attendees roared in disapproval. Cabot was most vocal among them.

"How are we supposed to defend our shores against the Russians without our armed forces?"

"Please, everyone, let me finish," replied Sarge. "First of all, through our usual means of communication with Putin and the Chinese, we have prevented any immediate threat to the nation from outsiders. Despite the President's inaction on this issue, we have effectively put the world on notice not to take advantage of our brief moment of weakness."

"That's good to hear," said Endicott, "but where did all of our soldiers go?"

"Sir, many of them are with us or like-minded patriots around the country. For years, libertarian-minded thinkers, tea party activists, and self-reliant individuals became painted with a broad brush as domestic extremists and terrorists. In fact, a narrative was established in the media and liberal think tanks like the Southern Poverty Law Center that these individuals represent a clear and present danger, alluding to the doctrine allowing the government in times of national crisis to prosecute almost any citizen giving material support to enemies of the state. Material support has included verbal opposition to government policies, while enemies of the state included anyone in vocal opposition to this administration. Under martial law, that definition has broadened to include, arguably, anyone who has survived."

Sarge paused to take a drink of water and then surveyed the group. Sometimes he wondered if it made sense to provide all of the details to the Boston Brahmin. In the end, he determined that they were capable of taking the truth.

"But to finish answering Mr. Endicott's question," added Sarge, "the soldiers who have left their posts have, in large part, joined groups like ours throughout the country. These groups are made up of organized and patriotic citizens. Some are military; most are not. They are all committed to fighting for our country."

Sarge decided to move on to financial matters. *This was something they would all be interested in hearing.*

"World financial and commodity markets are collapsing," said Sarge. He referred to a sheet of notes provided to him by Donald. He would continue to lean upon Donald for navigating the financial stratagems employed by Mr. Morgan. "The dollar is no longer trading on the FOREX. Hyperinflation has set in, and our Federal Reserve Notes are becoming worthless."

"What about gold prices?" asked Lowell. Sarge looked towards Morgan, who provided him an imperceptible nod. *Okay.*

"At the time of the cyber attack, gold traded at about eleven hundred dollars an ounce. Today, it's trading at seventy-three hundred dollars an ounce, with no end in sight."

Lowell and Cabot couldn't contain their excitement with back slaps and handshakes. Sarge smiled and shook his head.

Let's end today's briefing on a high note, shall we?

CHAPTER TWENTY-THREE

Wednesday, October 26
4:00 p.m.
Huntington Avenue near Northeastern University
Boston, Massachusetts

The four soldiers of J-Rock's gang remained hidden as they watched the young couple scurry past the entrance to the Northeastern University School of Law. They laid in wait as the pair—probably students of the university, based upon their backpacks bearing a crimson *N*—worked their way up the sidewalk from Wollaston's Market. Each of them carried a pack full of what remained from eight weeks of looting.

The white couple was unaware of their observers. It was still daylight, and besides, why should they worry? The United Nations troops were now patrolling the streets and providing them protection.

The tallest of the men, nicknamed Jacko for his proficiency in carjacking, was adorned with gold jewelry boosted from prior home invasions. As a high-ranking member of the consolidated black gangs of South Boston, he was also extended the privilege of sporting the gang's colors—a Raiders jersey. In a city which loved its hometown New England Patriots, there were not enough Raiders jerseys available to go around for the new recruits. Only senior leadership was afforded that honor.

The other three gangbangers, relatively new hires, had not yet earned their stripes. The approaching couple provided Jacko a teachable moment for his newest protégé, fifteen-year-old Latrell, a former honor student at the Brooke Mattapan Charter School.

"You ready to do this thing, Latrell?" asked Jacko.

Latrell was shaking and looked nervously toward the couple as they reached the intersection. The two students hid behind an empty newspaper stand as a van roared through the intersection.

Latrell's dreadlocks stood in stark contrast to his soft, innocent hazel green eyes. He still proudly wore his navy blue hooded sweatshirt bearing his school's logo. He rose from his crouch and pulled up his oversized blue jeans. It was his weight loss, and not his desire, which resulted in his looking like the stereotypical gangbanger.

"Yeah, I'm ready, I guess," he replied hesitantly, which earned him a slap across the back of the head from Jacko.

"Damn right you're ready, kid. This is your time." Jacko handed him the thirty-two-ounce steel framing hammer.

Latrell, hands shaking, accepted the tool-turned-murder-weapon. It still contained the bloodstains of the old Asian man one of his associates had bludgeoned to death earlier in the day. They'd stolen the man's watch.

Although he was visibly nervous, his heart thumped with adrenaline-fueled excitement. Jacko had introduced Latrell to the thrilling rush of crystal meth. Free drugs were considered a perk for being part of J-Rock's crew. Methamphetamine was a white, crystal-like drug produced in hidden laboratories from amphetamines contained in over-the-counter cold remedies mixed with a variety of chemicals such as battery acid, drain cleaner, lantern fuel, and antifreeze. Despite the collapse of the power grid, the meth labs were still in full production.

The drug user snorted meth through the nose, smoked it, or injected it with a needle. Crystal meth created a rush in which the user felt euphoric, confident and full of energy. Jacko used the drug to keep his recruits ready to do his dirty work. He provided them enough during the day to keep them high. He didn't need his soldiers binging out of control or tweaking because they ran out of crystal meth. It was a controlled high. *Mostly.*

Latrell's drug-induced adrenaline kicked in and was in full effect. This was his final challenge before being fully accepted into J-Rock's gang. In addition, he had learned over the past two months that killing white people would earn him extra props. He'd been given plenty of examples of how white privilege still existed, even after the collapse. Jacko showed him that it was white people who were receiving all of the food and supplies from the government.

J-Rock's gang had grown in numbers and began to thrive after it was given the green light by Governor O'Brien to raise hell throughout Boston. The gang expanded because it was profitable to steal, at first. But as the pickins became slim, as they say, the leaders of the unified black gangs of Dorchester, Roxbury, and Mattapan turned to another motivational tack—hate.

Hate-filled speeches and a focus on racist rap music from artists like Common and Azealia Banks, who infamously wrote lyrics claiming the President hated white people, riled up the gang members to seek outlets for their frustrations. It became an initiation ritual for J-Rock's gang to kill a white person. This was going to be Latrell's rite of passage.

Jacko looked down at his three underlings. "Now, remember this is Latrell's turn. He takes the first hits. I don't wanna see nobody else involved, but our job is to jump in if he can't handle it."

The other three gangbangers laughed and Latrell managed a smile as well. "I don't need no help. That white boy ain't gonna do nothing but cry."

"I know you got this, kid," started Jacko. "I tell you what, leave the white girl alone. You boys grab her. After you do your bidness, we'll party with the white ho and have some more of this chalk. I'll let you have at her first, after me of course."

Latrell nodded and gripped the claw hammer tightly in his left hand. He gave it a couple of awkward swings to indicate he was ready. "Let's do this," he pronounced.

Jacko nodded and waved his new recruit toward the intersection. He emerged from the bushes alone as the young couple, blissfully unaware, turned their backs to the gang and walked east on Huntington.

Latrell stalked his prey while Jacko and the others walked fifty feet behind him. As Latrell got closer, he could see the couple more clearly. Both were in their early twenties and appeared to be neatly dressed. *Clean clothes. They're doin' better than us black folk.*

He then assessed the young woman. She had long blonde hair, worn straight so that it hung well past her shoulders to her waist. She was attractive and her figure was athletic. *He liked blondes.* Jacko had promised him a party.

Latrell gripped the hammer and gauged the distance between himself and the couple. They were thirty feet away and wedged onto the sidewalk by the fence guarding the commuter rail stop on their left and the elevated guard rail protecting pedestrians from eastbound traffic on Huntington Avenue. The time was almost right.

As the couple reached the midway point of this stretch, the girl glanced behind her and saw Latrell's approach. The plan was to bury the claw end of the hammer in the guy's back while his boys grabbed the girl. *He'd beat the dude down while his boys, and the girl, watched.*

The young woman grabbed her boyfriend's arm and picked up the pace. Latrell started running toward them and he glanced over his shoulder to see his gang brothers closing the gap. He raised the hammer and let out some type of guttural yell. The throaty sound was indiscernible, but it frightened the couple and caused them to drop their belongings. At first, they broke into a sprint up the sidewalk, which turned into a run for their lives.

"Get the white dude," shouted Jacko as he and the other two men were almost upon them. "We'll take care of the ho for you!"

Latrell focused his attention on the guy, who lost his footing and stumbled in his effort to observe his attackers. This brief slip caused the couple to slow, and Latrell was nearly upon them. His heart was pounding. He thought he could fly. He had reached *the shoulder*, the highest level of the methamphetamine-fueled rush. *Die, white boy!*

As the final few feet between them closed, Latrell raised the claw hammer over his head and swung at the man, but …

CHAPTER TWENTY-FOUR

Wednesday, October 26
4:09 p.m.
Rooftop of the New England Conservatory
Huntington Avenue near Northeastern University
Boston, Massachusetts

One shot, one kill.

The crack of the sniper's rifle reverberated off the canyon walls of the buildings flanking Huntington Avenue. The .308 round penetrated and exploded within the target's chest, immediately stopping his forward momentum with a clothesline effect.

He quickly loaded another round into the chamber of his standard Gladius .308 rifle, although it was far from *standard*. The bolt-action tack driver was his favorite post-service rifle. His muscular right arm, bearing a tattoo which read *1S1K*, effortlessly operated the bolt and readied another round.

Two of the attackers stopped, but one continued toward the young girl. The expert killer took a deep breath and focused on his next target through the Nightforce scope. In daylight or properly set up, it would've been an easy shot. But with darkness limiting his scope's range, he ran the risk of being less accurate.

He exhaled and gently squeezed the trigger of the powerful rifle.

CRACK!

"Hit," he muttered to himself, continuing to look through his scope at the remaining assailants.

Two shots, two kills.

Real time stands still for the sniper, but the mind races at lightning speed. His mind always found its way back to a mountain ridge high above that village in Afghanistan. He and his spotter, a young guy nicknamed Eagle Eyes, had been dropped off the night before by a Chinook helicopter. They made camp several klicks away from their position before getting set up in the early morning hours.

Eagle Eyes earned his nickname when the members of his scout sniper unit found out he had been an editorial intern for Random House books. He was also deadly accurate at the game of darts. His combination of attention to detail and a good eye made him an excellent spotter for a scout sniper.

The sniper team wore heavy ghillie suits designed to obscure their position. Together with strategically placed vegetation, the suits made them nearly undetectable to the enemy, and their target. The team spent a considerable amount of time customizing their ghillies. There was always the potential of spending long hours or even days in these outfits as they waited for the perfect opportunity to complete their mission. A bureaucrat's idea of a one-size-fits-all suit wasn't acceptable. Their lives depended upon comfort and concealment.

He and Eagle Eyes had determined the optimal position that provided the best line of sight to their target. Based upon the intelligence report they received, their mark would exit a mosque in the center of town. Once they reached the top of the hill overlooking the village, they hit the ground and crawled into position. The extra layer of canvas on the front of their suits provided a cushion from the hard rock and dried brush typical of the Afghan landscape.

Eagle Eyes checked his watch and announced that they should get ready. The team completed their range card and made the necessary adjustments. Then they turned their attention to the village. He observed the dusty streets through the eight-magnitude Nightforce scope mounted on his beloved .300 Winchester rifle.

"Overseer in position," Eagle Eyes reported over the comms as he searched for their target through his finder. The team was far enough away from the village that their shot would reverberate through the valley below them, helping shroud their location.

Several groups of men began to emerge from the mosque. Briefly, they congregated not far from the entrance and then began to slowly drift away.

The sniper team undertook this mission without the benefit of a drone flying overhead. This was a high-value target and command didn't want the Taliban leader to go back into hiding in a cave somewhere.

Eagle Eyes found their target. He announced this into his comms for the benefit of the interested eyes and ears in safer parts of the world.

"Target identified, sector B, right forty, add fifty."

Eagle Eyes continued. "Single target, light-colored khet partug and Peshawari cap, smoking cigarette."

The sniper shifted slightly, the ground crunching underneath him. He sought out the target through his scope. *There!*

"Roger, single target, light-colored Afghan clothing," repeated Eagle Eyes as he looked through his spotter scope.

"Repeat, target identified. I have two mils crotch to head, confirmed!" the sniper exclaimed.

"Roger, two mils crotch to head, dial five hundred on your weapon."

He made the adjustments called for by Eagle Eyes and confirmed it back to him. Eagle Eyes continued. "Wind left to right, four miles per hour, hold one-eighth mil to the left." He made the final setting, dialing it in with precision.

The factory setting on the Remington trigger was tuned to two pounds, which was a fairly light pull compared to others in his unit. When he was a boy, his dad taught him to respect the gun. *Don't jerk it when you fire.* He became accustomed to a light trigger that didn't offer any resistance.

Ready. Set. Squeeze. Boom.

The recoil hammered the folding stock into his shoulder. The ground vibrated beneath him. The feeling was exhilarating, powerful.

The long-range, high-velocity round left a slight vapor trail as it flew through the air, creating a distortion.

"Hit. Center mass, stand by," said Eagle Eyes. The target collapsed in a heap, generating a smile from the duo.

Then a young boy, not more than nine years old, who was concealed behind the target, stood stunned, dumbfounded. Blood poured out of his mouth as he attempted to reach for his throat, which was punctured by a bullet fragment that passed through the target's body. His empty eyes looked in their direction before he fell to the earth, convulsing. He held the boy in his sights for a few seconds before Eagle Eyes pried him away.

It was his first *and second* kill.

In his debrief, he was told the boy's death was collateral damage, a casualty of war. He was ordered to *shake it off.* He would never forget that child twitching in the dirt next to his dead father.

A shriek coupled with the sound of gunfire brought him back to the present. During his brief moment *away*, the other two thugs could have escaped, but they didn't. Oh no, they were stupid. One of the men ripped a handgun from his waist and began firing wildly in the air. He never had a chance to identify the hidden lair of the sniper.

CRACK! The sound was deafening in the still of the approaching darkness.

Three shots, three kills.

Finally, the fourth man got the message and hurdled over the barrier. He crossed Huntington Avenue into an alley, and he was gone.

He finally exhaled, relieving the tension. Three lifeless bodies bled out on the sidewalk. No cars. No trains. No bustling students scurrying off to their next destination. Only a cool gust of wind washed across his body. Then he heard it, faintly, but noticeable.

A woman's voice.

"Thank you!"

Now, that was a first.

CHAPTER TWENTY-FIVE

Thursday, October 27
4:00 p.m.
630 Washington Street
Boston, Massachusetts

Katie and Steven made idle conversation with some of the more familiar members of the Mechanics before the meeting got started. This was the last time the unit leaders would gather in this location. Because of the increased presence of UN troop patrols, they didn't want to be caught returning to the same location repeatedly.

Steven, with Katie's assistance, divided the city into logical sections. A unit leader was assigned to each section based upon their familiarity and ties to the neighborhood. Local knowledge provided the Mechanics a significant advantage over O'Brien's people. This was a critical advantage when fighting an insurgent war.

"Gentlemen, let's get started," said Steven. "First, let me reiterate that this will be our last meeting here. I've gotten together with all of our unit leaders and you know your territories. Our ability to communicate is solid. Face-to-face meetings, especially in the same location, are just too risky. If it becomes necessary for all of us to plan a major operation, we'll rotate to another place."

The leaders of the Mechanics mumbled between themselves as they nodded in agreement. Almost all of them wore some type of jacket or headgear that bore the stitched patch of the Rebellious Flag. It was the closest thing they had to a uniform, but it was symbolic of the modern patriot movement they were proud to be a part of.

"Does anybody have any questions about their neighborhood assignments?" asked Steven.

A hand came up from the rear and a stout ex-grunt approached the front of the room. "We haven't seen Sarge at our last few meetings. He's been a real inspiration to us. Is he okay?" Several voices in the room could be heard agreeing that the question was valid.

Katie bristled. *Assert yourself, Steven. These are your men.*

Steven snapped back, "Sarge has a lot on his plate, as do we. I've got a ton of experience in black ops, and he doesn't."

The former Army infantryman backed off the question. "I didn't suggest anything by that, sir. Some of us were wondering, that's all."

Steven took a breath and continued. "Listen, Sarge is my brother. We took different paths growing up. When we were kids, he was winning spelling bees while I was sailing a skiff around the Charles. He went to college to become a *brainiac*. I went to college to learn how to destroy things. We're about to enter the blowing-everything-up phase of our resistance. I'm better suited for this."

Steven took some time to relay events from around the country. The men seemed to be motivated by the fact that other parts of the country were experiencing success in their insurgent operations. They covered what had been working against the UN roadblocks and established a neighborhood warning system for when door-to-door searches were imminent.

Finally, they discussed recruiting, and several new faces were introduced. Because this was the last meeting at the former site of the Liberty Tree and no specific ops were to be discussed, Steven had allowed unit leaders to bring some of their prized new recruits.

"Why don't some of the new guys come forward, introduce yourselves, and tell us what you did before the collapse," said Steven.

One portly fellow stepped forward and introduced himself. "My name is Isaac Grant, and I was a delivery driver for a meat packin' company. Now I'm packin' heat."

The group laughed as Steven nodded his head in approval. Humor was good.

"I remember you. Weren't you one of the drivers on the Food Bank job?"

"I was," he replied.

"Well done. Who else?"

Another man stepped forward. He was thin, balding, and spoke like he had a mouthful of nails. "My name is Rory Elkins. I was an audio-visual security enhancement specialist."

"A what? A TV repairman?" The room burst into laughter. Steven laughed, but he didn't wait for a response. "Oh, sorry, you were being serious."

CHAPTER TWENTY-SIX

Friday, October 28
10:00 a.m.
1PP
Quabbin Reservoir, Massachusetts

The post-collapse operation envisioned by the Loyal Nine was in full swing. Like any plan, there were improvised revisions. Plan A was only the first letter of the alphabet; there were another twenty-five options waiting in the wings. It was the Scottish poet Robert Burns who wrote *the best-laid plans of mice and men often go awry.* The same principle applied to their meticulously conceived preparedness plans.

One of the most important aspects of their plan was communications and information gathering. Julia had won a Marconi Award for the development of the Boston Herald Radio Network. It was hailed as a brilliant solution to a dying form of media—the printed newspaper.

Building upon her success, Julia's thoughts turned toward the possibility of a catastrophic collapse event, like last month's cyber attack, which could collapse the nation's power grid and its complex interconnected communications system.

Julia's forethought provided the Loyal Nine the ability to gather information, monitor government transmissions, and broadcast to ham radio operators and AM band listeners across the globe. She was dialed into information resources and like-minded patriots.

She first unveiled the Digital Carrier Pigeon to their group in April. It achieved several goals. First, it helped satisfy a basic characteristic of human nature—the quest for knowledge. In the first few moments following the cyber attack, Americans turned to their smartphones for answers. Millions of calls were initiated, text messages sent, and attempts to download web pages were astronomical. The inability to access these basic functions of an advanced society caused a panic, resulting in societal collapse. *Within hours!*

As the chaos subsided, America looked for answers, and then hope. The government provided the nation little of either. While communications initiated by the administration were frequent, they were primarily dictates and directives. There wasn't a single broadcast offering solutions for those trying to survive. Nor were there any ideas advanced to restoring America to its former greatness envisioned by the Founding Fathers.

Tonight, as part of a broader plan, Sarge would begin broadcasting a weekly address to the nation. It would contain a message of hope and renewal. It would call on like-minded patriots to band together for the good of the country.

"Thanks, everybody, for making your way out here today," started Sarge. He looked at Steven. "I realize the UN forces have clamped down on routes in and out of the city."

Steven scooted Donald over on the love seat so that he could sit. "Hi, DQ!" He promptly put his arm around Donald's shoulder and started messing with his hair.

Donald swatted it off and said, "Get your manly arms off me!"

Steven laughed and removed his arm. He continued. "We've

created our own ways of ingress and egress," said Steven. "It's a little bit *over the river and through the woods*, but it works when necessary."

Sarge turned to Brad and asked, "Any more activity at Fort Devens?"

"Nothing major," he replied. "They are watching us. We take precautions when we head this way, but we'd be naïve to think that Prescott Peninsula wasn't on O'Brien's radar."

Sarge held a set of rolled-up maps, which he used as a pointer. A four-foot-by-six-foot combination blackboard and corkboard on wheels stood patiently behind him. He got down to business.

"This will be the last group meeting for a while," said Sarge. He was standing in the center of the group and approached the board. "Steven has effectively aggravated the UN contingent. For the past week, they've set up roadblocks and focused on curfew violators. This has been more of a law enforcement function. They are now searching house-to-house, but the extensive network established by the Mechanics allows the residents to stay one step ahead."

"And, I might add, our insurgent activities keep them on their heels," said Steven. "They are trained to be a peacekeeping, reactionary force. We're giving them what they want."

"Tell us some of the tactics that have proven successful," interjected Sarge. "We will try to share our experiences with others around the country via the Pigeon."

"The what?" asked Katie, who stood behind the love seat with her arms crossed.

"Julia's Digital Carrier Pigeon network," replied Susan. "We found that to be a mouthful, so we settled on the *Pigeon*."

Katie shrugged, indifferent.

Steven continued. "We are undertaking a plan in the city that frustrates the Citizen Corps while gaining favor with the locals. It seems to be working."

"Give us some examples," said Julia.

"We've conducted a variety of surprise attacks on individual groups of UN troops, installations and roadblocks. We plant IEDs in homes that are raided by the UN. The element of surprise is critical."

"Believe it or not, Steven and I have studied this in college," said Katie dryly. "We learned from the Viet Cong."

"Nice." Brad laughed.

"Well, I mean we followed their blueprint for establishing political and military wings during the Vietnam War," she added. "We can thwart the enemy and receive the loyalty of the residents at the same time."

Steven continued. "By dividing the city into manageable parts, we've been able to establish an organizational structure and defined lines of communications. Each neighborhood has its own administration, security, and recovery sections."

"Government was intended to be based upon a pyramid structure," added Sarge. "Local governments are closest to their communities. They know their neighbors and what their needs are. As you go higher up the pyramid—county, state and then federal— the impact on our lives should diminish."

"The pyramid has been turned upside down in our country," said Donald.

"That's right, Donald," said Sarge. "By focusing on neighborhoods and local communities first, we can build on these successes and apply this principle regionally and then nationwide."

"What about the gang threat?" asked Brad.

"We have effectively chased the rats back into their nest," replied Steven. "Between our increased sniper activity and foot patrols, J-Rock and his buddies have stayed out of our way."

"And the MS-13?"

"My new friend, the White Devil, has driven them back to East Boston, Hell, I had to call him back because the Asians wanted to invade the Easties. Besides, I've got plans for his crew."

"What is it?" asked Brad.

"We've been capturing some of the UN soldiers," replied Steven. "We strip them of their gear and uniforms. After some interrogation, we drop their naked asses off in the middle of the city to find their way back to the Seaport."

"Hilarious!" shouted Brad.

"Yeah. A large part of the UN force is of Asian descent. We've been using the Asian gang members to infiltrate their ranks and gather intel."

"Well done, Steven," said Sarge. "This keeps Chinatown involved in a big way. The idea behind classic guerilla warfare is to keep the people emotionally tied to your movement. Conventional warfare focuses on territory gained and casualty counts. The insurgent movement led by the Mechanics is gauged by the support of the population. As long as we can provide them, or assist them in producing, food, clean water, shelter, and other necessities, we will win their loyalty."

"What's the big picture?" asked Katie.

Sarge pushed his sleeves up and replied, "The biggest mistake a movement or insurgency operation can make is alienating the population. Once you alienate the population, you're finished. I believe the administration, through its heavy-handed approach, has lost the support of the American people."

"I can say this, from an armed forces perspective," interjected Brad, "morale couldn't be lower. Those soldiers who've stayed on post are doing it out of a sense of duty and honor or, in rare cases, opportunism. In some regions, the military is conducting the same types of functions as the UN is in our region. The bad apples in the military are taking advantage of their newfound power for personal profit and gain."

Sarge moved to the corkboard and pinned up his first map. It revealed the regional headquarters of the Citizen Corps governors.

Headquarters - *Washington, DC*

Region I - *Boston, MA*
Region II - *New York, NY*
Caribbean Area Office San Juan, PR
Region III - *Philadelphia, PA*
Region IV - *Atlanta, GA*
Region V - *Chicago, IL*

Region VI - *Denton, TX*
Region VII - *Kansas City, MO*
Region VIII - *Denver, CO*
Region IX - *San Francisco, CA*
Pacific Area Office Honolulu, HI
Region X - *Bothwell, WA*

"Similar to what we discussed a few moments ago, we need to establish a national game plan," said Sarge. "This is a map indicating the divisions of the country established by the Citizen Corps. Typical of a government bureaucracy, it is divided by state lines, not like-minded people."

Sarge paused to allow the group to study the ten regions created by the President. A large red dot depicted Washington, D.C., as the headquarters. He directed everyone's attention to this point first, using his rolled-up maps.

"Washington, as our capital, was originally envisioned as the headquarters of the Citizen Corps. That's not gonna happen. The city has descended into anarchy."

"But we saw them secure the city early on," said Katie.

"Scary fast, in fact," added Steven.

"From the reports we're receiving, a large part of D.C.'s population fled as riots broke out," said Julia. "The government was effective in preventing an influx of people, but they couldn't control the population that lived there. Government buildings were overrun and razed. It's a war zone reminiscent of Georgia and Estonia."

Sarge brought their attention back to the map. "Region IV, which encompasses the Deep South, has enjoyed the greatest success. Its state's governors have taken control and reestablished their legislatures and governments. Brad can confirm that the military in this region has backed the state governor's efforts."

"We've talked about Region IV previously, something about the Confederacy," said Susan.

"That's right," said Sarge. "Citizen Corps Governor Cooper, a Tennessean, refused to obey some of the more onerous directives from the President, and he was replaced. That, coupled with an ill-conceived raid on homes outside of Atlanta, resulted in a coup of sorts. Patriots came from five states, banded together, and ran the Citizen Corps out of town. The entire southeast region is now preparing to govern itself."

"That's great news!" exclaimed J.J., who had remained silent thus far.

"It is, but there is still uncertainty," said Sarge. "There isn't a coordinated effort among the states. The ejection of the Citizen Corps and takeover by local governments is in its infancy. But their effort does bolster my hope that this can be duplicated. Fellow patriots are moving into other regions of greater Appalachia, which includes Oklahoma, Virginia, Missouri and the lower parts of Indiana, Illinois, and Ohio. They are prepared to take the fight to the Citizen Corps as well."

"We're winning," said Steven.

"Yes, in some parts of the country, we are," said Sarge. "It's time for us to win our own neck of the woods, and then we'll assist and advise others. The battle will begin here, in Boston, where it started two hundred and fifty years ago."

Sarge circled the city with his fingers. Then he added, "*Choose freedom* is more than a slogan. It will become a nationwide political movement."

CHAPTER TWENTY-SEVEN

Friday, October 28
8:00 p.m.
Prescott Peninsula
Quabbin Reservoir, Massachusetts

On this date in 1787, a series of eighty-five essays were published in the *New York Independent* newspaper under the pen name *Publius*. The authors, including Alexander Hamilton, James Madison, and the first chief justice of the United States, John Jay, set out to promote the ratification of the Constitution by providing a comprehensive and cogent explanation of the nation's most sacred document. It was a series of both practical and philosophical dissertations.

Sarge scrolled through *The Federalist Papers*, which Donald had downloaded onto a spare iPad. He had read the essays many times and incorporated their principles into his lectures and his bestselling book, *Choose Freedom or Capitulation, America's Sovereignty Crisis*. Concepts of limited government, separation of powers, and the freedoms enumerated within the Bill of Rights were all addressed in these documents.

Tonight, Sarge would incorporate some of these precepts in his first address to the nation via the Pigeon. This was an opportunity to raise Americans' aspirations beyond survival or avoidance of oppression. He wanted to encourage them to bind together and return to the principles espoused by the Founding Fathers.

He settled before the microphone, waiting for Julia's signal. She had announced the speech to her vast network of patriotic groups across the country during the week. There was no way to know how many people would be reached via ham radio and across the AM band. It was a start that hopefully would grow legs each week. At eight o'clock, Sarge began.

"My friends, my name is not important, but what I have to say is. Like you, I am an ordinary American who has survived the deliberate terrorist attack upon our nation. Like you, I have experienced death among my friends and family. And like you, I've survived.

"I'm coming to you as an American who foresees a bigger threat —a threat that seeks to take our freedoms under the pretense of protection and recovery. While the attack on our nation has shaken our resolve, it has not broken our freedom-loving spirit. While the attack has prompted a suspension of our Constitutional rights, it has not permanently taken them away.

"In the aftermath of this vicious attack, our President responded by implementing certain emergency responses and executive actions. I want to believe that our government's response had our nation's best interests in mind. However, rather than focusing on helping our injured or taking efforts to protect us in our homes, our government sought to gut our Second Amendment by confiscating our weapons.

"Rather than marshaling its recovery assets across the country, our government used the attack as an opportunity to level the playing field and right perceived social injustices. The President is picking and choosing who receives aid and who gets power restored based upon political alliances.

"Rather than rebuilding our communities from the ground up,

our government has undertaken to impose its oppressive controls from the top down.

"My friends, America has stood down enemies before, from both within our shores and around the world. It's now time to address the enemy within.

"Tonight, I'm calling on my fellow patriots, freedom-loving Americans who value the sacrifices made by our Founding Fathers, to join me in saying enough is enough. Seek out like-minded friends and neighbors. Work together to stop the exercise of absolute power that has been employed pursuant to the Declaration of Martial Law.

"Together, we can stand up to tyranny. We can bring our nation back to its former greatness. We can restore the freedoms granted under the Constitution."

Sarge paused, caught his breath, and looked at Julia for support.

"I want to add the words of Thomas Jefferson. *Experience has shown that even under the best forms of government, those entrusted with power have, in time, perverted it into tyranny.*

"I will conclude with this. When given the choice between tyranny and freedom, my friends, I ask you to choose freedom!"

And with that first anonymous address to the nation, the political career of Henry Winthrop Sargent IV was born, as was the nationwide political movement with the rally cry *choose freedom*.

Sarge also unknowingly became a fugitive from justice.

CHAPTER TWENTY-EIGHT

Saturday, October 29
10:12 a.m.
Prescott Peninsula
Quabbin Reservoir, Massachusetts

"I think you nailed it last night, Sarge," said Donald as he sipped his second cup of coffee. The raid on the Food Bank allowed for an extra cup now and then. *The spoils of war.*

"I hope so," said Sarge. "Julia has been monitoring global news networks through the Hughes Gen4 Internet, and supporters abroad are cheering. I hope those cheers translate to support and action here."

"How long will you have to remain anonymous?"

"We need to gauge the government's response. If drones start buzzing overhead, we'll know we've got trouble. Besides, I want the movement to center on the message, not the messenger."

"Choose freedom," said Donald.

"Exactly."

Mr. and Mrs. Lowell began to approach them when shrieks

came from near the boat launch. Susan's cries for help grabbed everyone's attention.

"The girls!" shouted Donald as he broke out into a run so fast that he stumbled over a loose branch and rolled down the hill toward the path before he struck a log.

"C'mon," yelled Sarge as he passed Donald, who quickly regained his footing. There were more cries for help from Susan.

"Mommy, it hurts," cried Penny as the two men got closer to the boat launch clearing.

"Susan!" shouted Donald. "We're coming, honey!"

"Hurry!"

They entered the clearing and found Penny sitting on the ground with Susan hovering over her. One of the Marines stood nearby, wiping blood off his knife.

"What happened?" asked Donald.

"Snakebite. It's bad."

Donald leaned down and took Penny's face in his hands. "Try to stay calm, baby. I need you to relax, okay."

Sarge ran over to the Marine and found the source of the blood. A three-foot-long timber rattlesnake, now cut into three pieces, was still writhing on the pine needle floor of the woods.

"Are you sure this is the snake?" asked Sarge.

"I believe so, sir," he replied. "I was standing watch by the dock when the little girl screamed. I ran up the bank and found the snake working its way to those fallen trees. I cut off its head and then sliced its torso in half. There's the head."

The snake had a rough-skinned appearance that contained dark brown cross bands. The rattlers broad, triangular head was unmistakable. This was a venomous pit viper. Penny was in trouble.

"It burns, Daddy!"

"Donald, her leg is swelling up."

"Daddy, it hurts and my mouth tastes funny, like quarters and dimes." Penny was trying to flex her leg as it became tighter.

Donald had to calm her down. Stress increased the flow of

blood, which would speed the process of sending venom throughout her tiny body.

"Okay, my little punkin', I know it hurts. But you have to be still and stay calm. We'll get Uncle J.J. to fix you right up."

Donald turned his attention to Sarge. "Hey, get J.J. ready. I'm gonna carry her up to 1PP."

"Okay," said Sarge before he ran through the woods.

"Penny, honey, I'm going to gently pick you up. I want you to wrap your arms around my neck and your legs around my waist. Can you do that?"

"I'm sorry, Daddy. I didn't see it on the log."

Donald wiped her tears away and gave Susan a reassuring smile. He hoisted his daughter up and moved quickly up the path. A crowd had developed at the clearing, but they quickly gave way as Donald ran up the slight incline.

J.J. was waiting for them on the front porch. "We're ready, Donald. Penny, let's get you inside and fixed up, okay?"

Penny didn't respond as she held her father's neck tight. Inside J.J.'s medical room, Donald sat her on the examination table, which was propped upright like a dental chair.

"We need to keep the bite below the level of her heart," said J.J.

Susan entered the room. "Let me help!"

J.J. looked at Donald for assistance as he prepared a soapy water solution using antibacterial soap. He began wiping the area around the bite wound.

Donald tried to calm Susan. "Honey, you're pretty emotional. Abbie is right outside. Let her handle this with J.J."

"No way!" Susan bulled her way into the room and immediately brushed the hair out of Penny's face.

"Okay, Susan. While I'm doing this, create a diluted iodine solution."

"How much of each?" she asked.

"Half and half, until the dilution is iced-tea color. We'll flush the wound several times and then rinse it well with clean water. This will help remove any venom that isn't deep in the wound."

J.J. nudged his way past Donald to a cabinet opposite the room. He emptied a shelf of its compression bandages. He also grabbed a tube of Neosporin.

Penny began to cry again and wiggle in the chair. Donald moved to comfort her.

First, he pulled a Sharpie out of a drawer and drew a circle around the bite. J.J. applied the antibiotic ointment, and then he systematically wrapped the compression bandages around her leg as if he were treating an orthopedic injury.

"Bandaging begins two to four inches above the bite, winds around and then back down and past the wound. We have to be careful to avoid overtightening. This would cause her to reflexively move her leg and cause the venom to spread."

"J.J., chopper?" asked Brad through the doorway.

Donald answered for him. "Yes."

Brad didn't move. The Loyal Nine had an unspoken rule—don't let an emotional decision overcome the best decision.

After thinking for a moment, J.J. responded, "Yes, get the chopper ready. We'll go to Mass General."

"One more thing," started Brad. "While we're being exposed, do you need to check out Mr. Morgan? Might as well get our money's worth from this hospital visit."

"Good idea," replied J.J. "Would you mind getting Abbie and her dad together?"

"On it," said Brad as he spun and headed toward the front door.

J.J. continued to wrap Penny's leg, going further up the leg than he might for other types of injuries.

"Doesn't she need a shot or something?" asked Susan.

"How much does she weigh, roughly?" asked J.J.

"Around eighty-five pounds."

"Listen, the dosage of antivenin is tricky with children. I have a one-hundred-milliliter adult dose I can give her initially, but some tests need to be run at the hospital to determine follow-up doses."

J.J. administered the shot and put a Mickey Mouse Band-Aid on the spot. He checked her pulse and blood pressure. He also checked her for a fever.

Brad returned and announced that the Sikorsky was ready.

Donald approached him and whispered, "What about security?"

"I've got Shore and three of my best men," replied Brad, putting his hands on Donald's shoulders. "Sarge and Julia will hitch a ride as well. Your girls will be in good hands, I promise."

Donald turned to Susan and gave her a hug. Her eyes welled up with tears.

"She's so small, Donald. I should never have let this happen to her."

"Honey, don't worry. We live in the woods now. These things happen. J.J. will be with you. Sarge and Julia will be there also. It will be safe, and Penny will be okay." Donald looked into J.J.'s eyes for reassurance. He didn't want to make hollow promises, but J.J.'s smile confirmed his hopes. Venomous snake bites could be deadly especially for a young child. But Penny was treated within minutes of the bite, giving her a far better chance than others. A few hundred dollars' worth of antivenin courtesy of the family's vet probably saved his daughter's life.

Susan nodded and sniffled. "I love you."

Donald kissed his daughter on the cheek, and she managed a smile. "You get to ride with Mommy on a helicopter. J.J. will be there with you too."

"Is Becca going too?"

"No, she'll stay here and keep me company."

"Ha-ha. Stuck like chuck."

CHAPTER TWENTY-NINE

Saturday, October 29
8:26 p.m.
99 High Street Rooftop
Boston, Massachusetts

Ineffectual. Unproductive. Insufficient.

The words seared through O'Brien's brain. Earlier in the day, a courier had delivered his thirty-day performance review. Compiled by the staff of DHS, O'Brien received overall poor reviews. The report concluded that *he failed to achieve the minimum requirements of knowledge, skills, abilities, and behaviors required for an individual to perform the role and occupational function to which he or she was assigned.*

"Really? Well, screw you!" he screamed as he threw an empty glass of bourbon thirty-three floors to its death.

The rooftop access door closed and La Rue approached him cautiously. It was pitch black on the roof except for the glow of lights coming from the UN encampment at the Seaport.

"What's got you riled up?" asked La Rue, who poured himself a drink. Before he took a swig, he noticed O'Brien wasn't drinking. "Are you not havin' one, Jim?"

"Yeah, I mean, I just threw the damn thing overboard, along with the rest of my *new career*," replied O'Brien.

La Rue walked around the table and handed his old friend the glass. He topped it off.

"I know things have been rough goin', but we're just getting started with the UN boys. There has been some progress."

"Apparently not enough progress to satisfy those bureaucratic idiots in Washington or Hawaii," said O'Brien. "They gave me some kind of performance eval that pretty much calls me incompetent."

"That's pretty ballsy considering you're up here bustin' your ass to keep it together. At least you're on the job. That guy in Atlanta tucked tail and ran back to Tennessee. There is no Citizen Corps in the southeast."

"That's true," said O'Brien, as he began to feel better. "Hell, there isn't a Citizen Corps in D.C. either because there isn't a D.C. The place has been ravaged by their own."

La Rue reached into his jacket pocket and pulled out a handful of tube-sealed Romeo y Julieta cigars. He handed them to O'Brien, who greedily accepted them. He fired up his lighter to read the label.

"Wait, these are Cubans," he said.

"That's right, boss. Some of my guys found them in a humidor at this place they hit on Chestnut Street. Liquor too. I had them deliver the boxes to your office a few minutes ago."

O'Brien lit up the woodsy cigar and took in the aroma. He relaxed as he savored the spoils of victory. *Things are looking up.*

He let out a deep breath and downed half the glass of bourbon.

"I need a win, Marion," he started. "I've been at this for nearly eight weeks, and all I have to show for it is an army of misfits and now, thanks to you, a resupply of cigars and whiskey."

"What else is there?" La Rue laughed.

"I wouldn't mind gettin' laid," replied O'Brien.

"Why didn't you say so?" asked La Rue, who lit up a Marlboro.

"There are plenty of young girls out there who *will work for food*, if you know what I mean."

"Great, just what I need, a hooker."

"No, seriously, it's not like that. They call it *bartering*. People are doing whatever they have to do for survival."

"Well, no, thanks," said O'Brien. "At least not right now anyway."

The men remained silent, taking in the night air. O'Brien refilled his glass and then La Rue took a swig out of the bottle. They returned to the roof's edge and looked at the spectacle below.

"Look at 'em," said O'Brien, shaking his head. "What do they do all day?"

"Believe it or not, they are gaining control of large parts of the city," replied La Rue. "Their roadblocks are effectively cutting down on traffic in and out of Boston. Anyone who leaves must pay a toll of sorts. They have to give up their weapons, food, and valuables. In exchange, they get to pass and stay alive. If they resist, their stuff is taken anyway and they get their asses beat."

"That's all well and good, but what do we get out of that? I don't see Zhang delivering any boxes of goodies."

"Letting them have a little taste is serving a purpose," replied La Rue. "It's buying us time to get our own force together. I've recruited some good people, and they're not gangbangers."

"That's good, but we need our boys out of Fort Devens," said O'Brien. "I want Zhang to attack Bradlee now!"

O'Brien saw Brad as the cause of his problems. He'd put too much trust in him initially, and that set him back a month. Now, because of Brad, the administration was up his ass. There had to be a way to turn things around.

"Order him to do it."

"What?"

"Lie. Tell him you received orders from the President to storm Fort Devens, release our prisoners, and take the base over."

Why not? "We've got the numbers and probably equal firepower. Let's strike directly at the heart of the beast, which is that smug colonel and his beloved Fort Devens."

"Now you're talkin," said La Rue. "Let me tell you something else that might help you gain favor with the President."

"What's that?" asked O'Brien, now fully relaxed as he enjoyed his cigar. He gestured for La Rue to proceed.

"I was at Mass General today, following up on a tip from one of my boys who got stitched up. He's sharing a room with a guy recovering from the gas line explosion. The guy, a professor, claims he knows about the cyber attack."

"We all know about it; look around us," interrupted O'Brien.

"What I was gonna say is the guy may have been involved somehow. I went to the hospital today to visit my man, and I spoke with this professor today."

"Did he tell you anything?"

"He was hesitant, even scared," replied La Rue. "Jim, I've made a living out of reading people and *encouraging* them to see things my way. This guy knows something, but he wasn't gonna reveal it to strangers."

O'Brien perked up. This could make a difference on his next evaluation. "Bring him in to talk to me. Surely he'll spill what he knows to his governor."

"He can't really be moved right now. The explosion messed him up pretty bad. But I'm keeping my man in place even though he's scheduled to be released tomorrow. I want this professor to be monitored and protected. We'll become his new best friends."

"Outstanding, Marion. I'll tell Pearson tomorrow and let that snitch report this back to the President's people. Maybe my *performance* will be appreciated then."

"Jim, can you hold off on that? This professor may be our golden parachute. This President and his do-boys in Hawaii won't appreciate what you've done for them. Let's hold onto this information in case we need it as leverage or a larger payout in the event he leads us to somebody, or something, even bigger."

"That makes sense," said O'Brien. "Now, enough business. Let's talk some more about this *barter* thing the ladies are embracing."

"Almost done, Jim. There's one more thing."

"C'mon, what else?" asked O'Brien as he walked to a roof scupper and peed into the downspout.

"While I was at the hospital, a helicopter arrived with a number of passengers onboard," replied La Rue.

"Was it military?" asked O'Brien as he zipped up his pants.

"No, it was private, and it was big. It looked like it could've been owned by Trump or someone like him."

"So what's the deal?"

"Apparently, a little girl got bit by a rattlesnake," La Rue replied. "They brought her in for those anti-venom shots. There was also an old man who was checked out for a stroke."

"Any names?" asked O'Brien.

"Nothing at all. The doctors and staff were tight-lipped. The two patients were placed in a recovery room at the end of the floor I was on. They had their own armed security guarding the hallway. I caught a glimpse of them as I left the professor's room today."

"Whaddya make of it?"

"It could be nothing, except for the fact that there is obviously some money behind the whole thing—a big chopper, special privileges, private security. It's worth watching."

O'Brien considered his options. He could always use a helicopter for himself, especially since someone shot down his UN choppers.

"Tell you what, Marion. You get me the N-number off that chopper. I'll have Pearson run it through the FAA Registry. We'll find out a little more about our mystery guests."

CHAPTER THIRTY

Sunday, October 30
11:08 a.m.
Citizen Corps Region I, Office of the Governor
99 High Street
Boston, Massachusetts

O'Brien and Pearson leaned over the conference table in the offices of the Citizen Corps and studied the maps provided to them by Zhang. The UN commander stood quietly to the side while the two men soaked in the information. Pearson spoke first.

"If I understand this correctly, the areas indicated by the light blue crosshatched markings are wholly within your control. Is that right, sir?"

"Affirmative," he replied. "Each day, we expand the grid outward from the center point, which is indicated by the red star. Our focus has been the residential areas to the south and southwest. Moving through populated areas first enables us to flush out the opposition and to accomplish our goals of gun confiscation."

O'Brien stood up and turned his attention to Zhang. "How's that coming along?"

"I am pleased," said Zhang. "We have confiscated over one thousand guns and many more thousand rounds of ammunition. I have them stored securely within the confines of the Convention Center. In hindsight, confiscated and stored food should have been held there as well."

O'Brien bristled. He didn't appreciate the passive-aggressive body slam. Zhang had wanted to empty the Food Bank facility and transfer the contents to the Convention Center. O'Brien refused, in part because he didn't want to give up control over his most precious asset at the moment. The decision cost him.

"Well, good for you, General Zhang," commented O'Brien. *Now, let's talk about some of your failures.* "What are you doing to tamp down this insurgency?"

Zhang moved to the map and pointed out yellow highlighter markings across several arterial roads leading in and out of the city. "We've cut off access to the north and—" started Zhang before being interrupted by O'Brien.

"You mean the gas pipeline explosion cut off access to the north."

"Yes, of course," said Zhang. He continued. "Access to the east has also been cut off."

O'Brien interrupted him again. "The access has been cut off by those Chinese gangs while we stood by and watched. We don't control those tunnels, they do."

He wanted the high and mighty general to realize that he wasn't performing up to *O'Brien's performance standards.* That he, too, was *ineffectual and unproductive* and he was making the boss look bad!

"Continue," said O'Brien brusquely. He glared at the map, with his hands on his hips.

"Thus far, we have concentrated our efforts to the south towards Roxbury, Dorchester and Mattapan. These neighborhoods are being subdued."

O'Brien could feel the heat rise into his face. *Subdued?* We didn't want those neighborhoods subdued. We wanted them to run wild in the streets! But he couldn't admit that to Pearson and Zhang.

"Listen up. The money is here," shouted O'Brien, slapping his hand on top of Newton and the neighborhoods representing the western part of the city. Then he caught himself and he thought about La Rue's words from last night. *It's buying us time to get our own force together.* Let the UN *subdue* the poor parts of the city and save the good stuff for me.

"I understand, Governor, but there is a logical—" started Zhang before he was interrupted.

"Never mind, General," said O'Brien. "Keep up the good work. Let's talk about something more important. I've received a directive from the President's office." O'Brien ignored Pearson's puzzled look. Any directive from the President would come through his liaison—Pearson.

Zhang stood and looked at O'Brien. "Yes?"

"The President has ordered us to free the prisoners located at Fort Devens and to seize the base. I am told this is of the utmost priority."

"What shall I do about the U.S. Marines protecting the facility?" asked Zhang.

"Disgorge them," replied O'Brien.

"Disgorge? I'm not sure what you mean by—"

"I want you to take all of your soldiers up there and kick them the hell out!"

"But—" started Zhang before an urgent knock at the door interrupted him.

"Come in," said O'Brien.

One of Zhang's aides entered the room, holding a military telephone. He quickly approached the general. "Sir, an urgent call for you from the Braintree checkpoint," announced the aide.

Zhang took the phone. "Yes." Zhang listened intently as the situation was explained to him. O'Brien and Pearson grew impatient as the one-sided conversation lingered.

"Hold the line," said Zhang. In Chinese, he dismissed the aide and instructed him to close the door behind him. He turned and addressed O'Brien. "We have someone entering the city claiming to be from Barnstable on Cape Cod. He identified himself as a member of your General Court—a state legislator."

"Why is he coming to Boston?"

"He claims to be on official business upon orders of the governor," replied Zhang.

"I don't have any need to meet with somebody from Barnstable. Did you request this, Pearson?" asked O'Brien.

"No, sir."

O'Brien turned to Zhang. "Did he say anything else?"

"Yes. When our unit at the roadblock pressed him for a letter of authorization, he claimed he did not have one. He was directed to return to Boston and the State House. He said the governor was reconvening the legislature at 9:00 a.m."

"Tomorrow?" asked O'Brien.

Zhang returned to the call and asked the soldier what day he was referring to.

"Yes, 9:00 a.m. tomorrow morning," replied Zhang. "Shall I have him detained and brought in for questioning?"

"Absolutely!" But as Zhang raised the phone to give further orders to his men, O'Brien reached for his arm and stopped him. "Wait."

O'Brien paced the floor methodically with his hands in his pockets. His back was turned to Pearson and Zhang when a smile came across his face. *This is a gift from God almighty himself.*

He regained his composure and turned to Zhang.

"No. Let him pass without further discussion," instructed O'Brien. "In fact, tell him to have a nice day and safe travels."

"Sir," Pearson began to object but stopped when O'Brien raised his hand.

"Go ahead, General, tell them."

General Zhang gave the instructions and then disconnected the call. Pearson was agitated and immediately questioned O'Brien.

"Why didn't you detain him?" he asked.

"No," replied O'Brien, smiling again. He was unable to contain himself. "Why the hell not? Let them convene."

"But, sir, this open act of defiance would potentially undermine your tenuous authority and would not be well received by the President," said Pearson.

"Let them convene," repeated O'Brien as he directed the other two men to sit at the conference table. He spun the map around and studied it. "We'll be ready for their treasonous assembly."

CHAPTER THIRTY-ONE

Sunday, October 30
8:49 p.m.
100 Beacon
Boston, Massachusetts

Julia and Sarge were standing guard on the rooftop of 100 Beacon until their relief came at midnight. Despite Sarge's new status as the head of the Boston Brahmin, it was difficult for him to set aside certain day-to-day responsibilities. Plus, it gave him an opportunity to be alone with Julia where they could talk.

The two huddled under a blanket as they sat Indian-style on top of the dormant heat and air unit, which elevated them another eight feet above the rooftop. The clear skies and lack of wind would probably produce a frost, their second of the unseasonably warm fall. As always, fires were burning throughout the city. Attempts to stay warm resulted in buildings catching on fire. The charred remains became commonplace.

Steven and Katie were going to remain at 100 Beacon full time to oversee the activities of the Mechanics. Julia and Sarge would be spending their last week here for a while. After Election Day, they would remain at 1PP permanently. It was safer for them there.

The conversation quickly turned to Steven and Katie, who had become aloof over the last several weeks. Julia and Sarge rarely had the opportunity to talk without being overheard, so now was a good time to broach the subject.

"I believe it stemmed from Mr. Morgan putting you into his position," started Julia. "Over the next several days, I saw a noticeable difference in Katie's attitude towards us. It's easy to explain things like this away as typical jealousy."

Sarge sighed and gave his opinion. "I don't have any other explanation. Steven and I have always been tight. We were brothers and partners. I never felt like either one of us considered ourselves to be superior to the other. He has his strengths, and I defer to him on certain matters. Likewise, I have my strengths. We always struck a good balance." Sarge got quiet and shook his head. The whole thing puzzled him and he'd strained for an explanation.

"Then you reached a higher level of success," said Julia. "When you were handed the reins of the Boston Brahmin, you garnered the attention of the entire group. Although not by design, you were elevated above Steven. Maybe he didn't appreciate that?"

"I guess," replied Sarge. "I'm not sure it is him. I think it may be Katie chirpin' in his ear. Whenever Steven and I are together, alone, it's like old times. But when she's influencing him, I see a noticeable difference."

"Like what?"

"Well, his attitude towards me changes," replied Sarge. "I don't want to use a word like insubordination because we've never had that kind of a relationship, nor will we. It's more like insolence."

"I've noticed this in Katie too," said Julia. "Her behavior is more nonverbal—folded arms, sighs, and eye-rolling. I thought about confronting her, but I feel we have bigger fish to fry."

"I'm afraid it's gonna build up into something hard to overcome," said Sarge. "I can talk to him man-to-man, but I can't compete with someone undoing our conversation."

"Under the circumstances we live in, it's more than two brothers needing to work out a disagreement. In a way, both Steven and Katie are employees who have a job to do. You have to be able to give them direction and have confidence that your orders will be carried out. Do you have that right now?"

Sarge hung his head to where his chin touched his chest. He was losing confidence in Steven. Sarge was excluded from the meetings with the leaders of the Mechanics. If it wasn't for the interaction with the top lieutenants who lived at 100 Beacon, Sarge would have no direct involvement in their activities. Granted, he needed to be protected because of his role as head of the Boston Brahmin, but he felt like Katie and Steven were pushing him out. It had bothered him for days.

"I don't know, honey," replied Sarge. "For right now, if all of this does stem from jealousy, which is the only logical explanation, I'll have to diffuse it before the situation becomes disruptive."

The two sat in silence for several minutes, interrupted by the sound of an occasional gunshot or a siren. After eight weeks, Boston was largely abandoned. The UN troops were effectively instigating a mass exodus from many neighborhoods. Perhaps that was by design. Word of atrocities began to surface—executions, rapes, and theft. The Mechanics continued to grow in numbers, but there weren't enough to take on the trained UN forces head-on. For now, the insurgent activities were the best tactic, but eventually a plan to drive the UN out of the city would have to be put into place.

"By the way, in just forty-eight hours, HAMRs across the country have exploded with excitement over your speech Friday night," said Julia, breaking the silence.

"I didn't really say much. It took all of five minutes."

"Don't underestimate yourself, Sarge. People out there are starving for a leader. They crave someone who thinks like they do. They need someone who isn't afraid to stand up for what's right, especially against tyrants like the President and the Citizen Corps."

Sarge sat up and stretched his arms. "I've just taken the reins of what is arguably the most powerful and wealthy cartel in America, if not the world. I'm still digesting that. I have to leave this part of my life hidden while I try to convince the masses that I'm one of them and a patriot to boot."

"Yes. Welcome to politics. If you only could muster up a Southern drawl on command like Hillary, you'd be unstoppable."

"Very funny, Julia. She's probably gonna be elected President on the eighth and this whole exercise will become moot."

"I don't know about that. There hasn't been any discussion out there about the elections. I suspect the President has something up his sleeve."

"Yeah, a coronation. He will anoint himself King of the Americas!"

"Don't laugh," Julia said. "Would it surprise you?"

"Nope."

Sarge pushed himself up and offered his hand to Julia to help her as well. "Let's walk around so I can stretch my legs a little bit. I'm getting stiff."

"Old fart," Julia laughed.

As the two descended from the top of the HVAC unit, Julia asked, "Are you worried about tomorrow?"

"You mean Governor Baker's shindig? No, not really. It's all for show anyway. I believe the politicians are simply showing their voters they are doing something, even if it's all talk."

Julia stuffed their blanket into a storage cabinet near the hot tub. The city remained strangely still. The two walked the perimeter of the rooftop, taking a moment to glance at the sidewalk below from time to time. The majority of the UN activity had been to their south, and the gangs remained in South Boston. Their Back Bay neighborhood, which now contained a couple of hundred families from the Mechanics, was fairly safe.

"Are you taking security with you?" asked Julia. She appeared to be apprehensive about his attending the impromptu legislative session.

"Of course, babe. We have to remember nobody except our group knows who I am and what I do. Unlike Mr. Morgan, who had been in the political limelight for years, I'm just a humble professor from Harvard that happens to control seventy percent of the world's gold reserves and countless billions in dollars or marks or something of value." They both laughed at Sarge's attempt to downplay his importance.

"Okay, Mr. Big Shot," said Julia. "Call it a hunch, but I think it would be a good idea to take a handful of the guys from downstairs with you. Dress just like them so you blend in. Don't wear a suit like the politicians. If something is going to happen, they'll go after the suits."

"Fine." He laughed. "I'll wear a Halloween costume. Tomorrow, I'll go as Darth Vader!"

The well-earned shove almost knocked him on his ass.

CHAPTER THIRTY-TWO

Monday, October 31
9:00 a.m.
Massachusetts State House
Boston, Massachusetts

"Now, this is a day to die for," said Sarge to the entourage that escorted him up Beacon Street toward the Massachusetts State House. The temperature was in the upper forties, but the sun rising over the deserted skyscrapers of downtown Boston provided a warm glow on his face. Most of the leaves had fallen on Boston Common to his right, creating a carpet of fall color. Gone were the rotting corpses that were strewn about. The UN troops had systematically cleaned up the streets and moved abandoned vehicles out of the way. The scene still resembled one from *The Walking Dead*, minus the zombies, of course.

"I'm surprised at the number of people out this morning," said Captain Kurt Branson, who had been assigned to head up Sarge's newly formed security detail. Branson was the lone active-duty Marine who, coupled with six of the Mechanics residing in 100

Beacon, would provide Sarge protection whenever he was in the city.

"Me too, Captain. This was planned for a couple of weeks, but I don't know how Governor Baker would've gotten the word out. There must be four or five dozen people headed toward the State House."

Sarge and Branson were flanked by men roughly twenty paces in front of and behind them. Across Beacon, walking along the wrought-iron fence, were two more members of the detail. All of the men dressed casually, with winter jackets. They didn't want to stand out for any reason. Each of the men, including Sarge, wore a shoulder holster.

Branson and his detail also carried AR-15 pistols confiscated by the Mechanics from UN troops. For all practical purposes, the 5.56 NATO Tactical pistols were identical to a ten-and-a-half-inch AR-15 rifle. The only difference was the absence of a stock. The compact profile made it easily hidden under a jacket while attached to a single-point sling.

As they approached the grounds of the State House, the sun reflected brightly off the gold-leaf dome and temporarily blinded Sarge. Standing high on Beacon Hill, the gleaming gold dome of the State House actually had a humble beginning—gray, weathered wood. Just a few years after the State House was completed in 1798, Paul Revere's company covered the wooden structure with copper to preserve it and prevent water leaks.

Seventy-five years later, the entire structure was covered with 23-carat gold leaf. The cost at the time was $2,863. Today, the price to regild the dome would be in excess of a million dollars. The golden-domed State House was a joyous sight to Bostonians in the late nineteenth century. Oliver Wendell Holmes, who coined the phrase *the Boston Brahmin*, referred to the State House as *the hub of the solar system*. The State House was such an important influence in the governing of Massachusetts and surrounding New England states that signs were erected on major roadways leading into the city, which read *Boston, 26 miles.*

For days, legislators and their families made the trip to the famed Massachusetts State House. They were inspired by their governor, Charlie Baker, to show the citizens of the state that their government was intact and prepared to function. After nearly sixty days, it was apparent that the crisis would not be resolved quickly. Bay Staters needed to see their government in action. Governor Baker hoped to start the process today.

Two members of the security detail led the group through the wrought-iron gates and up the steps toward the bright white Doric columns that stood atop the entry. The other two joined Sarge and Branson.

"I don't see any building security, do you, Captain?" asked Sarge.

"No, sir. It seems odd under any circumstances."

Before entering, Sarge turned and surveyed Boston Common and the street below. This was where Abbie had stood when she announced her senate re-election campaign. A lot had happened since then. Her career had taken off when she was named the running mate to Hillary. On the surface, it was an odd coupling. Hillary was decidedly liberal, and Abbie was a libertarian. But, as Sarge learned, like many political pairings, theirs was not a match made in heaven. Rather, it was made in a back room, under suspicious circumstances, between John Morgan and Bill Clinton. *Will I be able to maneuver in the world of politics like John Morgan?*

"Sir," said Branson, grabbing Sarge's attention, "it's almost time."

Sarge turned and joined the group. "Yeah, okay."

The men moved into the open hallway and passed through a security checkpoint of sorts.

"Gentlemen, are you carrying weapons?"

Branson responded, "We are."

"Governor Baker has instructed us to inform you that weapons are acceptable under the present circumstances. However, you are admonished to keep them obscured from view. Also be aware that you are not the only visitors carrying weapons today. We ask that you remain orderly during these proceedings. Understood?"

"Of course," said Branson.

The men made their way into the building and were awestruck at the ornate architecture and beautifully painted murals. Of the group, only Sarge had been inside of the building. However, Branson had briefed his team on the layout of the building and surrounding grounds, using a history book from Donald's prepper library at 100 Beacon.

Walking up the grand staircase to the third floor, Sarge attempted to estimate the number of people milling about on the main floor. He was amazed at the crowd. Granted, a large number arrived in Boston from out of town, but this was more people in one place than he'd seen in a month—combined.

They entered the State Representatives Chamber, where Governor Baker was going to speak. Statues, paintings and marble busts adorned the walls. The flags of the United States and Massachusetts flanked the Speaker's chair. Well-dressed men and women made small talk as they awaited the governor's speech. Except for the .45-caliber handgun pressed against his ribs, Sarge thought this looked like any other day when the General Court was in session.

Sarge began walking toward the front, but Branson gently grabbed his arm. "Sir, let's sit toward the rear, near one of those side exits."

Sarge looked at him and nodded.

Branson spoke to the detail, who immediately took up positions behind them and near each of the closest exits. Sarge relaxed. His detail was well prepared.

After sitting in silence, and as the crowd began to shuffle into their seats, Branson asked, "What's the deal with the fish up there?"

Branson was pointing to the five-foot-long carving of a codfish. One of the most visited items in the State House, the revered Sacred Cod was a reminder of the state's survival and success.

Sarge explained, "The story goes that in the mid-seventeenth century, local fishermen caught three hundred thousand cod and it quickly became the biggest source of revenue for the locals.

According to the colonists' journals, the cod were clustered so thick in the bay that you could walk across the water on them."

"That's a real fish story," said Branson.

"Here's another one for you," started Sarge. "Back in the thirties, some of my predecessors at Harvard entered the Chamber, pretending to be visitors. They armed themselves with wire cutters and clipped the wires holding the Sacred Cod to the wall. Then they smuggled it out in a flower box."

"Undercover cod-nappers?" asked Branson.

"You got it," replied Sarge. "It created such an uproar that the legislators claimed they couldn't conduct the state's business without their beloved Sacred Cod. They did, however, pass a law stating a suitable punishment for the cod-nappers, as you say. The Harvard police ultimately recovered the Sacred Cod, and there it is, safe and secure."

"I feel better, don't you?" Branson laughed.

"Yes, and by the way, the Senate chamber has its own fish too," said Sarge.

"What kind?"

"A mackerel," replied Sarge.

"Let me guess, a holy mackerel." Branson laughed.

"It is indeed."

They were startled by the rapping of the Speaker's gavel. The Massachusetts General Court was being called into session.

CHAPTER THIRTY-THREE

Monday, October 31
9:20 a.m.
Massachusetts State House
Boston, Massachusetts

Sarge listened respectfully to Governor Baker's speech and admired him for his fortitude in calling the session. But his mind continue to wander to his own speech. Baker, a Republican, used phrases intended to instill confidence in government. Phrases like *public trust*, *working hard for you*, and *protect and provide* were used repeatedly. Sarge contrasted this with his own words—*fellow patriots, freedom loving, stand up to tyranny*. Baker was making a political speech designed to pacify constituents. Sarge's address to the nation last Friday night was designed to be a call to arms. *Am I, or have I become, a revolutionary?*

"Sir, I need you to remain calm," started Branson as he sat in the seat next to Sarge. Sarge was so engrossed in thought that he hadn't realized Branson had left.

"What's wrong?"

"Sir, after the governor began speaking, several late stragglers entered the Chamber. They've begun to take up strategic positions throughout the hall. I recognize two of them, sir."

"Who are they?"

"Citizen Corps," replied Branson. "I wasn't sure at first until I saw that man with the Bruins cap on." Branson nodded toward a heavyset man who'd found the only available seat on the front row. He was wearing the logo hat of the city's beloved hockey team.

"Maybe it's a coincidence?"

"No, sir. I just went into the hallway and had my man check the street. UN security vehicles are patrolling Commonwealth. They were noticeably absent thirty minutes ago. I have a bad feeling, sir. We really need to go."

"Okay," said Sarge, who was now genuinely concerned. This had been too easy.

"I'll wait a moment and then join you."

"Should we alert everyone?" asked Sarge.

"Sir, you are my priority. We can't help everyone, and I am not going to place you in the middle of a gunfight."

Sarge looked around the room one last time. *So much for democracy.*

He made his way through the north exit, where two of his detail stood vigilant. Their eyes were darting back and forth, and their weapons were protruding through the front of their jackets. Voices and the sounds of fast-moving footsteps could be heard from the south where the grand staircase was located.

Branson and the other two members of the team emerged. "Weapons ready, gentlemen. I'm afraid we're a few minutes too late. Sir, you stay close to me."

Branson moved them against the wall toward the state library. In the back of the library was a spiral staircase, which would allow them access to the staff offices on the second floor. They moved quickly but quietly as a unit. The activity was happening behind them.

"Dammit," said Branson. "It's locked."

"I've got this, sir," said the only black member of the security detail. Standing six foot four, the man had arms like Thor. He pulled up his pants leg, which revealed a sheath and a six-inch fixed-blade knife.

He pulled the knife and approached the door. He worked the blade between the door and the door jamb's striker plate. Applying steady but forceful pressure, causing the wood to splinter, the bolt made an audible *SNAP*. They were in.

Branson closed the door behind him and instructed the men to barricade the door with a table.

"Look through the windows to the west and tell me what you see," he shouted as he went to the east wall of the State House. He shook his head. "They're getting into position in the courtyard. What about over there?"

"I've got a Humvee down on Hancock Street and another one parked below us on Myrtle."

Branson started running towards the rear of the library and into a storage room. "This way. We'll take the stairs to the second floor. They'll be focusing their efforts on securing the main floor, but I think their real prize will be in that House Chamber."

"They're here to kidnap, not kill," said Sarge. "Do you think O'Brien is behind this?"

"No doubt about it," said Branson. "I'm sure that was his man in the front row."

The group arrived in a hallway on the second floor. There were frantic people running back and forth, ducking in and out of offices, seeking cover.

"We've got to make our way to the west wing. There isn't a street adjacent to that part of the State House. We could lower ourselves out of a window, or maybe there's a back stairwell to the first floor."

They began working their way along the landing overlooking the main floor. They had to get past the main staircase until they reached the corridor on the west side of the building. Just as they reached the double doors leading into the west wing, gunfire erupted on the main floor and bullets flew wildly into the ceiling of the State House.

"Here we go," said Sarge. They broke into a sprint as screams echoed throughout the State House. More gunshots could be heard.

They reached the end of the corridor, and the men frantically searched for a stairwell or fire escape. With the doors to the offices closed, the light was dim. Sarge cautiously moved down the dimly lit hallway to the south and looked toward the ceiling until he found the *fire exit* sign. *There!*

He ran back and retrieved the security detail. "This way!"

Branson took a moment to look out the window and announced, "Clear outside."

As they worked their way down the stairs, gunmen suddenly burst through the first-floor doorway and started up towards them.

Sarge's detail didn't hesitate and opened fire. Three quick bursts and the UN soldiers dressed in maintenance-worker coveralls were dead. Only the open door saved Sarge from a concussion from the report of the gunfire.

"C'mon," shouted Branson. "That'll draw a lot of attention."

Taking two steps at a time, they bolted down to the first floor and burst through the exit door into the bright sunlight. All of the men needed a moment to adjust their eyes.

"Follow me," yelled Branson as he led them across a short stretch of lawn to the ivy-covered brick walls of the row houses on Joy Street. He used the leafless oak trees to provide them some cover until they reached an alley leading away from the State House grounds.

Glass broke in a third-story window of the Capitol and bullets penetrated the brick above them. A body fell out of the window and was impaled on the spires of a black iron fence behind them.

"Run!" They sprinted away from the body and turned the corner in the alley until they were able to crouch behind a disabled delivery truck. All of the men were breathing heavily.

This was Sarge's neighborhood, and he had to get them back to 100 Beacon. He could hear the sounds of trucks parking near the entrance of the State House and at Boston Common. Returning on

Beacon Street was out of the question. In fact, all of the streets seemed like a really bad idea.

"Everybody good?" asked Branson.

"Yes, sir."

Sarge spoke up. "The streets are too dangerous and it would be crazy to hide out here and wait."

"I agree," added Branson. "They'll be moving quickly to secure the perimeter. We've got to boogie."

"This is my neighborhood, guys, I've jogged these streets a thousand times," said Sarge. "We need to slip through the backyards. If we go down any of these streets, we're screwed."

"Lead the way, sir!" said Branson.

CHAPTER THIRTY-FOUR

Monday, October 31
12:00 p.m.
Massachusetts State House
Boston, Massachusetts

O'Brien was pleased with himself. He'd caught these treasonous jerks off guard. He walked past the security checkpoint and stepped over the dead security guard. He stopped in the middle of the lobby and looked around. This was more like it. *Maybe I should relocate my offices here.*

He pulled out one of the Cuban cigars given to him by La Rue. He lit it and allowed a large puff of smoke to exhale out of his lungs toward the ceiling. He approached a woman and child cowering in the doorway of an office. They were both crying.

"Miss, are you a traitor?" he asked.

"A what?" she replied in broken English with a Spanish accent.

"*Traidor, traidor!*" he shouted at her.

"No, *señor*. We are hungry."

O'Brien stared down at the mother and daughter and studied the frail women. He reached into his coat pocket and pulled out a

Snickers candy bar. He tossed it towards the child, where it landed in her lap. After the little girl didn't make a move towards it, he spoke.

"Food, there you go."

The girl buried her head in her mother's shoulder.

O'Brien finally lost interest. "Screw it. Let them go!" he shouted. "All of these people need to be questioned; then let them go. I'm interested in the traitors upstairs."

O'Brien finally reached the top of the stairs where La Rue was waiting.

"Welcome, Governor," said La Rue formally, and loud enough to be overheard by anyone in the hallway outside the House Chamber.

O'Brien dismissed his welcome with the wave of a hand. He was out of breath from the trip up the stairs. He could hear the crying and occasional raised voices coming from the Chamber.

"How many?" he asked breathlessly.

"I think about two hundred, including the visitors," replied La Rue.

"Deaths?"

"Several. We had some cowboys in there who tried to shoot their way out of the room. We piled the bodies in the House Majority Leader's office over there. He joined them, by the way, when he refused to relinquish his own weapon."

"So you've secured the room?"

"Yes, you can go in when you're ready. But I have to warn you, a lot of these people pissed themselves when the bullets started flying. It reeks in there."

"Yeah, well, they're about to piss themselves some more. Let's go."

O'Brien relit his cigar and led a procession including La Rue and four uniformed UN troops that represented his new security detail. He waddled down the ramp and climbed the steps to the Speaker's chair. The crying continued and the murmur of voices rose.

He took another deep draw on his cigar and then pounded the gavel directly on the Speaker's desk, disregarding the sound block.

"Hear ye, hear ye, hear ye. Everyone shut the hell up!"

When the noise persisted, O'Brien pounded so hard that the gavel broke.

"Enough! I'd be just as happy to shoot the noisiest among you, if you'd rather." The room gradually became quiet.

"My name is Governor James O'Brien, the real, duly appointed by the President of these United States, governor of Region I, which includes, by the way, Mr. Baker, the good state of Massachusetts." Governor Baker sat in the front row and was held at gunpoint. He wouldn't make eye contact with O'Brien.

"I'm not gonna beat around the bush with you people. What you have done here today is not only a mistake, but a violation of the law. A big one, in fact. Short of murder, there isn't a crime in this country more vile than treason. All of you are under arrest for treason!"

The Chamber erupted in shouts of anger.

"You can't do this!"

"We are the government!"

"Under what authority?"

O'Brien gave them a moment to vent. Nobody liked to be accused of a crime. But when the protests continued too long, he moved to quiet them again—except the gavel was broken. He got the attention of his security detail. He formed his right hand to look like a gun and moved his thumb to mimic dropping the hammer. Then he pointed up. The soldier understood and immediately fired three shots into the ceiling, causing plaster to rain down on Governor Baker and the other front-row inhabitants.

Following a moment of screams, the room became quiet again.

"That's more like it," said O'Brien as he reached into his jacket and pulled out a folded piece of paper. He began to read.

"By the authority vested in me by the President of the United States pursuant to Executive order 13777 titled *Declaration of Martial Law*, I hereby charge you with the following high crimes and misdemeanors.

"You are guilty of the unlawful assembly of more than ten

persons. In furtherance of such unlawful assembly, you have entered into speech that is deemed intended to incite a riot and hostilities against the United States. The sum of these activities constitutes treason!"

Once again, fits of anger erupted in the Chamber. Nobody was crying anymore. Now they were all threatening. For a brief moment, O'Brien stepped back. His men were outnumbered ten to one. But his guys were armed, and these people were not. *Screw the Second Amendment.* He chuckled and regained his composure.

He looked to his security guard again and nodded. Three more rounds into the ceiling got the people's attention.

"Let me continue so that we can go about our business," he started as calm was gradually restored.

"In accordance with the Declaration of Martial Law, if you are found guilty of these charges, the following penalties shall include, but not be limited to ..." O'Brien paused and stared at Governor Baker until he finally made eye contact.

"Death!"

PART II

NOVEMBER 2016

CHAPTER THIRTY-FIVE

Tuesday, November 1
10:15 a.m.
Citizen Corps Region I, Office of the Governor
99 High Street
Boston, Massachusetts

"No, I'm not gonna kill them," replied O'Brien to General Zhang's demands for answers. "They're more valuable alive than dead. Plus, we don't need a couple of hundred martyrs on our bloodstained hands."

"That's good news, sir," said Pearson. "I received quite an earful this morning from the President's chief of staff." Pearson poured himself another cup of coffee. *Earful* was an understatement. Valerie Jarrett had ripped him a new one as if the raid on the State House was his idea. He made the mistake, after a heated barrage of criticism from Jarret, of reminding her that James O'Brien was nothing more than a thug who rose through the union's ranks by being good at his job—thuggery. The President should not be surprised by the fact O'Brien had fallen back on his usual playbook.

Naturally, as was true in D.C. politics, or Hawaii politics under present circumstances, crap flowed downhill, and O'Brien's poor decision making was Pearson's fault. *"That's what you're there for. Fix it!"* she had screamed into the phone before slamming down the receiver.

"I don't give a tinker's damn what that Iranian thinks," responded O'Brien. "Let her come out into the trenches and out of the President's bed for a day to see what it's like." Pearson couldn't argue with that.

"Sir, the White House is under tremendous pressure right now," started Pearson. "We're nearly sixty days into the martial law declaration and the Citizen Corps initiatives around the country are failing." Pearson sipped his coffee and sat in a chair across from O'Brien. Other than a few initial questions, Zhang had remained quiet. Pearson got the sense that Zhang was not one hundred percent on board with the State House raid.

"I get that," said O'Brien. "We're holding our own up here. With Zhang's help, Region I is nearly secure. We can't let the people question our authority. There can only be one boss in the northeast, and I'm it." O'Brien poked his chest twice with his thumb.

"That's true, sir. The entire southeast consisting of Region IV is beyond the President's control. He is contemplating a major military offensive, but to do so, he would have to send troops around Texas and the adjoining states that make up Region VI. Other than pockets of Citizen Corps loyalists in New Mexico, the state governments comprising Region VI are being systematically restored."

O'Brien pulled out a cigar and lit it. "I don't get it. The federal government worked overtime to help those people, and they spit in their face. If the South isn't interested in the feds' help, we are. Let Jarrett and all of her cronies send help our way. It'll be accepted with open arms." He exhaled a huge puff of smoke and began coughing. He then mumbled, "Damn things are dried out."

Zhang was compelled to speak, finally. "Our troops have performed admirably in securing the city and we are now moving into the outlying areas. The curfew is being enforced and the roadblocks are effective. The looting has subsided as well."

"And the rapes are increasing exponentially," interjected a smug O'Brien.

"Excuse me?" questioned Zhang.

"Don't play dumb with me, General," O'Brien snapped back. He waved his cigar toward the window, leaving a contrail of smoke. "I've got eyes and ears out there."

"I protest the use of the term *rape*," he replied.

Pearson wasn't surprised. Stories of atrocities perpetrated by the United Nation's Peacekeeping forces had existed for years. In 1997, Belgian troops making up a UN force in Somali roasted a young boy alive. Ironically, the operation was dubbed *Operation Restore Hope*. The two soldiers were reprimanded by a military court, which sentenced the two paratroopers to a month in jail and a fine of roughly two hundred dollars. During the same operation, a young Somalian, Muslim by faith, was forced to eat pork, drink salt water, and then eat his own vomit.

Over the years the reports of rapes and sexual abuse became common, so it didn't surprise Pearson that the UN troops would undertake the same behavior on U.S. soil.

The general, still bristling, continued. "I am not going to apologize or be criticized for the methods my officers and soldiers utilize to take control of this city. Strong-arm tactics are needed at times to gain the respect of the people. In my country—"

O'Brien cut him off. "In your country, you drive up to somebody's grass hut and throw them in the back of a truck, never to be seen again. I get it. You don't put up with any crap from the dissidents. We should've treated Republicans the same damn way in this country. We'd be better off."

Then Zhang surprised both Pearson and O'Brien. "It was your General William T. Sherman who once said *should the inhabitants burn bridges, obstruct roads, or otherwise manifest local hostility, then army commanders should order and enforce a devastation more relentless.*"

"Okay," said Pearson quietly, impressed with the general's

knowledge of General William Tecumseh Sherman, who infamously drove his Union armies from Chattanooga, through Atlanta, and to Savannah in what became known as the *March to the Sea*. It was Sherman's *scorched earth* approach to war with the Confederacy that earned him both criticism and praise.

"Impressive. Listen, General, I don't give a damn what your boys do out there as long as they do their job," said O'Brien. "But when you're tooting your own horn, just know that I'm the one driving the bus. Keep doing as I request, and I promise not to throw you under it."

Zhang didn't respond and seemed puzzled by O'Brien's statement. While proficient in English, he didn't quite understand the figure of speech used by O'Brien.

O'Brien changed the subject, thankfully. "Let's get back to yesterday's brilliantly orchestrated maneuver. Not only have we secured the State House, which I should have done to begin with, but we now have a couple of hundred valuable assets at our disposal."

"What are you thinking, sir?" asked Pearson. Pearson continued to refer to O'Brien as *sir* and *Governor*, not out of respect, which was lost long ago, but out of fear of the governor's wrath. O'Brien didn't bother earning the respect of others, he demanded it—*continuously.*

"It's time to get our boys back from that traitorous Bradlee. I propose a simple exchange. He gives us Fort Devens and my men. We will give him the governor and the rest of those wusses. I'll even throw in their beloved State House to boot. I oughta strip the gold off the dome first, however."

"My troops can move their encampment into Fort Devens," said Zhang.

"Yes, General," said O'Brien. "We'll give you what you couldn't take for yourself."

Zing, thought Pearson. "It sounds like a straightforward proposal. Should I contact Colonel Bradlee?" he asked.

"Do that, Pearson. I also want to look at some other options."

"Like what, sir?" asked Pearson.

"I want to take one step at a time here, but we need to deal with this Prescott Peninsula situation. I believe the activities at Prescott, the insurgent problems Zhang has experienced, and Fort Devens are interconnected. Bradlee might be the common thread."

"Do you think he's behind all of this?" asked Pearson. Pearson had wondered the same thing but learned not to offer up any suggestions. His suggestion to raid the Massachusetts Guard Armories had failed miserably, and O'Brien made a habit of reminding him of the debacle.

"It's a good possibility," he replied. "Why don't you go up there and run our proposal up the flagpole. Gain his confidence. He might provide us an opening to get back more than our forty-four friends."

"What would that be, sir?" asked Pearson.

"The head of the snake."

CHAPTER THIRTY-SIX

Wednesday November 2
12:07 p.m.
Prescott Peninsula
Quabbin Reservoir, Massachusetts

Sarge scratched his scruffy beard. Unlike his brother, who could grow a beard in a matter of a few hours, Sarge took weeks to have a full beard. He scruffed it again.

"You got fleas in that thing, brother?" Steven laughed. Steven's beard was in perfect, trimmed shape. The last time he'd sported a beard was almost a year ago during his Ukraine mission.

"No, it's just slow growin'," replied Sarge. "I can't grow them as fast as you do. I guess I've evolved more than you have, Neanderthal."

"Hey, we're spawns of the same apes, pal!" He and Steven exchanged high fives. It was a rare moment of joviality between the two in what seemed like a month of tensions. Sarge immediately felt the connection again.

"I'm glad we were able to get everyone together today," started Sarge as he waited for the last of the Brahmin to return indoors.

Katie finally joined the group after fetching her coat from their bungalow. It was a brisk forty degrees, but the lack of wind and a cloudless sky made conditions ideal for an outdoor meeting. "I'm especially glad to have Susan and her little storm trooper, Penny, back here at the ranch."

"Thanks, Sarge," said Susan. "Dr. Daugherty took very good care of Penny, and I thank God for J.J. and his ability to keep me from losing it. I'm the one that needed to be admitted to the hospital."

"You did great, Susan," said Donald, giving his wife a reassuring hug.

"There was a time when I despised the sight of that helicopter," said J.J. as he glared at Morgan's Sikorsky. "It did an admirable job as our version of LifeFlight."

Sarge continued. "Soon, Steven and Katie will remain in Boston for an indefinite period of time as Steven directs the activities of the Mechanics. Brad will continue to command the Marines from here while maintaining a presence at Fort Devens. The rest of us have our jobs to do at 1PP as we contemplate taking the fight to a regional or even national level."

"We're winning," interjected Julia.

"The war? Is there a war?" asked Katie brusquely.

"No, we're winning the ideological war—the most important battle," replied Julia, glancing at Sarge.

"Julia is right," said Sarge. "I have spent a considerable amount of time on the Pigeon. Patriot groups from around the country are forming and are encouraged by the results being achieved. We've decided to step up our broadcasts to include news and information from around the country."

Donald nodded his head and smiled. "Do you guys remember how infuriated we'd get at the mainstream media?"

"Yeah," replied J.J. "I tore that one reporter a new one, remember that?"

"I do," replied Donald. "Now is our opportunity to become the alternative media and the one with the broadcast coverage and listening audience. Sarge's statement was inspiring and the perfect length for the initial broadcast."

"It was very well received," added Julia. "We want Sarge to incorporate specific examples of successes to give fellow patriots across the country hope and confidence."

Sarge looked around to be assured they were alone and then stepped forward into the group. "We are winning the ideological battle, but we cannot underestimate this devious President. Before the collapse, most pundits referred to him as naïve or incompetent. I disagree. I think he is a brilliant strategist who has achieved a lot for his liberal, even socialist, agenda. As his term comes to an end, I expect more from him, especially under these circumstances."

"What can he possibly do?" asked Katie.

"I believe he plans to suspend the elections," replied Sarge. "In case you haven't noticed, Abbie isn't on the campaign trail. Most Americans are trying to stay alive. The November 8th election is the last thing on their minds."

"I haven't heard anything from the campaign, and they know how to reach me," said Abbie. "It's possible they know something I don't, or won't be made privy to."

"How can he do that?" asked J.J.

Sarge continued. "If you recall, in the Declaration of Martial Law, the President cited National Security and Homeland Security Presidential Directive 51 signed by President Bush in '07. They call it Directive 51."

"I remember that," said Brad. "President Bush put it in place towards the end of his administration. It was hailed as a good thing by the talking heads, but it's really a huge power grab by the Executive Branch."

"Exactly right, Brad," said Sarge. "Pushed by the Republicans, the purpose of Directive 51 was to provide for certain national essential functions in the event of a catastrophic national emergency."

"How do you define *catastrophic*?" asked J.J. "Obviously, the collapse of the power grid is catastrophic."

"The problem is not a matter of definition," replied Sarge. "The issue is the power Directive 51 gave the Executive Branch. Today, our President is the functional equivalent of a dictator."

"Thanks a lot, Dubya," said Steven, who was never a fan of the former President.

Sarge continued. "When Presidents do these things, they don't contemplate the potential use of these powers by their successors who might have ulterior motives. This is one of the legacies of the Bush administration. Directive 51 turned national emergencies into a power-grabbing tool in the hands of a President desperate to hold onto power."

"If this is true, what can we do about it?" asked J.J.

"I'm not sure we can stop it, but we can certainly get people fired up in advance," replied Sarge. "Many patriots around the country are expecting this to happen. I'll remind them, point out the consequences, and prepare them for a call to arms in a subsequent broadcast."

"You're setting up the next phase of the ideological war," said Donald.

"That's right," said Sarge. "Anticipate your opponent's move before it is taken, and vocally define his ill intent. It sets the tone of the debate."

"Only on Friday nights?" asked J.J.

"For now," said Sarge. "Now, what else do you guys have?"

Brad spoke up first. "Pearson has reached out to me about the State House prisoners. He indicated O'Brien has a proposal."

"I've got a proposal for him," chimed in Steven. "Let me take him out. Assassinate the guy and be done with him."

Sarge crossed his arms and said, "That's not a good idea. What do you think he has in mind, Brad?"

Before Brad could respond, Katie nudged Steven, who spoke up. "Why the hell not? We need to show that SOB that he can't screw with people!"

"I agree, Steven," said Sarge, trying to calm his brother down. "Let's hear what the man has to say before we *take him out*, as you suggest."

"That's what the old man would do," responded Steven defiantly.

Sarge was taken aback by Steven's brusque attitude. One minute Steven was his joking, man-child brother. The next minute, he was in Sarge's face. He'd become about as predictable as a wasp on speed. Regardless, this kind of confrontation in front of the others was unacceptable and needed to be shut down.

"Well, that's not me," Sarge pushed back, startling Steven and the group. He moved to soften the response. "I agree there is a time and a place for a strategic killing. But not here, not now. Some of America's greatest foreign policy successes were mostly the result of skilled diplomacy, not military force. Having a big stick is nice, but speaking softly may be more effective, especially in a volatile situation like this one. Trust me, Steven, there will be a time very soon to use our stick. Just not yet."

Steven stared at Sarge and then looked to the ground. He shook his head.

Sarge continued. "Let me add this. The fact that O'Brien is willing to negotiate so quickly tells me he is receiving pressure from above, probably directly from the President. There must be something big coming, and the President doesn't need something like the kidnapping of the Massachusetts government gumming up the works."

"The elections," added Julia, touching Sarge on the shoulder for support.

"That's right," said Sarge. "If word of O'Brien's attack on the legislative session reached the rest of the nation, suspension of elections would be the least of his problems."

"I think Sarge is right," said Donald, who had become an invaluable member of the Loyal Nine. Other than Julia, he was the most important confidant to Sarge.

"Plus, we don't want O'Brien to do something rash," continued Sarge. "The man has a propensity for hasty, ill-conceived decisions. There are a few hundred lives at stake over there."

"Okay, got it," said Steven. "You're the boss. I just don't believe in negotiating with terrorists. You just kill 'em."

Steven always has to get the last word. "However—" Sarge paused for effect "—that's not to say we can't potentially use this to our advantage. Brad, set up the meeting as soon as possible. Hear Pearson out, but don't beat his ass."

"I'll be the model of restraint." Brad laughed.

CHAPTER THIRTY-SEVEN

Thursday, November 3
11:00 a.m.
1st Battalion, 25th Marines HQ
Fort Devens, Massachusetts

Brad had no use for Pearson. Not back in the spring when they first met and certainly not today. He knew Pearson played a role in the Belchertown attack of a month ago. He'd lost a couple of good soldiers that day. He wasn't pissed off anymore, because death was a part of war. It was the cause, not the death itself, that bothered Brad the most.

"So we meet again," said Brad, gesturing for Pearson to sit down. He then turned his attention to CWO Shore, who had become Brad's constant companion. Corporal Morrell had assumed the duties of security at Prescott Peninsula, and Shore became the head of Brad's security detail. "I assume he's been frisked."

"Yes, sir, clean."

"After all we've been through, you still don't trust me, Colonel?" asked Pearson, attempting to make a joke.

Brad didn't laugh. He stared a hole through the man's head. *Maybe I am still pissed off.*

After an awkward moment, Pearson continued. "Colonel, I'm going to stick my neck out here a little bit. A lot, actually. While I understand you have others to confide in, I don't. I need assurances from you that our conversation will remain confidential, at least as it relates to the people on my side of the equation."

Brad thought for a moment. He was not going to let Pearson entrap him. Brad was a man of few words when dealing with a potential adversary and that had always served him well. He'd listen to Pearson and engage cautiously.

"Fair enough."

"Colonel, O'Brien is unstable. He's trying to do his job like he's undertaking a wildcat strike."

"Without a doubt," said Brad.

"The stated purpose of my meeting with you today is to propose a prisoner swap. Formally, O'Brien is offering the two hundred plus civilians locked in the State House for the forty-four men in your Federal Prison Camp over there." Pearson pointed out the window to the housing facility.

Without acknowledging Pearson's intel, Brad responded, "Why should we do that? The forty-four men you refer to violated the law by breaking into fully stocked armories. You played a very big part in that operation, if I'm not mistaken. Maybe I should lock you up with them!"

Pearson sat back in the chair and took a deep breath. "Colonel, I'm trying my best to diffuse a dangerous situation. I realize you and I have been at crossed-purposes in the past. Please understand, I'm trying to keep a bad situation from getting worse."

Truthfully, Brad knew the prisoners he was holding were not dangerous. They were union guys, but mainly they were family men induced to raid the armories by promises of food, shelter, and power. After sixty days in captivity, all they cared about at this point was finding their families alive, hopefully.

"I'll consider it," said Brad, who wanted to leave the impression with Pearson that he was the proverbial *decider*.

"There is one more thing," added Pearson.

I knew it!

"The governor also proposes to swap the Massachusetts State House for Fort Devens."

"Hell no!" Brad snapped back. "The Massachusetts State House belongs to the people. Fort Devens belongs to the United States armed forces. Non-negotiable."

Pearson began to explain O'Brien's position, but Brad tuned him out. As Pearson spoke, Brad gave it some thought. It didn't make sense for the UN troops to leave their primary theater of operations to take control of a facility an hour away. Gas didn't grow on trees. Traveling back and forth could be costly and dangerous. On the road, you opened yourself up to IEDs and insurgent activity.

"... primarily concerned about housing for his troops this winter," finished Pearson.

"Okay."

"What?" asked Pearson.

"I said okay, we'll agree to the facility swap," replied Brad, catching Pearson off guard. "I'll need a few days to remove all U.S. military equipment and personnel. We'll de-identify the base. I don't want any of the local citizens misunderstanding what this really is—a foreign occupation of a United States military installation. But for the good of the people of Massachusetts, I'll make it happen."

"That's good news, Colonel. I'm glad we could reach an agreement. You know, it just shows that you and I can work—"

"Shut up!" yelled Brad as he leaned forward in his chair.

Pearson was frightened by the outburst.

"We're not best buds! I know you were involved in the Belchertown raid. God knows what you said to those people to give them the courage to die for nothing."

"But it wasn't just—"

"I don't care," Brad shot back. "What's done is done. Here's a message for your boss. I'm unstable too. He needs to focus on taking care of the people within his charge who are trying to survive. This collapse, or whatever you wanna call it, is not O'Brien's opportunity to get rich, powerful, and famous. He's tried that for nearly sixty days, and he's a complete failure."

"Colonel, I didn't come here to make you angry. I simply wanted to help."

"Fine, then here's how you can help. You and I can keep the lines of communication open. We're not friends, got it?"

Pearson nodded sheepishly.

Brad continued. "I believe it's possible people with different points of view, with good intentions, can come together for the good of the country. Maybe you fall into that mind-set. Maybe not. Either way, I know O'Brien and his type. He only cares about his personal gain."

"I don't disagree," said Pearson.

"Good. We have something we can build on. But make no mistake. If O'Brien doesn't quit or the President doesn't fire him, then I will remove him from his governor's throne, and the result will not be pretty. Are we all clear, Pearson?" Brad leaned back in his chair and locked his eyes on Pearson.

"Crystal clear," replied Pearson, adding with respect, "sir."

CHAPTER THIRTY-EIGHT

Friday, November 4
7:15 p.m.
Prescott Peninsula
Quabbin Reservoir, Massachusetts

"Tonight, we rally the troops," said Sarge as he walked through Donald's workshop, admiring some of the interesting projects on the drawing board—including the handheld EMP device. He examined it while he spoke. "My goal is to convince like-minded Americans there is hope, and a means, to pull ourselves out of this disaster. It all starts with them, as individuals."

"What are you going to suggest?" asked Donald as he took the EMP device away from Sarge like a father would retrieve a dangerous tool from a child. "Let me put that over here before you fry the place."

"Yes, please," said Brad. "Keep him away from the big-boy toys."

Julia laughed. At that moment, she envisioned Sarge taking away a toy airplane from little Henry. *Henry? Is our child going to be a boy? When do I tell Sarge?*

She joined the conversation. "There have been some

developments, Donald. The government is beginning to restore power in parts of the country. The locations are telling."

"Julia is right," said Sarge. "I'm learning as I go. Morgan has a wealth of knowledge, and his resources are endless. As you guys know, the Boston Brahmin are heavily invested in the industrial-military complex."

"That's an understatement," said Donald. "They *are* the industrial-military complex. After World War II, defense spending skyrocketed and the Brahmin's investment in armament manufacturers followed the trend. As the U.S. military budget increased accordingly, the privatization of the production and invention of military technology followed suit."

"Our benefactors have been an integral part of that growth," said Sarge. "As the relationship between the public sector and private defense contractors became more complex, an agency of the Department of Defense was created to act as a liaison between these technological innovators and the military."

"DARPA," interjected Brad.

"Yes," said Sarge. "It's an acronym for the Defense Advanced Research Projects Agency. For our purposes, a program initiated via DARPA has surfaced. Mr. Morgan asked the President for permission to set the wheels in motion back in September, and the President refused."

Sarge glanced at his watch and tapped his wrist. He led Julia, Brad, and Donald out of the room and down the dimly lit corridor in the bowels of 1PP. It was almost time for his *Choose Freedom* broadcast. He continued to speak as they walked.

"One of the projects initiated in the past year was known as RADICS—Rapid Attack Detection, Isolation and Characterization Systems. The project was designed to provide early warning of impending cyber attacks on critical infrastructure as well as rapid forensic identifications of cyber threats."

"It didn't work," said Brad.

"Well, the advanced warning aspect of RADICS was still in its infancy," replied Sarge. "The primary focus was in disaster relief response efforts."

"Is that part of the project online?" asked Brad.

"Yes," replied Sarge. "The RADICS project was designed to include mitigation and damage control following a successful attack by isolating unaffected networks, repairing damaged ones, and coordinating efforts to replace damaged electricity transmission components, like transformers."

Sarge paused as the four made their way up the spiral staircase to the main floor of 1PP. The living area was empty except for two soldiers who were eating bowls of oatmeal, which had become everyone's favorite meal as the weather turned colder. As the group entered the living area, the soldiers quickly finished and left.

"Why would the President refuse to implement a disaster relief option that could restore the power grid, at least in part?"

"It's complicated," said Sarge as he turned to Brad. "I know what the President's agenda is. It hasn't changed since the day he announced his run for office in 2007. He promised a *fundamental transformation of America*. There are those who criticized his presidency as out of touch. I see his actions as brilliant and calculating when taken in the context of a fundamental transformation. He used the mandate given to him by the 2008 election to effectuate radical left-wing political ideologies that have been on the drawing board for decades. These policies, like government-mandated insurance, open borders, and correcting social injustices, relied upon a permanently agitated and divided population to create the sense of crisis that is the only context under which people are willing to accept radical change."

"The cyber attack took away those tools," said Donald.

"That's true, but his presidency was nearing an end," said Sarge. "The collapse of the grid has presented him with new opportunities to reshape America in his vision. The President will bring America back online, but he'll do it by rewarding his constituency."

Sarge gave Julia a kiss on the cheek as he approached the

broadcast room to prepare for his Friday night address to his fellow patriots.

"How does RADICS play into all of this?"

"The President has been restoring power to areas loyal to him," replied Sarge. "I have Donald comparing the information we've received to the voting results of the last two presidential elections, but it appears he's playing favorites based upon voting districts that overwhelmingly supported him."

Donald added, "It's very strategic. Northern California, parts of Oregon and Washington are the primary West Coast areas. Chicago is the only Midwest city. On the East Coast, New York and Washington are getting power restored. Nothing in the South or Southwest."

"The heartland has been left behind," said Julia.

"Tie it all together for me, Sarge," said Brad.

"First, we have to anticipate the President's next move," began Sarge. "I've been reaching out to people loyal to us within the government. Donald has been establishing a pattern. The President has been establishing power in regions within the country that are strategically located."

"Let me add this," said Brad. "My friends are telling me troop movements have escalated toward the West Coast. I'll inquire about more activity."

"Good," said Sarge. "Listen, I've got to get ready, but let me say this. The President used the media to stifle dissent before the collapse. I think he plans to use the military and those citizens who are willing to support him to stifle dissent in the post-collapse world. We have to be ready for the inevitable war between Americans."

Sarge was bringing his broadcast to a close.

"Fellow patriots, revolutions are brutal affairs. In most cases, they don't end well. But in America, free men will always succeed.

Our forefathers shed blood for us. The result was a stable and prosperous nation.

"Today, our freedoms are under attack by an oppressive and controlling federal government that is picking and choosing who it wants to survive. For those of you in the Southwestern United States and throughout the Southeast, you are to be commended. You've acted bravely and with conviction. You've taken back your homes, your communities, and your states.

"For the rest of the nation where hope is in short supply, look to your patriot brothers in Little Rock, Tallahassee, Atlanta, and Nashville. They recognized the clear and present danger posed to our freedoms by the Citizen Corps. Patriots across those regions rose up despite being hungry and ill-equipped. They had pride and commitment. They overcame a greater force using their love of country.

"Start at home by making sacrifices for the country we love. Talk to your neighbors and other members of your community. Reach out to surrounding communities and then establish a network within your state. Seek out like-minded patriots whom you can trust. There are more of you than you might realize. The successes I've described today will be your successes tomorrow.

"Be inspired. Be brave. Choose freedom!"

CHAPTER THIRTY-NINE

Saturday, November 5
3:00 p.m.
Belchertown, Massachusetts

"Hey, take it easy up there, driver!" shouted Sarge as he playfully cajoled Steven about the bumpy ride to Belchertown. It had been five weeks since the failed raid by the Belchertown residents. They had captured one of the group, the teenage son of the town's leader, Ronald Archibald. Following last night's *Choose Freedom* broadcast, Sarge decided to try diplomacy close to home. He intended to make peace with Belchertown by returning the boy and extending an olive branch. Just in case, he brought a contingent of heavily armed Marines to back him up.

"Yes, sir," replied Steven. "Remind me to file a formal complaint with the road commissioner while we're in town. That's if, of course, we don't get our asses shot up while here."

"Let's hope that isn't the case," said Sarge. "J.J. has bonded with the boy. In fact, it was borderline Stockholm syndrome. There have been several occasions when J.J. has suggested his release. I believe the time is right for a dry run of our big prisoner swap on Tuesday."

Katie and Julia sat in silence as they rode along Daniel Shays Highway southward into Belchertown. Shays, a farmer and Revolutionary war hero in the 5th Massachusetts Regiment, became famous for leading Shay's Rebellion against controversial tax policies instituted after the Revolutionary War. *This country needs more patriots like Daniel Shays.*

Steven looked at Sarge in the rearview mirror. "You got your body armor on, Chief?"

"I do." Sarge was wearing his usual kit with ballistic plates installed. When in public, he wanted to blend in with the rest of the group, although today he planned on taking a risk by dealing with Archibald directly.

Steven continued. "I've never been a big fan of protection."

"It's amazing I'm not an uncle," said Sarge, drawing a laugh from Julia and a sharp glare from Katie.

"They didn't hesitate in their attempt to kill us all five weeks ago," said Katie dryly. Nobody responded, creating an awkward silence in the truck.

The convoy, led by two Humvees equipped with fifty-caliber weapons mounted on their turrets, approached the meeting point established by Donald and Archibald. Donald, and then J.J., assured Archibald the intended meeting was strictly peaceful and that no harm had come to his son. Over the past five weeks, Archibald and his wife had cautiously approached the front gate of Prescott Peninsula to inquire about Nate on several occasions. J.J. had established a rapport with them on the last two visits, which prompted Sarge to arrange this meeting.

They passed a looted hospital on their right as they approached the intersection of Shays Highway and, ironically, Sargent Street. A welcoming committee was set up in the parking lot of a small shopping center containing a CVS Pharmacy, a Dollar Store, and the newly opened, and now closed, Frozen Yogurt store.

"Look, Sarge," whispered Julia as she pointed to McDonald's across the street. "The American flag is still flying proudly."

Sarge shook his head. *Should I have reached out to these people sooner? Could the attack have been avoided and lives saved?*

"I don't like this," said Steven as he slowed the Humvee to a stop several hundred yards behind the lead vehicles. A third Humvee sped around them, which contained Donald and J.J. with the boy.

Archibald and his wife stood directly under the traffic signals in the center of the four-way intersection. With their hands held high, the parents slowly turned to reveal they were unarmed. For a tense moment, nobody moved. The gunners manning the fifty cals slowly surveyed the crowd, pointing their powerful weapons menacingly at the entire contingent.

"We're ready, sir," came the voice of CWO Shore over the comms.

"Okay, Sarge," said Steven. "You know the drill."

"I do," said Sarge as he leaned over and kissed Julia. "I'll be right back."

"I know," she replied. "Sarge, one person, one town, one state, one country at a time." He kissed her again.

Steven and Katie exited the vehicle first and scanned all sides of the intersection with their M4s. Steven rapped the fender twice, indicating to Sarge that it was safe to exit. As he exited and began walking towards the intersection, Marines exited the front vehicles and shielded J.J. and Donald as they emerged as well.

Steven said to Sarge as he passed, "You know I've got your six."

Sarge hesitated and looked Steven in the eyes, probing. "I need to know that you've got me around the entire dial."

Before Steven could answer, Archibald yelled, "Where's my son?"

His wife added, tears streaming down her face, "Where's my Nate?"

Sarge didn't wait for a response from Steven and began walking toward the intersection.

Donald, standing behind two of the soldiers, responded, "Mr. and Mrs. Archibald, your son is safe and with us. But there are a lot of people here. We need assurances from you that there won't be any trouble."

"No trouble! No trouble!" yelled Archibald. "They just came because, well, we're a tight-knit community. We're not armed. They're not armed."

Sarge caught up to Donald and J.J.

Archibald turned to the townspeople. "Show them. Everybody! Show them we're unarmed!"

Nearly three hundred people standing at the Mobil station on the right and across to the McDonald's on the left slowly raised their arms and spun around in unison.

Contrition, thought Sarge. "Remove the boy's restraints and let him go," instructed Sarge to Shore. "I don't want his mother to see him in wrist cuffs."

He walked past the Marines and into the open intersection. The soldiers immediately raised their weapons to thwart any potential trouble.

"My name is Henry Sargent," he said as he extended his hand to greet Archibald. Mrs. Archibald was sobbing. "They're getting your son now, ma'am."

She nodded and calmed down somewhat. Nervously, she said, "This is Sargent Street."

"It's probably named after my family."

"Really?"

"Yes, ma'am," replied Sarge, but Mrs. Archibald was off in a flash, running toward her son, who ran past the Marines and into her arms.

"Mom!" he shouted as the two crashed into each other in an embrace. Archibald tried to restrain himself and maintain some sort of leadership decorum, but he broke into tears and ran toward his teenage boy as well. Sarge stood alone in the intersection bearing his family name and surveyed the crowd. They were weak. Eyes were sullen. Clothes hung on them like rags. Their faces screamed despair.

The tearful reunion continued for another moment while young Nathaniel introduced his parents to his captors. J.J. and Donald spoke a few words to the Archibalds before the group returned to Sarge.

"Mr. Archibald—" started Sarge before being interrupted.

"Please, call me Archie," he said. "All my friends do."

"Are we friends, Archie?" asked Sarge, who towered over Archibald by six inches. "We got off to a rocky start, as I recall."

"Let me explain. I am very sorry that—"

Sarge cut him off by raising his hand. "Mr. Arch … Archie, we've put that day behind us. Have you and the rest of Belchertown?"

"Absolutely."

"Let me ask you this," started Sarge as he surveyed the crowd once again. "What's the population of Belchertown?"

"Before the lights went out, around fourteen thousand. Now we're down to a little more than a thousand."

Sarge ran his fingers through his beard but resisted the urge to scratch it. *This has to go.* He wondered if the CVS store had any razors.

"We've used up the harvests and removed anything from the local stores."

"How are you surviving?" asked Sarge.

"We've sent groups into Amherst and Northampton to barter markets on Saturdays. After we attacked, um …" Archibald became emotional and then composed himself. He whispered, "I'm sorry."

Sarge reached out and placed his hands firmly on the man's shoulders as his wife and son watched Archibald break down.

Containing himself, he spoke again. "We began trading our weapons and ammunition for food. It's all anybody wants at these things. A handgun might bring a bag of rice in trade. Fifty rounds of ammo gets you a bag of beans."

Sarge waved Shore over to the group and whispered in his ear, "Call them up."

"Yes, sir," said Shore, who double-timed it to the Humvees.

Within moments, two five-ton M928 Cargo Trucks drove along the shoulder past the parked Humvees. Sarge waved them in front of the Mobil station, where the onlookers parted to make way.

"What's this?" asked Archibald, who had overcome his emotions.

"Archie," said Sarge, "we're neighbors now. We're no longer enemies. We want to help our neighbors the best way we know how."

The soldiers inside the M928s lowered the side gates and removed the canvas covering of the oversized six-by-six military vehicle, revealing boxes of food, bottled water, hygiene supplies, and medical necessities.

"Is that for us?" asked Mrs. Archibald.

"Yes, ma'am," replied Sarge, which earned him a big hug from both Archibalds.

"God bless you, Mr. Sargent," she said tearfully.

He repeated Julia's words in his mind—*one person, one town, one state, one country at a time.*

"Call me Sarge. All my friends do."

CHAPTER FORTY

Sunday, November 6
8:30 a.m.
310 Washington Street
Boston, Massachusetts

Dubbed the *Sanctuary of Freedom* in the eighteenth century, the Old South Meeting House still stood in the heart of downtown Boston. The Puritan meeting house, or church, had been an important gathering place since it was built in 1729. Sons of Liberty leader Samuel Adams and Founding Father Benjamin Franklin were some of the more infamous members of the church.

In the early morning hours of December 16th, 1773, Samuel Adams called upon thousands of colonists from the region to attend a political meeting at the Old South Meeting House to discuss the British Crown's onerous tax on tea. As ships entered the harbor loaded with tea, they were told that the tax must be paid, or they could not be unloaded. For days, colonists from all walks of life listened to Samuel Adams as he protested the actions of the royal governor. When the third ship arrived and was refused its request to unload, the colonists unloaded.

Whipped into a frenzy by Samuel Adams, hundreds of colonists, led by the Sons of Liberty, left the hall and made their way to Boston Harbor. The story is well known. The tea was thrown into the harbor in open defiance of British rule. The covert gatherings at the Old South Meeting House sparked and ignited a revolution. Historians will always look to the Boston Tea Party as the catalyst and the turning point in the history of America that led to its independence.

Steven began to rotate the meetings of the Mechanics from one location to another each week. He chose churches because they were exempt from the martial law declaration's prohibition on large assemblies.

O'Brien, out of sheer laziness, signed an order that permitted church services in any designated house of worship between eight in the morning and noon on Sundays. O'Brien appointed four of his men to act as designated agents to supervise the program. The Mechanics kept tabs on their activities each Sunday morning and quickly learned that the agents rarely reported for duty.

The Old South Meeting House, while operating as a museum, was technically designated as a church. It provided the Mechanics the perfect cover for their own form of revolutionary meetings. This morning, no fire-and-brimstone preacher was necessary to inflame passions. They came in the door with smoke coming out of their ears.

"We can't let this stand!"

"When are we gonna take the fight directly to those UN invaders!"

"Screw them, I wanna take out O'Brien!"

"Hell yeah!"

"Choose freedom!"

"Steven! Where's Sarge?"

It was this last outburst that caused Steven to quieten the crowd.

"Listen up. Hey, calm down, everybody. This is an old building. We don't need to bring the roof down."

Steven surveyed the room. This was by far the largest group of the Mechanics assembled to date. Nearly six hundred sets of eyes stared at him for guidance and leadership. He wanted to give them what they demanded—O'Brien's head on a pike.

"Okay, thanks. Listen up. Like I've said, Sarge will not be attending these meetings anymore."

"What are we gonna do? Tell us!" shouted a voice from the rear of the room.

"I know you guys are pissed off and anxious to do something," replied Steven. "Just hear me out. We'll get to all of this."

The room was filled. Makeshift Rebellious Flags had been created out of torn sheets stapled to tree limbs and split two-by-fours. The five red and four white vertical stripes were created with paint, permanent markers, and in one case, the blood of some type of animal. The crowd wanted blood and Steven desperately wanted to give it to them.

"Steven, the people are with us. Right, everybody?"

"Yeah! Choose freedom!" The demonstration continued again.

"Let's storm the State House. We outnumber the UN!"

Screams of approval filled the Old South Meeting House.

Katie beckoned him over while the Mechanics rallied. She cupped her hands over her mouth and spoke into his ear. "They need this."

"Katie, Sarge was pretty direct. He doesn't want a bloodbath out there."

"Can you do it without a bloodbath?"

"Maybe," replied Steven. "We still have a couple of days to plan it out."

Steven looked at Katie seeking guidance, who began to smile. She mouthed the words, "Go for it."

"I will. Does he think he can do this thing without me? Does he think Tuesday's prisoner swap is gonna be some kind of lovefest like Belchertown?"

Steven stood up and returned to the lectern. The time for debating the use of force versus diplomacy was over.

CHAPTER FORTY-ONE

Sunday, November 6
7:00 p.m.
Western White House
Honolulu, Hawaii

This was only the second nationwide address by the President during this time of crisis. His other public appearances were confined to one-on-one interviews with foreign news media. The White House press corps was starved for information. Press briefings were minimal and particulars were scarce. When the President's chief of staff announced this national speech, rumors were plentiful. Homeland Security briefings provided the most insight into how the nation was recovering.

However, the reporters were skeptical about the source. DHS painted a rosy picture, consistently touting the accomplishments of the Citizen Corps. The media, including those outlets typically favorable to the President, suspected otherwise. Their ranks had thinned, and only a single camera was allowed. *Today's Q and A following the statement should be interesting.*

In the President's first address to the nation on September 7th, the slightly elevated stage contained the large blue podium adorned with the seal of the President of the United States, together with two flags—the United States flag on the right, and the flag of the President of the United States on the left. Today, a third flag appeared. The blue and white flag of the United Nations stood on the left next to the flag of the President.

The President approached the blue goose, the large blue podium bearing the official seal of the President of the United States. His previously jet black hair had grayed. His wrinkles were more pronounced. He was decidedly thinner. The President looked exhausted.

"My fellow Americans and citizens of the world, it has been two months since the devastating, unprovoked attack upon our nation.

"Although it may seem like an eternity to some, it is a brief period of time under these circumstances. I do not wish to diminish the pain that most of you have endured. I feel for your loss and your hardships. Know that your government is working hard to provide the basic necessities to as many of you as possible." He paused, distracted as his communications director abruptly left the room.

"In this short period of time, we have accomplished quite a bit. Through the valiant efforts of our Citizen Corps governors and their teams that are made up of people like you, our Citizen Corps team leaders and members of the public worked together. Side by side, you've helped save your neighbors and those among us who are vulnerable. As a nation, we've come together, and now it's time to move to the next phase.

"I have set forth a plan for my agency heads to follow. It is designed to take us into the next phase of the recovery process. The plan has two strategic imperatives. First, I want to establish a whole community approach to the recovery effort. By that, I mean every member of the American public must participate for the greater good. Those who are physically able will be able to assist in the rebuilding of our infrastructure. Those who are not may provide goods or other services deemed necessary by the Citizen Corps. This will be looked upon as a team effort.

"Second, I want to foster commitment and loyalty to this great nation of ours. In the past, political rancor and disagreement ruled the day. This is not who we are. I intend to use this catastrophe to bring us together as a nation. We simply do not have the time to argue amongst ourselves, creating bitterness and resentfulness. In addition, we do not have the governmental resources to waste at a time of national emergency."

The President paused again, this time for effect. "On Tuesday, November 8th, a presidential election was scheduled. Pursuant to my authority under the Declaration of Martial Law, Executive Order 13777, I am hereby suspending elections until further notice, and the Twenty-Second Amendment is also suspended until such time as our nation is able to properly conduct and monitor the electoral process.

"Let me be clear. This decision did not come without serious thought and counsel. These actions are appropriate under these catastrophic circumstances and are necessary to heal this nation.

"Now, I'll address a few questions. Dan Balz, *Washington Post*, is first up. Dan."

"Thank you, Mr. President. Is your canceling of elections and the suspension of the operation of the Twenty-Second Amendment effectively giving you a third term in office?"

Balz remained standing as the President replied, "The office of the President is the only office elected by all of the citizens of the United States. The Twenty-Second Amendment to the Constitution, enacted in 1947, provides the term of office for the President shall not be greater than two terms, or eight years. There are many, including President Ronald Reagan, a Republican, I might add, that believe the Twenty-Second Amendment is an infringement on the democratic rights of the people."

Balz continued with his questioning. "Mr. President, a follow-up, please. The Twenty-Second Amendment was ratified by every state. Doesn't that speak to the will of the people?"

"Dan, I consider the Twenty-Second Amendment to be an invasion of the people's democratic rights to vote for whomever they want to vote for and for however long. Now, I wasn't on the ballot this Tuesday, so it was never my intention to run for a third term. It is my intention to unify this nation in its time of need. Leaders lead, and that's what I am doing by this executive action."

"Mr. President! Mr. President!" came the shouts as hands sprang up around the room.

"Jonathan."

Jonathan Karl of ABC News addressed the President next. "Mr. President, with respect to the second part of your statement, when do you anticipate holding elections?"

"At this juncture, I can't answer that, Jonathan. As soon as practicable."

"Any time frame at all, Mr. President?"

"No," the President replied curtly. "Over here."

"Thank you, Mr. President. Luis Ramirez, Voice of America Radio. The United Nations Peacekeeping forces have multiplied exponentially on U.S. soil. Reports are rampant of atrocities committed by their troops. Have you been informed of the details of their misdeeds, and how do you respond to calls for the removal of the UN?"

"We are pleased with the partnership established with the United Nations Secretary-General Ban Ki-moon. The UN has provided aid throughout the nation and has been especially helpful in stifling tensions in our highly populated urban regions. While there have been rumors of so-called atrocities, I've received no credible evidence from the Department of Homeland Security that these atrocities are the norm rather than the exception."

"Next up is Peter Baker, *New York Times*."

"Thank you, Mr. President. A follow-up to my question at our last press conference. Are our intelligence gatherers any closer to determining who is responsible for the cyber attack?"

"No, Peter, they're not. Attribution—or lack thereof—is another major obstacle that prevents any nation from defining when a perpetrator initiates a cyber attack. If a government cannot determine who carried out the attack, it's difficult to know who to blame and whether the attack warrants retaliation. Without definitive evidence leading to identification of the offender, a nation-state can't formulate an appropriate response without knowing who was involved."

"Mr. President, at one point, the Russians appeared to be on the radar of our law enforcement agencies. Is Russia still the focus of their investigation?"

"Just like any criminal investigation, if law enforcement could somehow figure out the assailant, then a lot of issues go away. If you know who's conducting the cyber activity, you also get an insight into their intent. If it's the Russian government, you know they have the ability to take things a step further. If it's some hacker in his mom's basement, you know there's no intent or ability to raise the level of force that's going to be used. Ultimately, the issue of attribution is not a legal problem; it's a technical problem."

The President continued, this time addressing all of the media present. "It is human nature in a stressful situation like this to seek answers. It is important to know who and why. There have been justifiable outcries for this administration to respond militarily. So let me be clear. Attribution, the process of detecting an adversary's fingerprints on a cyber attack, will always be a challenge. Establishing any degree of confidence in determining guilt may always stand in the way of a military response. Will the United States government require a beyond all reasonable doubt standard as it might in a criminal prosecution? Time will tell."

"Mr. President, a question about Fox News."

The President glared at the reporter from the UK *Daily Mail*. "Go ahead."

"Fox News has been barred from press events by your communications staff. They are the fifth news organization to be excluded from direct questioning of your administration. Do you feel this has a chilling—"

The President interrupted the reporter. "Our administration will no longer grant press credentials and access to the highest level of government to any media source that has no journalistic integrity.

Our nation is in a crisis, and it doesn't need the flames of emotion stoked by false or misleading reporting."

"But, sir," the reporter continued at the risk of losing his credentials, "all of us in the media recognize the inherent conflict between the official statements released by the administration and our desire to press the government for more accountability and transparency. Wouldn't you agree the media's job isn't to write down what you or members of your administration say and regurgitate it. If that were the case, we could limit this room to one person."

The President was incredulous. He looked over for his communications director twice and caught the eye of an aide, who tried to melt into her chair.

"Well, perhaps we should do that. I believe in a free press. I also believe our country is in dire straits. Before the cyber attack, the public's confidence in the media was at record lows. *Perhaps* you should look at each other to determine whether you are being sensationalistic or acting for the greater good of our nation."

The President began to walk away from the podium, but the reporter persisted as Secret Service agents moved toward him.

"It's a slippery slope, Mr. President," he said, raising his voice. "If there are no objective points of view to say *this is true and this isn't*, then what are we left with? The American people will only be left with one set of facts—yours!"

As the young brit was wrestled to the ground, the second post-collapse press conference in sixty days came to an end as the single camera broadcasted the events to the world.

CHAPTER FORTY-TWO

Monday, November 7
8:30 p.m.
310 Washington Street
Boston, Massachusetts

"Tomorrow is a big day, my friends, so let's get down to business. I've met with all of you individually today, and I'm comfortable that we'll have the right personnel in place. I am pleased with the turnout from the Massachusetts State Defense Force."

Steven walked toward the front pews and gestured for a man to stand. "Props to Colonel Lancaster from the 1st Battalion Operational Support group out of Milford. You guys have done a tremendous job in bringing in new recruits with substantial training under their belt. Would you like to say a few words?"

"Thank you, Steven. The MSDF was formed by the Massachusetts General Court during the Civil War. For one hundred and fifty years, our all-volunteer military force, made up of members who have regular civilian careers, stood at the ready until activated by the governor. I regret that we weren't here to prevent this injustice against our Massachusetts legislators. We intend to make it right tomorrow!"

Cheers and applause rose throughout the Old South Meeting House. Steven thanked Colonel Lancaster and continued.

"As you all know, our President, the tyrant, went too far. The right to vote is the most important right granted to a U.S. citizen, as it acts as a preservative of all other rights we hold true. When we vote, we make our voices heard. We register our opinions as to who government should work for. This President has stolen that right from us!"

"Choose freedom!" shouted one of the Mechanics. He cajoled his fellow militiamen to join in, which resulted in a full-throated chorus. "Choose freedom! Choose freedom!"

Steven moved to quiet the crowd. "Tomorrow will be a big day in American history. Like other patriots around the country, we will band together to stand up against the tyrannical approach this President has implemented."

"Hear! Hear!" yelled someone in the back of the room.

Steven nodded, acknowledging the expression dating back to the seventeenth century. "In the name of protecting us, he has imprisoned our voices. In the name of rebuilding, he has torn down our freedoms! In the name of restoring order, he has invited a foreign army onto American soil!"

"This will not stand!"

"This is our land!"

"U.S.A.! U.S.A.! U.S.A.!"

Steven smiled. *So this was what a political rally looked like.* The Mechanics brought themselves under control.

"Tomorrow, some of us may die. I am prepared for death. We will mourn the fallen and thank God for those who live. If a revolution is to begin in this country, the time is now. If freedom is to be saved, it will be saved tomorrow. Against all odds, I choose freedom!"

And the group rose again, much like a partisan congress at a presidential State of the Union address. Steven didn't need to cheerlead further. His men were with him—live or die.

"Tomorrow is our opportunity. There may be others later, but as General Patton once said, *A good plan, violently executed now, is better than a perfect plan next week.* Or as I like to say, *It's time to get after it!*"

Steven spent the rest of the evening breaking the Mechanics into groups. He moved unit to unit, reminding them of their strategy.

Each had a defined purpose. The attack upon the UN forces would be slow and methodical. The element of surprise would be their key to success. The use of guerilla tactics was ideal for tomorrow's operation. The Mechanics would use their mobility to fight the larger, traditional militaristic UN forces.

He approached the group that contained the new guys Elkins and Grant. "This team will be using code name *Hammers* on the comms. There are only four of you, and we will monitor our own frequency on the radio. You guys have one job. Get as close to Governor O'Brien as possible. Elkins and Grant have provided us outstanding intel on how the prisoner swap is to go down tomorrow. Let's go over what you've learned."

Grant spoke up first. "Today, I was in a food line set up by O'Brien downtown at the government center. He was holding court, as you might say. Shaking hands. Chatting up his constituents, etcetera. I overheard him say to a woman who I assume was one of the wives of the prisoners that he hoped she looked forward to the reunion with her husband. He said he planned to be standing on the State House steps to greet his old friends home."

Elkins added, "They started assembling scaffolding this morning. I believe it's going to be an observation stand. It's behind the wrought-iron fence."

"Okay," said Steven. "We won't know until tomorrow whether this is even feasible. You men, as the Hammers, will have to find a soft spot, a breach in O'Brien's security detail. We may use a distraction to divert attention. Be prepared to react to conditions on the ground."

Elkins looked to Grant and then spoke. "I assume you've cleared this with the boss."

"I don't have a boss," Steven snapped back.

"Well, I mean Sarge," replied Elkins. "Sarge is pretty much running things, right?"

"Not tomorrow," Steven reacted defensively before walking away. "This is my baby."

Steven tried to shake off the reference to Sarge as his boss. *He's my brother!*

He rolled his neck and moved on. Steven held his final conversation with Colonel Lancaster's unit. "We will fight the UN because the will of the people demands it. We will not stand for the atrocities committed by them in the name of peacekeeping. More importantly, tomorrow we send a clear message to our brothers around the country. Stand with us. Together, we can take our country back!"

CHAPTER FORTY-THREE

Tuesday, November 8
11:25 a.m.
100 Beacon
Boston, Massachusetts

This would be their last day at home for many months. Sarge insisted upon being in town for the prisoner exchange even though he agreed joining the festivities was too dangerous. He enjoyed a level of anonymity for the moment. His regular appearances on Choose Freedom radio and his increased contact with both domestic and international political leaders increased his chances of being recognized. He believed he could walk among the people gathering on Boston Common undetected, but Julia wisely warned against it. It wasn't worth the risk. She was not going to orphan their child before the baby was born.

"I'll observe from here," said Sarge to a member of his security detail as he looked through the telescope toward the eastern end of Boston Common. All of the leaves had fallen and the streets were devoid of vehicular traffic. The southeast corner of 100 Beacon provided the perfect, safe observation tower.

"Yes, sir," replied the soldier, who withdrew to take up a defensive position at the north side of the building.

Julia moved to hug Sarge around the waist. "I know you wanted to be down there."

"This is a big step, honey," he said. "If we are going to move forward, there has to be a spirit of cooperation between the government and the people. At least for one day, despite the protests around the country due to the President's canceling of elections, Boston can raise the white flag and prove an orderly transition of some nature can occur."

"Even if it's the swapping of political prisoners," added Julia.

"Exactly. Throughout history, warring opponents can call a truce for the limited purpose of returning prisoners to their families."

Julia interjected. "Despite the fact that the prisoners may come back to fight you again?"

"You hope not, but that happens. This situation is unique because O'Brien committed the crime of armed kidnapping, in my opinion. And the victim happens to be the government of Massachusetts."

Julia laughed. "The symbolism is not lost on me. A so-called governor appointed by a tyrannical President has to kidnap the legitimate government in order to establish his own legitimacy." They both began laughing.

"That was a mouthful coming from a former political editor to a newspaper." Sarge laughed.

"Imagine if I wrote it and someone had to read it," she replied, giving Sarge a fist bump.

"LOL," said Sarge, utilizing his favorite acronym from Facebook. He turned serious again. "We have to win the battle of ideas first. Americans are looking for leadership, not oppression. Restoring our freedoms and rights under the Constitution are a prerequisite to revitalizing and restoring America to its greatness."

"How do you get everyone on board?" asked Julia.

"Not everyone, but at least most," he replied. "We need to convince patriotic Americans to reaffirm the principles of limited government, free enterprise, and the rule of law so that we can reemerge a nation where freedom, opportunity, and prosperity can flourish."

"Well, don't you sound like a politician." Julia chuckled. "Maybe you should run for office? President Sargent. I like it."

"Shhhh," joked Sarge. "Somebody might hear you and second the motion."

"Can we succeed in taking back our country and restoring democracy in your vision?" asked Julia.

"I have to say, the changes must start with our political parties. I believe the Republicans and Democrats became less interested in winning elections than in controlling their parties' candidates. History has proven that. When Barry Goldwater won the Republican nomination in '64, it was his fellow Republicans who destroyed his chances of success in the campaign against LBJ."

"What about now?" asked Julia.

"Libertarians have never had a chance within either of the two major political parties. I've always said that it would take a major reset of the political landscape to change that."

"Now, you have your reset," said Julia.

"Yes, courtesy of my predecessor, John Morgan."

Sarge thought quietly. "Our country was headed for a societal meltdown. The nation was unhappy all across the socioeconomic spectrum. During my lectures, I focused on external threats to our sovereignty. But over the past few decades, America began to rapidly decline. Our country was going to collapse eventually, like all of the great nations before her, but not from an existential threat. It was going to collapse from within. By that, I mean from within our hearts and souls."

"Are we talking a Civil War or a second American Revolution?" asked Julia.

"Perhaps a little of both," replied Sarge. "Before the cyber attack, most Americans didn't care to learn about, much less conceive, the concept of a world without a United States. Yet, it is inevitable. The signs are there as you see the foundations and principles established by our relatives disappear. We have a unique opportunity to return the country to a course of greatness, but it won't be easy."

Julia took in the words of the man she loved so much. Things happened for a reason. He was a great leader whose time had come. The time was also right for something else.

"Sarge, I want our baby to grow up in the country you envision. I want our baby to have the opportunities we had and to respect the meaning of freedom that most of the children in the world will never know."

"Julia, I agree, but what are you saying?"

"Our baby, Sarge. I'm pregnant." Julia began crying tears of joy. She'd been holding this inside for days, waiting for the right moment to reveal the news to the man she loved so much. There was never a perfect time to have a baby, and there was never a perfect time to tell a man he was going to be a father.

"You're pregnant! I love you. I love you. My God, Julia, really?"

Julia nodded with tears still streaming down her face. Sarge hugged her so tight it slightly hurt her tender chest, but she didn't care.

"Yes, Sarge. Is it okay?"

"Okay? Why wouldn't it be okay?"

"Look around us," she started. "We live in some kind of postapocalyptic, dystopian horror movie. How will we raise a child in a world like this?"

"The same way they did two hundred and fifty years ago, with morals and ethics and hope for the future. Our child will be with us as we sow the seeds of liberty across America. I can't think of a better motivation to make America great again."

Julia hugged him tightly. She was so proud of Sarge and would carry his child proudly. Their baby would be born under precarious circumstances, but she was confident Sarge was uniquely capable of making America that shining city upon a hill, as John Winthrop, Sarge's ancestor who founded the Massachusetts Bay colony, wrote in the early seventeenth century.

"Sir! Sir!" exclaimed Captain Branson as he abruptly interrupted their tender moment. "Sir, I'm sorry to interrupt you, but this is urgent."

Sarge broke away from their embrace, but not before wiping the tears off Julia's cheeks. "What is it, Branson?"

"Sir, we've been monitoring radio chatter. There appears to be an operation going on by our men."

"The Mechanics or the Marines?" asked Sarge.

"The Mechanics, sir. We're picking up a significant amount of communications across our frequencies, indicating they're planning an ambush of the UN forces during the prisoner exchange."

Sarge looked at Julia with a scowl on his face. "Dammit, Stephen.

"Branson, have you been able to raise my brother on the radio?"

"We've tried, sir, but there's been no response. We weren't sure if you were aware and didn't want to disrupt the flow of the operation."

"Dammit!" Sarge yelled out of frustration. He immediately moved to the telescope to get a better view. The long-range capability of the lens allowed him to focus in on specific groups of people. Steven was to set up the Mechanics in a defensive position, mainly to be a rapid-reaction force in the event O'Brien pulled a double-cross. Sarge had expressly prohibited the use of force on the UN soldiers.

"This was supposed to be a day of diplomacy, not conflict. There will be plenty of time for that."

"What are you going to do?" asked Julia apprehensively. She didn't want Sarge to go down to the Common.

"I can't put our guys at risk by a bunch of radio communications. I have to find him and call this thing off."

Sarge turned his attention back to Branson. "What's his codename?"

"Hammer One, sir."

"Have you established what the operation is?"

"Yes, sir. I can fill you in on the way. This is happening fairly quickly. The zone of action appears to be focusing on the steps of the State House. I believe O'Brien may be a target."

Sarge grasped Julia by the shoulders, and she began to cry again. "I love you. I know what you're thinking. Don't worry. I'll be careful."

"You better be," she replied. "I don't want anything to happen to our baby boy's father."

"A boy? Yeah, I like it—Little Sarge Junior." He laughed as he kissed her and turned to leave.

"The fifth," she yelled after him.

"Henry the fifth, I like it!" he shouted back.

Julia muttered, "I love you," but Sarge was gone.

CHAPTER FORTY-FOUR

Tuesday, November 8
12:00 p.m.
Boston Common
Boston, Massachusetts

It was a bright morning without a cloud in the sky. Last night's frost melted and the temperatures hovered just above forty. Steven exited the stalled van about a block away from the State House near the Beacon Street entrance to Suffolk University.

In his mid-thirties, Steven was as fit as any professional athlete. The poor food selection hadn't diminished his energy or physical abilities. He quickly emerged and was off in a sprint. Steven's team of Hammers followed him down the sidewalk until he took a sharp right turn and bolted down an alleyway between the university's buildings. Grant and Elkins struggled to keep up. They would not have been his first choice, or second or third, for that matter, to be a part of his Hammers team. The men claimed to know the State House and had learned that O'Brien planned a celebratory party for his returning union guys. Steven smelled an opportunity to take down O'Brien and his forty-some trusted men at the same time.

The inside of the State House would be an easy killing field for five men with full-auto M4s.

Steven zigzagged his way across an open parking area, using the stalled vehicles as cover. Every once in a while he would respond to a radio broadcast as the various teams got into position.

By the time he reached Ashburton Place to the east of the State House, all teams were in position. He motioned for his men to press themselves against the building while he ordered the perimeter units to begin their mission.

"Delta One, Hammer One. Over," said Steven into his handheld mic attached to his kit.

"Go for Delta One."

"Hammer down all Delta teams."

The Delta teams were dispersed throughout downtown Boston and had been monitoring the UN troops all night. The UN was preparing for a riot. Their troops were equipped with tear gas, pepper spray, and long-range acoustic devices. Their outfits consisted of riot helmets, body armor, face visors, and riot shields. When the water cannons and armored fighting vehicles rolled out of the Seaport, Steven knew O'Brien planned an ambush. Well, Steven had an ambush planned of his own.

Their job was to disable the riot personnel without alerting O'Brien. Steven expected them to be used after the prisoners were exchanged. The riot control soldiers were positioned in the side streets out of plain view, to the east, south and west of Boston Common. Because the primary focus of O'Brien's men was that location, Steven determined the north entrance of the State House would be most vulnerable.

Steven sent Elkins and Grant across the street to take up positions behind the concrete planters. He led the other two along the wall toward the State House. He ducked into the entry of the Capitol Coffee House. The men across the street behind the planters would be his eyes for any UN soldiers around the corner.

Steven keyed the mic. "Talk to me."

"You've got two Humvees positioned in a V. From here, we can see four UN soldiers in front, looking towards the Common. The park appears to be empty."

"Roger that."

Steven looked over his shoulder and scanned the faces of the men behind him. He held up four fingers. Each man nodded their acknowledgment. Steven poked his head around the corner and saw the four targets. Today, he was carrying an H & K MP7S with a suppressor and an extended, forty-round magazine. It was compact, light and ideal for this type of operation.

"All right, Hammers," he said. "Flip transmission on and move."

He ran into the street behind the UN Humvees undetected, quickly moving across the narrow road onto the sidewalk adjacent to Ashburton Park. The other men followed the wall to cover the left flank of the UN roadblock.

"Eyes on four targets," said Steven into the radio.

"Roger, eyes on four," came the reply.

"Fire." The four targets were dropped in seconds. "Pull the bodies under the vehicles. Grab the keys too." Steven waved for Elkins and Grant to join him.

After the bodies were secure, Steven led the team down the hill along the retaining wall supporting Ashburton Park. At the corner, he peered around the block planters to observe the Derne Street entrance to the State House's parking garage. The street was deserted.

"All clear," he said as they ran down the street and ducked inside the granite portico. For a moment, he debated whether to use the parking garage as a point of entry and thought about the lack of vehicles and security along the rear entrance to the building. *How are these forty-four prisoners getting out of here?* There weren't any vehicles on the street except a couple of broken-down trucks.

Then he heard voices and laughter coming from within the garage. *Chinese dialect.* UN soldiers.

"Let's stick to the plan and hit the service entrance," he said. He quickly switched his comms to the other frequency and received reports from the Delta teams. They had neutralized the riot squads of the UN.

All teams were awaiting the arrival of the school buses carrying the prisoners from Fort Devens. Once the prisoners from the State House descended into Boston Common, the forty-four would be allowed to enter the State House. O'Brien, via Pearson, had agreed to vacate the State House by the end of the day.

"Let's move," said Steven, anxious to get into position. He led the team into the bowels of the complex and veered to the right. He gestured toward the kitchen and then turned the team up a back flight of stairs to the first floor. Based upon information he'd received from Sarge during his debrief following the raid last week, Steven decided to use the same stairwell to the upper levels. This would give his team the high ground.

They reached the second-floor library and found it empty. The sounds of muffled voices could be heard in the grand foyer. Steven cracked the library doors and rolled the Bounce Imaging Ball onto the landing overlooking the first floor.

He studied the video pad on his wrist and reported his findings to the Hammers team. "They've got the prisoners kneeling down in the center of the building. There are guards on the second level."

"How many?"

"Four, two on each side. Their attention is directed to the prisoners, but they don't appear to be on alert." He studied the video pad for another moment until the sounds of feet shuffling could be heard coming from below.

"On your feet! Get up! *Arriba, arriba! Andale! Macht Schnell!* Let's go!"

Steven switched frequencies and was told the buses had arrived. He turned to his team. "It's almost go time. First, we'll use the activity below as cover as we take out the four men on this level. Elkins, Grant, we'll take the west side of the building. You men go left to the east. Take out your targets, and drag them out of view. Clear so far?"

"Yes."

"Second, and very important," continued Steven, "I came here to take out O'Brien. He's mine, got it? You'll know when to open fire—when that fat guy hits the floor. Clear."

The team nodded. Elkins and Grant followed Steven along the wall, ducking into the office doorways at each opportunity. A series of half-dead ficus trees contained in planters prevented him from taking a clear shot. Fortunately, the confusion downstairs supplied a perfect distraction. Steven aimed his weapon and shot the UN soldiers in the back with two rounds each. The other two members of the team followed suit.

"They're leaving," said Grant.

"Follow me," said Steven as he led the two men to the front windows overlooking Boston Common. Then he saw O'Brien standing on top of the makeshift scaffolding like a Roman king presiding over two warriors fighting in the Colosseum.

"They'll be coming in now. Shouldn't we get in position?" asked Elkins.

Steven looked around for the best vantage point. "There," he said, pointing to the entrance to the west wing. "That gives us a perfect vantage point and we can keep the guys below in a crossfire." As they carefully made their way back to the west wing where the balcony overlooked the entrance to the State House, Steven switched to the other frequency to monitor the transmissions of the Mechanics.

Reports were coming across the radio that the UN troops were converging onto Boston Common from Beacon, Park, and Tremont Streets. They were putting the squeeze on their people.

"It's an ambush! I knew it!" he unconsciously said aloud.

CHAPTER FORTY-FIVE

Tuesday, November 8
12:22 p.m.
Boston Common
Boston, Massachusetts

Sarge donned his gear and ran out the front door into the cool air. His security detail hustled to catch up.

Creeping up on the ripe old age of forty, he was about to be a father for the first time. Of all the times and of all the circumstances, becoming a dad wasn't the best idea, but it was one that he embraced wholeheartedly. He felt the same excitement as Julia when she told him.

Captain Branson rushed ahead of Sarge with two of the Mechanics in tow. A couple of Marines brought up the rear. Branson led them through the alleys and backyards of Chestnut Street along the same route they used to escape the State House a few days prior. *It worked before.*

As their pace quickened into a trot, Sarge turned up the volume on his radio and listened through his earpiece. Sarge picked up on chatter from the Mechanics that Steven was in place inside the State

House. He could not determine which channel his brother was utilizing in order to contact him. All that he could determine was that Steven was inside the building with his team.

As they ran up Chestnut Street toward Beacon Hill, none of his men attempted to conceal their weapons. Sarge wasn't sure they could arrive at the State House in time to help diffuse the situation or to help his brother with this *plan*, whatever it was. *But I have to try.*

Retracing their steps, the group reached Joy Street and made their way to the west side of the building. As they climbed the iron fire escape to the first floor, cheers rose from the front of the State House.

"Stand back," instructed one of Branson's men as he placed a small explosive charge on the steel door's frame. "Turn your backs to the door." A small explosion compromised the lock, and the door, still smoldering, flung open. The sound was barely heard over the shouts coming from Boston Common.

Once Sarge and his detail were inside, Branson asked, "Which way, sir?"

Sarge came to a realization. Steven was an assassin. That was what he knew best. He was there to assassinate O'Brien.

"Dammit, he's gonna take out O'Brien," said Sarge.

Branson didn't wait for further instruction. "Upstairs," he shouted as he quickly led the team up to the second level of the State House. Once in the hallway, Branson cautiously moved the team toward the grand foyer. As they approached the opening, Sarge ran past the team as Steven appeared from the right.

"There he is!"

Steven walked in a low crouch toward the railing to get a better look at the procession entering the building. He prepared his weapon and looked through the Elcan reflex sight, scanning the crowd for O'Brien. *How can I miss this guy?*

He raised up for a better perspective and then he felt the arm of Elkins around his throat. Before he could react, Elkins plunged a six-inch serrated knife into Steven's back, instantly severing several vertebrae in his spinal column.

"Governor O'Brien sends his regards," hissed Elkins into Steven's ear.

Steven landed face-first onto the marble floor, still conscious. In his peripheral vision, he saw Grant's chest burst into a mix of crimson and goo. Another round obliterated Grant's head.

———

Sarge saw Elkins drive the knife into his brother's back at the same time Grant pointed his rifle at Sarge. Without hesitation, Sarge put two rounds in his chest and a third in his head before his body hit the floor dead. Elkins looked toward Sarge and then ran, firing his weapon wildly into the air to create confusion. Sarge would never forget his face—the beady-eyes flanking an oversized nose. *Coward.*

"Get him!" he shouted as he ran to his brother's side. Branson's men gave chase for a moment, but Elkins rolled down the marble stairs toward the crowd on the first floor. Gunfire erupted in the hall as Steven's men and Sarge's detail exchanged volleys with the UN troops on the first floor.

Sarge was oblivious to it all. He slid through the blood to Steven's side and pulled him into his lap. "Steven, buddy. Hang on. We'll get some help." Sarge looked around him, frantically seeking answers, but there was a firefight going on and they were in danger.

"Listen, I've got to get us out of here. I've gotta move you, Steven."

Steven just grinned in response as he coughed up a little blood. "It's over for me, Sarge. I'm sorry."

"No, I'm sorry. You were right. O'Brien double-crossed us. I should've listened to you."

"It's okay, Sarge. We've all got our jobs to do."

"Steven, I can't do this without you. Can you hold on?"

"Dammit. I can't feel anything." He coughed up more blood and grimaced. "It's karma, you know."

"What is?" asked Sarge.

"My whole life has been in the shadows. I killed, and they never saw it coming."

He coughed again and his eyes began to roll back in his head.

"I love you, brother," said Sarge, ducking as a rapid burst of bullets sailed over his head. "Hold on for me."

Steven was whispering now. "You know what they say?"

"What's that?"

"Karma is just a polite way of saying ha-ha, screw you."

And Steven slipped into the darkness.

The saga will continue in CHOOSE FREEDOM.

Continue reading to get a sneak peek at the first few chapters.

THANK YOU FOR READING THE MECHANICS!

If you enjoyed it, I'd be grateful if you'd take a moment to write a short review (just a few words are needed) and post it on Amazon. Amazon uses complicated algorithms to determine what books are recommended to readers. Sales are, of course, a factor, but so are the quantities of reviews my books get. By taking a few seconds to leave a review, you help me out and also help new readers learn about my work.

WHAT'S COMING NEXT FROM BOBBY AKART?

Get on the list to find out about coming titles, deals, contests, appearances, and more!

Sign up for The Epigraph, my official newsletter, at BobbyAkart.com

VISIT my feature page at Amazon.com/BobbyAkart for more information on my other action-packed thrillers, which includes over forty Amazon #1 bestsellers in forty-plus fiction and nonfiction genres.

READ ON FOR A BONUS EXCERPT from CHOOSE FREEDOM, the thrilling conclusion to the Boston Brahmin Series. With over three thousand four and five star reviews, each of the books in The Boston Brahmin Series achieved #1 best seller rankings on Amazon.

www.BobbyAkart.com

International Best Selling Author

BOBBY
AKART

CHOOSE
FREEDOM

The Boston Brahmin Series . Book Six

CHAPTER ONE

Wednesday, November 9
9:00 a.m.
The *Miss Behavin'*
Marblehead, Massachusetts

The gentle wind billowed the sails as the *Miss Behavin'* skipped across the white-crested waves of the cold Atlantic Ocean. The forty-foot yacht bounced along the waves, sending cold spray onto the deck, invigorating Sarge as he thought about what his brother meant to him.

Corporal Morrell deftly guided them through the wind-whipped water. Sarge was reflective. No one was actually dead until the waves they caused in the world returned to the sea. His brother had left his mark on the world, without a doubt.

Sarge never liked sailing, yet sailing had been his brother's life. Steven would talk about the sea, the sun, and the cry of the birds, but Sarge only pretended to be interested. He regretted so many things, and not sharing Steven's love of sailing was one of them.

Steven would describe sailing as flying over the water, clearing a path through the waves with the goal of leaving the duties of the world behind him. Sailing into the vast, blue ocean was freedom to him.

"It's better than sex," Steven had once quipped, but then quickly added, "Nah, not really." He'd said the water called to him like a hot chick would whisper into his ear. He'd joke about this often, but Sarge knew he was sincere. Steven sailed in this life, and he would sail in the next.

"This is a good spot," instructed Sarge to Corporal Morrell, who adjusted the sails and slowly brought the *Miss Behavin'* to a slower pace within sight of nearby Bakers Island.

It was on Bakers Island during a family outing when Sarge and Steven were boys that they first met John Morgan. Although their father and Morgan were close friends, the Sargent brothers weren't around Morgan very often because the duties of politics kept him traveling abroad for many years as the two boys grew up. It was a weekend outing at the Bakers Island Light Station that set the course of the Sargent boys' lives, they just didn't know it.

Sarge's brother never talked about death despite the number of times he cheated it. Intuitively, Sarge knew Steven would want to be buried here so he could forever roam the ocean he loved so much.

Burial at sea was a time-honored tradition. For a Navy SEAL, there was no more exalted option for their mortal remains than being returned to the ocean.

The *Miss Behavin'* gently rocked in the ripple of waves on the leeward side of the island as Sarge gathered himself to speak. He was alone except for Brad and two more security personnel. Julia demanded to come along, as did Katie, but Sarge didn't want Julia to risk harm to their baby. As for Katie, they needed to have a talk.

Sarge caught his breath, cleared his mind, and started. "Steven's last words were 'Karma is just a polite way of saying ha-ha, screw you.' This is how my brother lived his life—balls to the wall with no regrets.

"Steven always said to me that a ship in the harbor may be safe, but that's not what ships are for. They are made to sail—attack the waves and conquer the unknown. Steven lived his life in the same manner.

"He was a warrior—made to protect and fight. For him, his death would not be a moment of sadness. Sadness comes from not living life to its fullest. The way of the warrior is the resolute acceptance of death. This was the way of my brother.

"There are so many things left unsaid between us. Now is not the time. This is the time to honor my brother, the warrior. I found these words in Steven's berth below. He lived by them, and he will be buried at sea with them."

Sarge wiped several tears mixed with sea spray from his face. As the seagulls cried above them and the surging waves washed onto the rocky shore, Sarge read the fitting tribute to Steven Sargent.

"Make no mistake. I will defend my brothers. I will defend the weak. I will defend our way of life. I will bring the fight to your home to keep you out of mine. I will pursue relentlessly all who threaten my family. I will sacrifice so that others may live. I am an American. I am a patriot. I am a sheepdog. If you strike me or those like me, you will lay upon the earth until you are buried in it."

Sarge, with the help of Brad and Corporal Morrell, reverently placed Steven's weighted body into the Atlantic Ocean to seek its final resting place. As it slowly disappeared into the darkness below, Sarge said, "Ashes to ashes, dust to dust. I love you, my brother. Godspeed."

CHAPTER TWO

Friday, November 11
10:00 a.m.
Prescott Peninsula, 1PP
Quabbin Reservoir, Massachusetts

Sarge joined Brad and Donald, who were waiting for him in the newly created war room located in the underground bunker of 1PP. When Donald had renovated the former astronomy complex over the summer, he'd fortified the bunker with a burster slab of concrete and steel. He'd also created an EMP-proof facility that included air filtration and blast doors. The facility was designed to withstand most explosive threats as well as biological attacks.

One room that had been used as a library became a war room of sorts. Sarge and Donald adorned the walls with maps Sarge had retrieved from 100 Beacon yesterday. A variety of colored Post-it notes were spread about, delineating a local, regional, and national strategy envisioned by Sarge. Donald had secured all of the documents and computers containing the intricacies of the Boston Brahmin's financial dealings inside the room as well.

Sarge needed a place to work without prying ears and eyes. He also needed to discuss the future with his two most trusted friends, besides Julia, of course.

Donald would become Sarge's financial *consigliere*. The Italian term for *chief advisor* suited Donald's role perfectly. The consigliere, although not officially part of the hierarchy of the Mafia, played an important role in a crime family. He was often the most trusted confidant of the family boss and typically the most knowledgeable of the Mafioso family's financial affairs. The concept was a throwback to medieval times when the king would place his trust in an advisor who could be summoned for strategic counsel.

Because virtually every decision, whether made by the king or the *capo di tutti capi*—the godfather of the Mafia—had a monetary aspect, the chief advisor was usually well versed in the organization's monetary affairs.

Brad was a brilliant military strategist who seemed to have a knack for dealing with this post-apocalyptic world. The rules of engagement were vastly different than the battlefields of the Middle East, where most modern commanders cut their teeth.

Following the cyber attack, the streets of America became the theater of war. Most Americans were reluctant to think about the ramifications of war, especially since they were typically fought abroad. The prospect of destroying their fellow man was not part of their psyche. In this post-collapse America, survival meant killing. The war zone was now Main Street, USA.

Brad, who was levelheaded except when he disliked someone, had a firm grasp on this concept. Politics was not his forte. It was Sarge's.

Sarge discussed the prospects of bringing Abbie into his inner circle of advisors. She was, after all, a sitting senator who just a few months ago was in line to become the next Vice President of the United States. However, her areas of expertise were grounded in the pre-collapse America. She was not cut out for the new normal, which required assassinations, insurgency operations, and attacks upon fellow Americans. Her time would come to lead if Sarge was successful in his strategy.

"Hi, guys," announced Sarge as he settled into a chair at the head of the table. He didn't waste any time getting to the point. "My brother's death leaves a huge hole in our hearts and our team. Allowing Steven to oversee the activities of the Mechanics freed up Brad to undertake more traditional military functions."

"I can handle both, Sarge, until we come up with a solution," said Brad.

Sarge had contemplated this and decided against it. The success of their future would depend upon political as well as military solutions. But politically, he couldn't taint Brad's stellar reputation among his peers nationwide by having him associated with the functions to be carried out by the Mechanics. These functions belonged in the world of black-ops, off-the-books operations.

"I appreciate that, Brad," said Sarge. "I can't have your fingerprints on these things. You need to maintain that separation so you can have plausible deniability. For now, I'll coordinate their efforts."

"No freakin' way, Sarge!" protested Donald. "You can't be out there risking your life."

Sarge started laughing, which enraged Donald more. His face turned red and he was about to let out another outburst when Sarge held his hands up to calm his dear friend.

"Donald, no worries, old buddy. No Rambo crap for me. Steven did an excellent job setting up and establishing regions of responsibilities for his top lieutenants. In fact, several of them now occupy the condos at 100 Beacon. I'll meet with them just like always, but only at the well-fortified 100 Beacon location."

"Sarge," started Brad, "at least let me beef up the security around there with my men."

Donald continued to noticeably shake his head in disagreement. Sarge didn't want to argue with his friend, especially when he knew Donald was right. But the group was already down one man and, as they were about to discuss, would be down another member as well.

"Okay, I'm on board with that. The military presence will provide a deterrent effect for any local thugs who might have designs on testing us. But keep a wide perimeter. I don't want to draw the attention of the UN forces unnecessarily."

"No problem," said Brad.

"Fine," muttered Donald. Sarge let Donald have his opinion because it was voiced out of concern for his friend.

"Okay. We'll meet here every day as practicable. This will give us an opportunity to share information and stay on top of planning. Also, it will continue to be our duty to keep the Boston Brahmin informed during the lunch hour. I believe this practice has helped us keep everyone within our charge as calm as possible. As odd as it sounds, this diverse group has assimilated into our new lifestyle. Let's not change things now because of recent adversity."

Sarge tried his best to discuss Steven's death in an impersonal manner. He vowed to share his emotional feelings on the subject in private, only with Julia.

"I agree," said Donald. "If you need me to take on that role, just say the word."

"Thanks, buddy," said Sarge, who turned his attention to Brad. "We need to contain the UN. What do you know about their casualties from Tuesday?"

"They took a real hit," replied Brad. "They lost quite a few men inside the State House during the firefight. But they sustained heavy losses of life and equipment around the perimeter they established. Steven was right. O'Brien and General Zhang planned an ambush and Steven sniffed it out. The Mechanics were very successful in taking out most of their units and confiscating weapons and vehicles."

"Good," said Sarge as he was once again forced to recollect the death of his brother. "Do you have a feel for Zhang's attitude. Did we kick a hornet's nest?"

"It's too early to tell. Thus far, they haven't undertaken any of their normal activities. My men entered the area after we deemed it secured and placed the dead in body bags. We returned the bodies of their deceased soldiers Wednesday afternoon. It was the right thing to do."

Sarge leaned back in his chair and quietly wished the humanitarian gesture by Brad's men would diffuse the tense standoff between the so-called UN peacekeeping forces and the Marines. Time would tell.

"If Zhang's troops are not interested in conducting more raids and roadblocks, then we've accomplished more than just freeing Governor Baker and the rest of the Massachusetts legislators. We may have broken the UN's spirit."

"It's possible," added Donald. "Or they're regrouping to come back with a vengeance."

"Very likely," said Brad. "Do you want me to reach out to General Zhang? I could find a way to bypass O'Brien and open up a dialogue. You know, soldier to soldier."

Sarge liked the idea of diplomacy. General Zhang didn't have a vested interest in this fight other than to achieve some type of accolades from his superiors.

"It's worth a try," replied Sarge. "Besides, O'Brien is probably hiding under a rock somewhere."

"I can't believe he got away," said Donald.

"Pure luck and an uncanny ability to take advantage of the chaos in the State House saved his dumb ass," said Sarge. "One of the guys reported that O'Brien used a woman and child as a prop to provide a cover story. He was allowed to leave because none of our guys knew what he looked like. Julia found some images of him and this ass-clown Elkins to disseminate to the Mechanics. They all know what to look for now."

Sarge slid the images of the two men to Brad and Donald.

"Well, O'Brien is a big one," said Donald. "And you can barely see Elkins's face behind that big schnoz. These two will stand out in a crowd next time."

"That brings us to the second order of business, which is finding O'Brien and that cockroach Elkins. I'm gonna meet with the

Mechanics day after tomorrow to assign teams to search for O'Brien. As for Elkins, I have a specific plan."

"What do you have in mind?" asked Brad.

"Katie."

CHAPTER THREE

Friday, November 11
4:00 p.m.
1 PP
Quabbin Reservoir, Massachusetts

Sarge had not spoken with Katie at length until now. There were several emotional outbursts since she was told of Steven's death, and he allowed Julia and Abbie, who were far more diplomatic than he was, to console Katie.

The Loyal Nine came together by fate, and their group was built on a foundation of trust. Family relationships and associations were part of it. Abbie, Julia, Brad, and J.J. were tied to the Boston Brahmin by lineage. Sarge and Steven were chosen at a young age by the handshake of two powerful men on Bakers Island one sunny day.

The Quinns came into the fold because of Donald's loyalty to a trusted friend of John Morgan's. Katie was allowed into the inner circle by virtue of her *special* relationship with Steven and her extraordinary analytical ability as a brilliant spook within the CIA.

Katie was the member of the Loyal Nine with whom the group

interacted the least. It wasn't because she was unwelcome. To the contrary, Katie was considered a vital asset to the team and an important mole for Morgan inside the White House. Katie's time was spent in Washington, so levels of trust weren't fully established.

As the Loyal Nine came together, there was no stated goal or formal association defined. They had common interests and a love for country. None of them ever contemplated a death within the group. Nor did they consider the possibility of expelling one of their own.

Sarge had seen the warning signs that emerged following his appointment to head the Boston Brahmin. Katie's love for Steven resulted in a jealousy of Sarge's success and attention. Naturally, she thought Steven deserved accolades of his own, so she set about to drive a wedge between the brothers.

When she saw the opportunity for Steven to shine, she'd guided him to undertake the risky operation on Election Day—despite Sarge's instructions. She admitted to Abbie and Julia that she had been blinded by envy, and the result had been Steven's death.

Sarge recognized there was a major change in the group's dynamics. The loss of Steven was huge. But now he had to deal with the possible banishment of Katie. He'd never mulled over the prospect of a traitor or malcontent within their ranks. Besides, Katie was hardly either of these. If she were, his decision would be an easy one. Traitors got shot. Troublemakers got straightened out. If the rabble-rouser didn't change his ways, he got shot too.

All of the members of the group were privy to the secrets of the Boston Brahmin, including their wealth, political power, and just as importantly, their location. Banishment was not the answer because an angry, rejected person was a potential liability.

Sarge had a solution to avoid the fate afforded a traitor or troublemaker. He hoped Katie would agree to take on her new role. Otherwise, the alternative was not a good one—for her.

"Katie, I want you to find my brother's killer. There's nobody more aware of Steven's dealings with Elkins and Grant than you."

"You're right, Sarge," said Katie sheepishly. Their conversation had been going on for ten minutes as Katie continued to apologize and pledge her loyalty to Sarge and the group. She admitted her mistakes and acknowledged responsibility for Steven's death. She was desperate to make it up to Sarge.

"Good. One of Brad's most trusted men, Second Lieutenant Kevin Bailey, is also very familiar with O'Brien and his operation. He was involved with the quasi-training session of O'Brien's top people early on at Camp Curtis Guild. Bailey will be a valuable asset to you, and you can count on him to have your back."

Sarge did not reveal to Katie that Bailey was under strict instructions to monitor Katie's activities. Sarge was giving her wide latitude in conducting this search. He wanted to make sure she stuck to the task at hand. If Bailey got the impression Katie was going off the reservation, he knew what to do.

"I know Bailey," said Katie. "We'll find the guys, Sarge. I promise."

Sarge wanted to keep this conversation short. He wasn't sure he'd ever truly forgive her for the role she'd played in Steven's death. Katie didn't stick the knife in his brother's back, but she was instrumental in clouding his judgment, which allowed it to happen. It was best that Sarge keep their interaction to a minimum until some time passed.

"Katie, this is very important. I want you to promise me you'll do everything necessary to bring Elkins back alive. I want to look my brother's killer in the eyes."

"Yes, sir."

THANK YOU FOR READING THIS EXCERPT OF Choose Freedom, book six of The Boston Brahmin Series. You may purchase CHOOSE FREEDOM on Amazon by clicking HERE or visiting www.BobbyAkart.com.

. . .

SIGN UP for Bobby Akart's mailing list to receive a copy of his monthly newsletter, *The Epigraph*, learn of special offers, view bonus content, and be the first to receive news about new releases.

Visit www.BobbyAkart.com for details.

APPENDIX A:

In the *Art of War*, Sun Tzu wrote, "Be so subtle that you are invisible. Be so mysterious that you are intangible. Then you will control your rival's fate."

Loosely organized guerrilla warfare and insurgent activities have been the dominant form of military conflict throughout history. Unconventional warfare dates back to the times of antiquity. From the nomadic rebels who fought to bring down the Roman Empire (detailed below) to the internet-savvy, to the plane-exploding jihadists who triggered America's global war on terror, irregular forces are a constant factor in the history of warfare. And fighting them has become tougher than ever.

Take, for example, Vo Nguyen Giap, the brilliant Communist general who succeeded in expelling first the French and then the Americans from Vietnam. Giap closely followed the teachings of Mao in planning a three-stage struggle—first, he utilized localized guerrilla warfare, then a strategy he called *the war of movement* and finally *general uprising*—which he waged with a three-tier force of village militias, full-time guerrillas and a regular army.

But where Mao was always cautious to avoid confrontations with more powerful forces, Giap's tendency to gamble on premature offensives in 1968, and again in 1972, could have proved fatal each time had it not been for the psychological and political frailties of the South Vietnamese. In guerrilla warfare, what matters most is the ability to shape the political narrative, not the facts on the ground. This is how guerrillas are able to win wars even as they lose battles.

How do the weak vanquish the powerful?

Because insurgencies pit the weak against the strong, most still end up failing. Between 1775 and 1945, an analysis of guerrilla warfare reveals that a quarter of insurgencies achieved most or all of their aims. But since 1945, that number has risen to nearly half. Part of the reason for the improving success rate is the rising importance of public opinion. Since 1945 the spread of democracy, education, mass media and the concept of international law have all conspired to sap the will of states engaged in protracted counter-insurgencies. Thanks to the internet and our complex, inter-connected world, in the battle over the narrative, insurgents have many more weapons at their disposal than before.

That's not to say that counter-insurgency in the twenty-first century is a losing game. But to prevail requires an understanding of the game's rules. Military strategists have returned to the so-called *population-centric approach* pioneered by the British during the twelve year, post-war Malayan Emergency, which lasted until 1960. The strategy was rediscovered by American generals such as David Petraeus and Stanley McChrystal in Iraq and Afghanistan after several setbacks in fighting the Taliban. There are several principals which make up the population-centric approach.

The first principle is to abandon conventional military tactics. *Clear and hold* replaces the normal approach of *search and destroy*. Most importantly, to defeat an insurgency you must provide enough security for ordinary people to live their lives. Winning the ideological battle is more important than military victories.

The second is that legitimacy is vital for both sides. Corrupt or excessively violent governments will always struggle, but so too will guerrillas who terrorize their own people. ISIS, for example, has failed in gaining legitimacy for this reason.

The third principle is staying power. Firepower is no substitute for patience and boots on the ground. The people you need on your side must believe that you are in it for the long haul.

The fourth is that most counter-insurgency campaigns abroad are lost at home. Liberal democracies have short attention spans, low tolerance for casualties and other calls on their sources of domestic spending. Unless voters believe that an intervention is necessary for their own security they will quickly withdraw support for it.

All of which explains why the wars in Afghanistan and Iraq never fully gained the support of the American people. The population-centric approach—and the troop surge needed to effectuate it—came too late in the conflict and with a foolishly rigid deadline imposed by Washington.

Insurgencies are the way of the future. Here are two examples of historic, successful guerrilla/insurgency campaigns:

The American Revolution: The Mechanics of 1767 - 1783

Although many of the engagements of the American Revolution were conventional, guerrilla warfare was used to a large extent during the War for Independence from 1775 through 1783, which made a huge difference.

However, guerrilla tactics were first used by the colonists, and then the Sons of Liberty via their insurgent arm - The Mechanics. As we wrote in *Seeds of Liberty*, America has a penchant for rebellion. Large scale insurrections began in the seventeenth century and continued until the Revolutionary War. Bacon's Rebellion, Culpeper's Rebellion, and King Philip's War are just a few examples explored in detail in *Seeds of Liberty*.

The Boston Massacre (1770) and The Boston Tea Party (1773) are other key events which led to the American Revolution. Later, at the Battles of Lexington and Concord on April 19, 1775, insurgent activities and unconventional methods were used by the patriots to fight the British.

During the War, George Washington sent militia units with limited Continental Army support to launch raids and ambushes on British detachments and forage parties, the militia and Continental Army support would skirmish with British detachments in small scale battles and engagements. Insurgent victories raised morale for the Patriots as their guerrilla operations against the British were very effective.

There are other Americans who used hit and run raids, ambushes, and surprise attacks against the British such as William R. Davie, David Wooster, Francis Marion, Shadrach Inman, Daniel Morgan, Morgan's riflemen, and over mountain men. All these American guerrilla fighters did their part by using unconventional tactics to fight the British and loyalists.

Nathanael Greene used a guerrilla strategy very effectively against Lord Cornwallis. First, Nathanael Greene would keep retreating to lure the British far from their supply lines, then send out his forces to fight in small skirmishes and engagements with British detachments to weaken them. Then fighting the conventional battle, Nathanael Greene fought Lord Cornwallis at Guilford Court House and gave him a severe blow. Although Lord Cornwallis was the victor, his victory was pyrrhic as he had too many casualties that he could ill afford. After the British surrender at Yorktown and America gaining their independence, many of these Americans who used guerrilla tactics and strategies became immortalized and romanticized as time passed.

Although guerrilla warfare was frequently used when avoiding battles, the Americans fought in conventional linear formations in decisive battles against the British. The American Revolution could be seen as a hybrid war since both conventional and guerrilla warfare were used throughout its duration.

Origins of Counterinsurgency in Assyria and Rome 1100 BC to AD 212

As we've written in *Economic Collapse*, all empires collapse eventually. Their reign ends when they are defeated by a larger and more powerful enemy, or when their financing runs out. In the case of the Roman Empire, all of the above applies.

Most ancient empires responded to the threat of guerrilla warfare, whether waged by nomads from the outside or rebels from the inside, with the same strategy. It can be boiled down to one simple word—*terror.*

Ancient monarchs sought to inflict as much suffering as possible to put down and deter armed challenges. Since, with a few exceptions such as Athens and the Roman Republic, ancient nations were primarily monarchies or warrior states, rather than constitutional republics. They seldom felt bound by any moral scruples or by any need to appease public opinion—neither *public opinion* nor *human rights* being concepts that they would have understood.

The Assyrians, who starting in 1100 BC conquered a domain stretching a thousand miles from Persia to Egypt, were particularly grisly in their infliction of terror. The Mongols would later become famous for equally grotesque displays designed to frighten adversaries into acquiescence.

But even at a time when there were no human-rights lobbies and no free press, this strategy was far from successful. Often it backfired by simply creating more enemies. Wracked by civil war, Assyria was helpless in the end to suppress a revolt by the Babylonians, inhabitants of a city previously sacked by the Assyrians, and the Medes, a tribe dwelling in modern-day Iran. They pooled their resources to fight their larger, mutual oppressors. In 612 BC the two enemies came together and managed to conquer the imperial capital of Assyria through insurgent warfare.

The Roman Empire, which faced and suppressed more rebellions than most of its predecessors or successors, developed a more sophisticated approach to counterinsurgency. But then it had to, because it faced more sophisticated insurgents—not just the type of primitive nomads that confronted then, but also rebellions led by men who had previously fought with the Romans or lived among them and knew how to exploit their weaknesses.

Many were originally barbarians who were *Romanized* to some degree, typically through military service. Yet, being foreign born, they were usually not able to share in the full fruits of Roman citizenship. This hardship was especially severe in the case of Spartacus, a slave from the Balkans who escaped from a gladiator training school and eventually led an army of ninety thousand freed slaves who briefly overran much of southern Italy.

Not only Spartacus, but many other semi-Romanized barbarians built up a lifetime's worth of perceived slights and grudges. They also sympathized with the plight of their native countrymen, who were often exploited by Roman overlords. The resulting tensions exploded in some of the worst revolts that Rome faced. Entire legions would be lost in the resulting wars. The Romans came back to conquer after many defeats, but the losses took a toll spiritually, and economically.

In response to insurrections, the Romans became just as savage and bloodthirsty as the Mongols or Assyrians. Witness the destruction of Carthage in 146 BC or of Jerusalem in AD 70 and again in 135. The Greek historian Polybius noted that in towns taken by the legions "one may often see not only the corpses of human beings, but dogs cut in half, and the dismembered limbs of other animals. . . . They do this, I think, to inspire terror."

To deter would-be rebels, the Romans spread news of their merciless conquests far and wide. After the fall of Jerusalem in AD 70, for example, new coins were minted all over the empire with the legend "Judaea Conquered," showing "a Roman soldier with a spear standing over a mourning Jew." As a result, Roman counterinsurgency warfare has understandably, if unfairly, come to be associated with the famous words: "They create a desert, and call it peace."

In addition to targeted assassinations employed in the latter periods of the Roman Empire, the Romans also employed psychological warfare. Those who praise the Romans for their ferocity in putting down revolts should realize that this was only part of the story. Rome's enemies were not always slain. Often they were accommodated. A succession of emperors maintained stability on the frontiers by reaching understandings with barbarian tribes—who consistently aggravated Rome with its insurgent activity, who were often bribed with favorable trade and what would now be called *foreign aid*. Neighboring kings became Roman clients, and many of their followers were paid to defend the empire or at least not to attack it. The Romans, like most successful imperialists, were skilled at exploiting political divisions among their enemies and using gold as a weapon.

If the Roman Empire had offered nothing but death and desolation to those it ruled, it could never have survived as long as it did: Rome ruled most of western Europe, the Balkans, Anatolia, and northern Africa for 450 years. The secret to the empire's longevity was that while the Romans punished revolts harshly, they generally ruled with a light touch.

Indeed, some historians argue that Rome was, like modern America, an *empire of trust* that was built and maintained with the implicit consent of its subjects. Another scholar suggests that Roman imperialism was primarily a *diplomatic and even social* phenomenon, not only or mainly a military undertaking. The Roman Senate even occasionally punished its own soldiers and envoys for dealing too treacherously or cruelly with subject peoples. As well it should have: the Roman legions could barely have functioned without the manpower and supplies provided by vanquished foes converted into slaves or unwilling allies.

The Roman version of counter-insurgency evolved from terror to a pacification over a period of several centuries. These transformations resulted in *Pax Romana*, which is Latin for *Roman Peace*. Pax Romana was the long period of relative peacefulness and minimal expansion by the Roman military force experienced by the Roman Empire after the end of the Final War of the Roman Republic and before the beginning of the Crisis of the Third Century.

The Crisis of the Third Century (AD 235–284) was a period in which the Roman Empire nearly collapsed under the combined pressures of invasion, civil war, plague, and economic depression.

Is there a lesson to be learned here for the governing of a nation-state? Can a nation's foreign policy, when faced with the threat of guerrilla warfare and insurgent uprisings, become too soft in its response? Time will tell.

To return to Chapter One of The Mechanics, book five in The Boston Brahmin series, click here: **RETURN TO BEGINNING**

COPYRIGHT INFORMATION

.